THE
FOSTER
FAMILY

BOOKS BY NICOLE TROPE

NICOLE TROPE

THE
FOSTER
FAMILY

bookouture

Published by Bookouture in 2022

An imprint of Storyfire Ltd.
Carmelite House
50 Victoria Embankment
London EC4Y 0DZ

www.bookouture.com

ISBN: 978-1-80314-480-1
eBook ISBN: 978-1-80314-479-5

For D. M. I. J.

PROLOGUE

'Police emergency, this is Ella.'

'Yes, hi... hi... Um, my... son is missing. My little boy, he's missing.'

'Right, okay, and where are you located?'

'Um... it's... Warren Road, Warren Road in Gilmore, number twelve... It's, um... a holiday home, I mean not mine, we rented it for the month. We rented it and he was playing in the garden and he's... We can't find him.'

'Okay, I'm looking you up now, I can see where you are. Police are on the way. How old is your son?'

'He's five, only five.'

'And his name?'

'Joseph, but my husband calls him Joe – we call him Joe.'

'And can you describe him for me? How tall is he?'

'He's about three and a half feet... and he has black hair and green eyes and olive skin.'

'And what was he wearing?'

'He was... Blue shorts and a blue T-shirt with a picture of a dinosaur on it. And sandals – he had his sandals on.'

'And he was playing in the garden, you said?'

'Yes, the front garden. It has a fence and he was there and I went to... put on some laundry, and when I came back, he was gone. He just disappeared. Are the police coming?'

'Yes, they should be there really soon. Did you see anything? Like a car you don't recognise or a person outside the house, anything like that?'

'No, no – nothing. It's a quiet street, there's nothing... Oh, wait, I can hear the sirens, I can hear them... They're here, thank God, they're here.'

'Good, I'll leave you with them.'

'Yes, thank you, thank you.'

CHAPTER ONE

When the man passes the bus stop the first time, on his way out for a drink with a friend, he chuckles to himself. Someone's had a bit too much tonight, he thinks. It's only 9 p.m., and the girl at the bus stop is slumped on the bench, her head resting on the glass. Passed out already. It's the season, of course. One Christmas party after another, drink everywhere and a festive feel in the air.

In the pub, where green tinsel glints in multicoloured fairy lights, he and his friend share a round of beers and play a game of pool. The man is not one for parties, despite being in his thirties, despite all the email invitations he receives. He has always preferred a quiet drink with a friend. They order another round, and then it's midnight, and the man bids his friend goodbye. He has work in the morning and a big presentation that will hopefully put him on the management track. He is ambitious, driven, even though he doesn't like his job much, or the people he works with.

He passes the bus stop again on the way home and glances at the bench where the girl had been.

Where she still is.

He is a street away when he stops the car. That can't be right, he thinks. The buses run all the time, every fifteen minutes at least. Surely someone would have noticed the girl and helped her, or tried to wake her up. It's warm enough in the Sydney December air, but it's not a place for a young girl to be. He is assuming it's a young girl because of the artfully ripped jeans and the long dark hair, though it was hard to see clearly as most of her was in shadow.

He debates with himself for a few minutes, and then he sighs, his mother's words ringing in his head: 'Never pass up an opportunity to do a good deed for someone, because one day you might be in need of a good deed yourself.' He needs to call his parents and have a chat, ask them what they want for Christmas. But right now, he can't leave that girl there. It's the rough side of town, close to where the man lives alone in a studio apartment.

He turns the car around and goes back to the bus stop, parking in the quiet street. He approaches her slowly, worried that he might scare her. He's a big man and the girl looks, even from a distance, very young. Her hands are on her lap, open.

When he is standing in front of her, his breath catches in his throat and his heart starts to pound. There is blood all over her clothes, all over her jeans and her pink T-shirt. Her face is a mess of bruises and blood from a large cut on her lip. He didn't notice the first time he drove past; didn't notice as he approached her because of the dim lighting at the bus stop. On the street behind him, another car roars past, and he turns quickly, wanting to signal to them to stop and help, but all he can see is the receding tail lights.

He takes his phone out of his pocket to call an ambulance, shocked that someone could hurt another human being this way.

'No,' groans the girl, her voice light and cracked.

It startles him, and he stops, leans down closer to her and

says, loudly, 'I'm just calling you an ambulance.' He speaks slowly, not sure that she can hear or understand him.

The girl must be in agony, but she opens her eyes and focuses on his face.

'Please,' she whispers, 'no police, no ambulance.' She sounds like her throat is scratched. He wishes he had some water for her.

'I can't just leave you here. You need help. You really need help. I'll stay until they get here,' he says, dropping his tone to match hers. He looks around him again, but there's no one on the street. He would like it if a woman came by – someone the girl could easily trust.

She starts to move, eyes scrunching and teeth bared with pain. 'Please, I'm begging you,' she says. 'No police, no ambulance.' She is more forceful now, and he worries that she will get up and walk off. He doesn't want to have to grab her and maybe scare her or hurt her more than she is already.

He hesitates. Why doesn't she want him to call the police? Is she running from someone? She looks so young, like she's still a child. He can't leave her here.

'You can come home with me,' he says. 'You can rest and then we'll figure it out. Okay?'

The girl looks at him, her bloodshot eyes struggling to focus.

'I'll keep you safe,' he says, the words coming to him from nowhere. He anticipates that she will say no, but she doesn't.

Instead, she nods and struggles to stand. He helps her, holding out his arm so she can lean on him, and they make their way back to his car. She climbs into the passenger seat with slow, steady movements, calculated to minimise her pain. He waits, his heart racing, wondering if he is doing the right thing.

Once she's in the car, she leans her head back, closes her eyes. 'Oh God,' she says softly.

'It's okay,' he assures her. 'It's okay.'

Only when she is lying in his bed an hour later, her face

bathed and cleaned, does it occur to the man that he may have made a mistake. The girl could be anyone, and she could be running from anyone. Any moment now, an angry boyfriend could show up at his apartment. He gets up from the bed he's made for himself on the sofa and checks that the door is double locked.

As he drifts off to sleep, he wonders at the girl coming with him so willingly. He could be anyone as well. He could be a rapist or a murderer, anything. And yet she climbed painfully into his car and came up to his apartment.

What terrible thing is she running from that would make her accept help from a strange man after midnight?

What terrible, terrible thing?

CHAPTER TWO

GORDON

Today, 7.55 a.m.

Gordon makes his way to the back gate and then onto the street that leads to Gilmore beach. He is determined to find the path that runs between two houses that will take him to the white-gold sand of the beach.

He stops next to his shed and takes a deep breath, adjusting his hat. There is something he needs to remember, something important, but he cannot recall what it is. He opens the back gate and walks out onto the street, his feet sure for the first few steps, and then less certain. He needs to find the path because Del will be here soon. Tonight. Del and Malcolm will be here tonight.

He stops walking and turns around, worried that he is going in the wrong direction. He stops again, mutters, 'Hell,' and turns back. He was going the right way in the first place. He keeps walking, following the road slowly and carefully, looking for something familiar, something he can recognise.

And finally he finds it – the path opens up before him, the slightly overgrown grass the most beautiful thing he has ever seen. The dark, salty smell of sea spray hits his skin and he breathes it in. He walks confidently through the space, his body warm in the heating morning. 'Did it,' he says to himself.

He stands looking at the ocean for a few minutes, and then remembers what he was supposed to do: latch the back gate. The latch is old and a bit tricky and needs to be pushed in a certain way or it doesn't work. 'Ah well,' he sighs. He'll be home soon enough. He turns and makes his way off the beach. 'Come on, old man,' he encourages himself.

It takes him another half an hour to make his way back to his house, relief running through his veins when he spots the familiar blue timber gate. There was a time when this walk only took him five minutes.

In the kitchen, he puts the kettle on to boil and goes to open his front door to let in the breeze. There's a police car parked across the road, silent in the sunshine.

Gordon shakes his head. He can't say he's surprised by that. Not at all.

CHAPTER THREE

ELIZABETH

Today, 8.10 a.m.

They are sitting on the sofa in the living room, close together. Howard has his arm around her shoulders.

She cannot quite believe how fast they have arrived at this point. Only ten minutes have passed since her call. The policemen look too young to be capable of helping. One of them, Constable Brown, has brown hair and light brown eyes. She won't forget his name. The other is Constable Fairweather, tall and thin with thick blonde hair and dark blue eyes. She wonders if anyone ever remarks on the suitability of their surnames, and then she wonders at herself for noticing such a thing now when she should only be consumed with thoughts of Joe. *Where are you, Joe?*

'I was in the kitchen,' Howard is saying, 'making breakfast,' and she opens her mouth to say that he wasn't, that he's lying, but she can feel the subtle pressure of his hand on her shoulder, so she closes her mouth again. This lie will be easily discovered. She told the woman who answered the phone for emergency services that she'd gone to put on a load of laundry. That was a lie as well, so it's probably best she keeps quiet. How soon before the constable asks a question about exactly who was where and they contradict each other? Which one of them will the police think is lying?

'Joe was out the front of the house, playing in the garden,' says Howard, his voice smooth, conscious he is being listened to – really listened to. Constable Brown is watching them, his gaze intense and concentrated. Elizabeth squirms a little, uncomfortable at being observed so closely.

'What was he playing with?' asks the policeman, a slight smile revealing crooked teeth, a little yellowed, which explains the thick, dark smell on the man. He's a smoker, and Elizabeth would like to tell him that he should know better. How can anyone who was born in the last thirty years or so be unaware of the horrors smoking can bring?

'His action figures,' says Howard with quick certainty. 'They're still there – Spider-Man and the Hulk and Batman, you know. He loves his action figures.'

'My son loves his figures as well. I'm always finding them in the strangest places,' says the constable conversationally.

'How old is your son?' Elizabeth asks quickly, seeking the human being behind the badge.

'Seven,' says the constable, and there is a slight softening of his face, a father thinking of his child. Elizabeth glances quickly at Howard, whose expression is perfectly neutral.

She looks away, swallows. The action figures are not all there, not all of them. He wasn't playing with them anyway. He was playing with his plastic fruit set that comes with a wooden knife. He was pretending to be a chef, before... Howard squeezes her shoulder a little harder.

'And Mrs Ealy,' says Constable Brown, directly to her, 'can you tell us exactly how long you looked for Joe before you called triple zero?'

Elizabeth takes a breath, unsure of how she should

answer. 'It was only ten or fifteen minutes. When we realised he was missing, I went through the house and Howard ran up and down the road, and we understood very quickly that he wasn't here at all. I didn't want to wait to call the police. I wanted—'

'We want as many people looking as possible,' says Howard desperately, his voice filled with concern. He is not just a father but the father of a missing child. She can hear how worried he is, and the constables can hear that too.

'And you didn't see anything unusual, like maybe a car out the front of the house that you hadn't seen before, or someone in the street?' Constable Fairweather has a high voice, and he doesn't look at Elizabeth when he asks his question, but rather down at his phone, where he is making notes with quick thumbs.

'No,' says Howard, 'but to be honest...' He stops speaking, waiting, using the pause to make sure both constables are looking at him. 'I've had a weird feeling about the man across the road, the old man named Gordon.'

'Can you explain what you mean by that?' asks Constable Brown, sliding slightly forward in the recliner he is sitting in.

Howard shrugs. 'He really seemed to want to talk to Joe, that's all. I found that kind of weird.'

Elizabeth feels her own words catch in her throat. *Stop it*, she wants to tell her husband. *Stop this right now.* But all she does is make a slight grunting noise. Howard squeezes her shoulder harder.

'Okay, we'll be canvassing the neighbours soon.' Constable Brown glances back at his colleague, who is standing as he makes his notes. Constable Fairweather offers him a barely perceptible nod. Elizabeth is conscious that an entire conversation just took place in a few gestures. These two men have worked together for a long time. They know each other well.

'We've already called the SES and they'll be sending volunteers,' continues Constable Brown. 'We might go through the house again, just to check, if that's okay.'

'Absolutely,' murmurs Howard. 'What should we do?'

'Just sit tight,' says Constable Fairweather. 'I'll start outside, Mark,' he says to the other police officer, and Elizabeth files away Constable Brown's first name. Mark Brown. Innocuous enough to be anyone, but he is not just anyone. He is the man who is looking for Joe.

The two men leave the room.

Elizabeth shrugs Howard's arm from her shoulders and sits forward, dropping her head into her hands.

It's begun. It's begun and nothing can stop this happening – nothing.

CHAPTER FOUR

GORDON

Two weeks ago

'And did I tell you about the fence, the back fence? Did I tell you it's fallen down and I tried to fix it, but I'm going to have to get someone out, although I don't know if I can this close to Christmas. I mean, the shops are crazy already, so I don't know if anyone will be willing to come out.'

Gordon pauses, and then he hears it, the soft, sad sigh, and he knows, just knows, that he's told Malcolm this before, that he's already had this conversation with his son, and his son – his good, kind son – is trying not to say so. He presses the phone harder up against his ear as though this will enable him to keep his thoughts straight.

'Maybe give Mr Hendricks a call, Dad, maybe he can help. Or it can wait until I get there. I'll be with you in two weeks. I'm coming up the week before Christmas and I'm going to stay for a month at least, and then I can get all the jobs done, everything that needs doing. All you have to do is put it on the list.'

Gordon nods his head, because he remembers the list. It's on the fridge and it's a mile long now. There is so much that needs doing, so many things that have broken or rusted away. It's an old house in a street near the sea, and it's a wonder it's still standing. The sea air is good for humans, not so much for metal, and as he looks out of his kitchen window, he can see the brown spots of decay on the railings that surround his front porch.

'Dad,' says Malcom, and Gordon pictures his son standing at the window of his apartment looking out over the city of Sydney. Malcolm works from home, something in cyber security, something that makes him a lot of money, but Gordon can't remember exactly what it is. Last year Gordon spent a week in the city with his son. He had to see a heart specialist and some other doctor, but he can't remember what that one was for. He remembers standing in Malcolm's living room and looking out across the buildings towards a tiny glimpse of harbour, and not understanding how Malcolm didn't find it hard to breathe that high up, surrounded by concrete and steel. They went to a few good pubs, though, had some nice steak dinners with fancy sweet potato fries and pepper sauce, so there were some good aspects to living in the city. The heart doctor recommended he keep away from steak and beer, but the man didn't even look old enough to have a degree, so Gordon took that advice with the salt he put on his fries.

'Remember the list, Dad?' asks Malcolm.

'Yes, the list,' Gordon says quickly. 'But you must be busy, so I won't keep you.'

'I'm never too busy for you, Dad, you know that,' says Malcolm softly, and Gordon feels a warmth in his stomach and chest because he knows it's true. He is a troublesome old man, but his son still loves him and really that's all that matters.

'And I'm bringing Del, remember? She'll be with us for at least two weeks and then Lila will come and get her.'

Gordon smiles, his body filling with a particular kind of happiness at the thought of his six-year-old granddaughter. She lives between her father's apartment and her mother's house, and has handled their divorce with grace and humour – probably because Malcolm and Lila have been so kind to each other, acknowledging that they have grown apart and remaining friends so they can raise Cordelia together. Cordelia, little Del, is a beauty, like her mother, with curly blonde hair and sparkling blue eyes, and she is the light of all their lives.

'We'll go to the beach every day,' says Gordon, excited at the thought.

Last year when Malcolm brought her to visit, Gordon would wake up early just like Del did, and the two of them would creep out of the house and stroll down the road to the beach for a pre-breakfast swim. This year might be different. Sometimes getting to the beach seems difficult, and Gordon finds himself wandering up and down the same street, looking for the path between the houses that leads there, despite having walked the same path most days for decades. He hasn't told Malcolm this because he doesn't want to worry him. But Del is a bright little thing, so she's sure to remember the way.

'I have to go now, Dad, but remember, just put everything on the list, okay?'

'Yes,' says Gordon. 'The list.' The list is on the fridge.

He turns around to find it, muttering, 'Put it on the list, put it on the list' to himself. He grabs it from the fridge and finds a pen on the counter, writes *back fence* carefully and returns the piece of paper to the fridge, fixing it there with a magnet that is a mini photograph of Del, taken at school this year. She looks very pleased with herself, her grin wide and showing her two missing front teeth.

Del loves it here, loves being in the house where her father was raised, where Gordon and Flora had sixty happy years of marriage, with a few bumps along the way, until she died two years ago. It's a good little house, with three nice-sized bedrooms, two bathrooms and a very modern kitchen. Last year

Malcolm insisted on updating the kitchen and bathrooms, and it was out with the old shiny brown tiles and in with white non-slip ones. Gordon protested that it wasn't necessary, but he does like the bath that's easy to get in and out of, and the railings everywhere are handy. At eighty, he is finding some things a struggle. Malcolm wanted to keep fixing things, but after two months of renovations, Gordon was tired and so now his son has to content himself with repairing the rest of the house when he comes to visit, if Mr Hendricks can't help.

'All right, Dad, is there anything else?' asks Malcolm.

'No... no... I'll see you soon,' says Gordon. He wonders if he should mention that the fence at the back has fallen down and he hasn't been able to repair it himself.

He opens his mouth to say something, and then turns to look at the fridge where his list of things he needs to get fixed is, and sees the words *back fence* written clearly. It's on the list, so he doesn't have to worry, and he turns around again to look out of the kitchen window. In the front garden, a couple of rosellas strut around at the bottom of the bird feeder as some lorikeets throw seed down, their beaks rifling through what's on offer. Gordon could watch the birds all day. His eyes are drawn to some movement on the street outside.

'Well, look at that,' he says.

'What is it?' asks Malcolm.

'A car just pulled up outside Dawn and Louie's old house. A fancy one like yours... what it is? A Mercedes, yes, it's a Mercedes – a black one. They must have sold it, but I didn't see the sign.'

'No, it hasn't been sold. Petra is renting it out as a holiday home, remember. That will be nice, especially if they have kids. Del will have someone to play with.'

'Yes, and look, they're getting out. Smart couple, very smart indeed, and they have a child, a little boy. He looks about Del's age. What luck. I wonder how long they're staying? I'll go and say hello later.'

'That's a good idea. Maybe give them some time to settle in, though. I've really got to go now, Dad.'

'Bye, son, love you.'

'Love you too.'

When Gordon ends the call, he realises that he forgot to tell Malcolm about the back fence, but he's sure he'll remember to mention it tomorrow.

He watches the family across the road unloading their bags. The man, tall and thin, with a head of thick brown hair and a neat beard, carries some big suitcases inside, and the woman brings in bag after bag of groceries. She's pretty, with long, curly black hair. The little boy looks a bit like her but not much. He has a much more olive skin tone and he runs back and forth bringing in toys from the back seat of the car. He runs like his feet have wings, darting in and out of the house, and then he stops and looks across the road to Gordon's garden, where there are now white cockatoos stomping around the seed patch, pushing all the other birds about.

The bird feeder was a project he and Malcolm completed together when Malcolm began high school and took a wood-working class. It's designed to look like a small log cabin, painted brown with a red roof and a wide circular platform underneath for birds to perch on. Inside the miniature house is a single piece of wood, so one or two birds can shelter in there. Gordon has happy memories of their time working together, of Malcolm's careful and precise use of the chisel and the hammer and nails. Before every step he asked, 'And what do I do now, Dad?' and then listened intently to the answer. At some point, 'What do I do now, Dad?' became 'Let me tell you what to do, Dad,' and Gordon has no real idea of when that was.

The grass underneath the bird feeder is covered in seeds.

Birds are messy eaters, but Gordon doesn't mind. The little boy seems fascinated. Del loves watching the birds as well.

His father comes to stand behind him and the little boy points at the birds. Gordon can see him saying something. He lifts his hand to wave in case they can see him through the net curtain across the window over the kitchen sink, but they don't wave back. He watches as the man rests his hand on the child's shoulder – well, pushes on his shoulder, pushes hard enough to make the little boy flinch. The man crouches down and Gordon can see him waving his finger in the child's face, his bearded jaw tense with anger as the boy's head drops lower and lower and then he wipes a hand across his face. He's such a little chap and he was only looking at the birds. Why would his father be angry? Why on earth would he be angry?

Gordon decides to put off saying hello for now. Perhaps they've had a long drive and tempers are a bit frayed. He'll go over and say hello tomorrow.

CHAPTER FIVE

ELIZABETH

Two weeks ago

Elizabeth pauses at the kitchen window, a tub of strawberries in her hand. In the front garden she can see that Howard has his hand on Joe's shoulder, can see the little boy cringing, and then she watches as Howard crouches down and lectures and points, and Joe looks down and she knows there will be tears. In her hand, the plastic tub begins to bend and crumple as she squeezes hard, standing frozen to the spot as she watches Howard and Joe – her boys, her lovely boys, except not right now. She feels a throbbing pain in her shoulder the way Joe must be feeling it. She is learning that motherhood can be a visceral experience. What she would most like to do is to go out there, just walk out and say, 'That's enough, Howard.' She would like to shout the words, bringing all her anger at her husband into the world, but she knows better than that. Joe shouldn't have stopped to look at the birds when he had a task to complete. That's a rule.

'He needs to know that once you start something, you don't stop until you have finished,' Howard explained to her last night when she questioned whether the little boy could be allowed to go to bed without having to restack the cupboard where all his plastic plates and cups were so that it was neat and tidy. He was only five, and so a task that would have taken Elizabeth a couple of minutes took him a lot longer. Howard ruffled his hair when he was done, said, 'That's my boy. I'm proud of you.' And the smile Joe gave him nearly broke her heart. Howard was good at that. His approval made you feel like you had stepped into a warm ray of sunshine on a bleak winter's day.

Her hand feels wet and she looks down. 'Stupid,' she mutters. The container of strawberries is crushed, the glistening red fruit squashed into pulp. She dumps the contents into the dustbin and washes her hands. Hopefully Howard won't look in there. And if he does, she will say that she packed them badly for the journey down from Sydney to this rented holiday home. She will accept the consequences of that; he told her over and over to be careful of how she packed the fruit.

Joe is back to taking things out of the car again. She can hear his small footsteps running in and out of the house, up and down the stairs and in and out of the bedroom that will be his for the time they are here.

'A whole month near the beach,' Elizabeth told her mother. 'There's an ocean view from the top level and it's just a stroll to the beautiful white sands of Gilmore Beach. It will be heaven.' She made sure to keep her voice light and infused with excitement.

'But you already live near the ocean,' her mother, Jean, protested. 'Why not just stay home and visit the beach every day?'

'Howard wants to get away. And it will be nice for Joe to see another town, to be somewhere different. It will be good for all of us.'

She was standing at her kitchen window at home at the time, looking out at the harbour, watching the sailboats getting ready to go out for the day. It was 5 a.m. and she had been up for half an hour. She always got up at 4.30, needing the time to get everything ready for when Howard and Joe woke up. Her mother was also an early riser, and they both enjoyed their morning phone conversations over their first cup of coffee. Right now, Jean was in Philadelphia, and that meant Elizabeth's 5 a.m. calls were actually at 1 p.m. for her mother.

'The house doesn't need to look perfect,' Howard always says, but she likes it neat, likes things in order, likes to feel that everything is under control. And she also knows that while Howard says things like this, especially in front of their friends, he likes it neat and under control too.

'I'm done now, can I go and play?' asks Joe, coming into the kitchen. He has pushed his hair away from his face, and his cheeks are flushed with the effort of bringing his things in from the car.

Elizabeth walks over and crouches down next to him. 'Well, you know the rules in my house,' she says.

Joe nods, his beautiful eyes serious in his beautiful face. 'Before I play, I need to get a hug and a snack and hear a joke.'

Elizabeth laughs, and Joe laughs with her, and she enfolds his small body in a long hug, making sure to hold on until he starts to move. Then she stands up and goes over to the worn cream kitchen bench and picks up a plate with some apple slices and carrot sticks and two chocolate chip cookies. Joe loves to eat. He is always just a little afraid that there will not be another meal, and Elizabeth hates that he feels that way.

'Knock, knock,' she says, and Joe jumps up and down. He loves knock, knock jokes.

'Who's there?' he giggles.

'Theodore,' she says, trying to keep a straight face at his glee.

'Theodore who?' His green eyes widen as he tries to guess the answer.

'Theodore wasn't open so I knocked,' she says, and she watches as his lips move while he repeats the joke in his head, making sense of it. And then he giggles. 'The door wasn't open, I get it, I get it!'

'That's because you are a very clever little boy.' She hands him his snack plate and walks with him to the small sitting room where the television is. The internet is working, and she quickly finds *The Garfield Show*, a current favourite, and leaves him there happily swinging his legs on a blue sofa that looks like it's seen better days. The whole house looks like it's seen better days. It's one of those 1970s red-brick houses, and driving through the small south coast town, she saw that the whole place had once been full of them. Now, every second or third lot is under construction. Big homes for holiday rentals are going up all over the place, and soon the small town with one coffee shop will blossom into a full tourist destination.

She searched for a long time on the booking website to find this place. Howard wanted somewhere far away from everything so he could really decompress from a hard year. He's in advertising sales, responsible for bringing in clients who will pay millions of dollars a year for their marketing. This year, the big clients have all been pulling back, dragging their feet on budgets, not interested in new campaigns. Howard has struggled with rejection, but in the last few months he's managed to bring in a brand-new client – a young woman who owns a clothing website that turns over millions and millions of dollars. She was impressed by his ideas for her social media presence. Elizabeth smiles as she remembers his triumphant phone call to let her know he had 'landed a big one'. That's when he suggested the month away.

She returns to the kitchen with its laminate bench top and wheezing fridge. The brown cabinets don't bother her, because everything is very clean. This is the first time the house has been rented out, according to the owner. *My parents are both*

*gone now and my brother and I were going to sell, but we
thought we would try this first. The house is old and needs to be
updated, but everything works and there is really good internet
connection and a new television.*

The woman, whose name is Petra, has made a real effort.
Aside from the place being clean, she has left a gift basket with
wine and fruit and chocolates on the old timber dining table,
and Elizabeth noticed that the towels in the bathrooms are
brand new, as is the bedding. There are three bedrooms, so she
and Howard can sleep separately if they want to. Elizabeth has
a feeling that she will get one of her headaches tonight. It's
easier for her to be alone, so Howard isn't disturbed as she fights
the tight band of tension that pulls at her ears and burns her
eyes.

'Car's unpacked,' says Howard, joining her in the kitchen
and sitting down at the table.

'Do you want something to eat?'

'Oh, you haven't made anything yet?' he asks, and she feels
her pulse rise just a little.

'I was unpacking and I made Joe a snack. I was going to start
right now. It's a bit late for lunch, but maybe cheese and
crackers and some wine?'

'Perhaps I should take Joe to the beach. I can get myself
some takeaway food if you're feeling tired,' he says drily.

'No, no, I'll make you a nice salad,' Elizabeth says quickly,
rushing to grab the ingredients, wanting to keep him happy but
mostly wanting to give Joe a little bit of space and time to enjoy
his TV show. Howard wants to teach him to swim properly on
this holiday, but Joe is afraid of the sea – afraid of water, actually – and swimming lessons have not been going well. Most
weeks when they return from the lesson, he has only managed
to be in the water for a few minutes without crying. Howard
thinks Elizabeth should just leave him with the teacher and
walk away, but she can't do that and his instructor, Ben, agrees.

'This little man will swim when he's ready,' he says every week. She is always conscious that Joe has fears that she may not know about. She doesn't want to push him to do things that might upset him. 'We can't mollycoddle him,' Howard said when she told him this. 'One day he'll regret not being able to swim. You don't want him teased at school, do you?' She couldn't argue with that.

'Great, a salad will be nice,' Howard says. 'I may just lie down for a bit.' He stands up to leave the kitchen, and she smiles, a perfect smile. She practises it in front of the mirror so she knows it's perfect. Howard is a good-looking man, with thick brown hair and light grey-blue eyes. He's at the gym every morning at 7 a.m., so his shoulders are broad and his stomach flat. He wouldn't tell anyone, but he uses an extensive skincare regime so that he always looks his best, artfully trimmed beard included.

If Elizabeth looks at photos of the two of them together, she is always struck by how beautiful they are. Her own hair is darker than his, curly but well managed by her hairdresser. She has it tucked behind her ears to keep it out of the way, and she wears it down when she's with Howard, because that's how he likes it. She has deep blue eyes and she works very hard to make sure she is still the same size she was on their wedding day twenty years ago. Neither of them looks their age. Howard is two years older than her, but he is wearing his forty-six years well.

She sinks down onto one of the chairs, tired from the long day after her early start. Howard will sleep for an hour, so there's no need for her to rush to make him something. He probably isn't even hungry, because they stopped on the road for brunch. He just needs to know that she's busy.

The other thing she thinks when she looks at photos of the two of them is that they would have created a beautiful child together. They would have, but they didn't – they couldn't.

CHAPTER SIX

The girl sleeps and sleeps, and each day the man wonders if he should call the police or a doctor. He has to go to work, so he leaves her in his apartment, making sure there is water by the bed and some things to eat. He comes home at night and there is evidence that she has gotten herself up, finished her water and, on the third day, had a shower. He finds her in bed, dressed in a pair of his tracksuit pants and a T-shirt, her bloodied clothes in the garbage.

At night he sits by the bed and tries to get her to talk to him.

What's your name? How old are you? Who did this to you? Are you afraid of someone?

He wants to call the police, to take her to the hospital, to get her real help, but each time he suggests it, her desperate, begging refusal prevents him from doing anything.

More days pass. Each night the man comes home expecting to find her gone, but she is still there after a week. He locks up his computer when he leaves, feeling bad, but it's all he has of value in the apartment and the girl could be anyone.

One night he comes home and finds her out of bed. She has cleaned, done a load of washing and cooked dinner. Over pasta with bottled tomato sauce, he asks the same questions he has asked every night. What's your name? How old are you? What happened?

The girl refuses to answer. 'If you can give me another week or two, I'll go. I just need to get a little stronger.'

'There are places to go, people who can help. I'll go with you and be with you when you talk to them,' the man tells her again and again.

'No, no refuges, no police. No one can help. I'll go if you want me to.' She is stubborn, and as the bruises fade, she becomes more stubborn, more vocal. He notices that she's pretty, and tries not to notice. He keeps asking his questions and finally she answers one.

'Fifteen,' she says, and he chokes on the cup of coffee he's drinking.

'You're a kid,' he says, and she looks at him, holding his gaze.

'I was,' she says, and he believes her. Whatever has happened to her has taken the last vestiges of her childhood, stolen them away forever.

'This doesn't feel right,' he says. 'I'm an adult and you're a child. Legally a child, at least.'

'I need another week. That's all. While you've been at work, I've been planning, thinking. I'll get a job. I'll make it work. Just don't tell anyone I'm here, please. I'm begging you.'

'Okay,' he agrees.

At night, on the uncomfortable sofa, he sometimes wakes in a cold sweat from a dream of being confronted by a faceless man, by the police, by anyone who could accuse him of doing the wrong thing. But he can see she is getting better every day, growing stronger. She even smiles every now and again. Soon it is impossible to tell that she was hurt at all.

'Thank you,' she says to him every day.

He keeps their secret.

CHAPTER SEVEN

GORDON

Ten days ago

It is 6 a.m. when Gordon walks out of his house to fill up the bird feeder. The gathered lorikeets scatter into the nearby tree, their blue heads turning this way and that as they watch him, far enough away so he can't touch them, but close enough so that he knows they trust him. They wait patiently while he scrapes off empty shells and then tops up the seed.

'There you go,' he says. 'That'll be nice, won't it. Come on then, tuck in.' He steps back a couple of paces, and the birds wait a moment before swooping down to feed, green wings fluttering.

Gordon smiles, looking around his little garden and across the road to the front garden of the house where the family arrived last week. Dawn and Louie kept it neat and tidy, a green lawn and a surround of English box hedging running along the timber fence on all sides. Flora preferred a profusion of plants and trees in her garden, but Dawn liked things neat and simple.

So far, he has not seen the family outside at all, and so he has stayed away. He doesn't want to intrude. He's been waiting to see the woman or the man outside so that he can call a greeting. But the house has remained silent, the blinds at the front kept down. He supposes that is to keep things cool as the days heat up. It's going to be a warm one today, getting to twenty-nine degrees, the young woman on the news has just informed him. He's glad about that. Last summer was nothing but rain, rain and more rain, so it will be nice to have a proper Australian summer filled with heat and sunshine. He adjusts his blue hat on his head, shading his eyes from the sun a bit more.

He studies the front garden of the house for a moment, trying to pick out what looks different, and then he sees the small lump near the black metal gate. It looks like a blanket of some sort. Curious and unable to help himself, he walks closer to his own gate so he can see better. As he watches, the blanket, which is brown with cream stripes, begins to move. Gordon pauses. It is most likely a possum, although how a possum got a blanket he doesn't know. But if it is a possum and he goes to try and free it, he is likely to get a nasty bite. The blanket keeps moving, and Gordon watches, staying firmly on his side of the gate, until suddenly a small head pops out and he can see it's the little boy. He starts to laugh. 'I thought you were a possum,' he calls, and the child jumps to his feet, looking startled and afraid.

'Sorry,' calls Gordon, and then he opens his own slightly rusty metal gate and walks out, crossing to stand by the gate on the other side of the road. 'I didn't mean to scare you.' An image of Malcolm at the same age flashes into his mind, so clear it could be yesterday. The past feels like it's right there all the time now. It's the present that he's struggling with.

The little boy crosses his arms and scowls. 'I'm not scared.'

'Obviously you aren't. It's very early for you to be up, isn't it?'

'*You're* up,' says the child, a touch of a smile on his face.

'I always get up early so I can give the birds fresh seeds.'

Behind him he can hear the clicks and whistles of the birds enjoying their breakfast.

'You've got thousands and thousands of birds.'

'I do, yes. I like to watch them.'

'Me too,' says the little boy wistfully. 'I was on the bench but I came down here to watch them.' He bends down and picks up the blanket and wraps it around his shoulders.

'Maybe you should go inside if you're cold. Ask your mum for a jumper. It's not that hot right now.'

'I'm not allowed inside,' he says.

'Oh,' says Gordon. He mulls this over and then says, 'My name's Gordon. What's your name?'

'I'm Joe,' says the little boy.

'Well, I'm pleased to meet you, Joe. How long are you staying here for?'

Joe shrugs his shoulders.

'Why are you not allowed inside?' Gordon asks, trying to remember if he and Flora ever put Malcolm outside in the mornings. Perhaps Joe's parents are having a lie-in, and that's fair enough, although he wouldn't have a child outside the front of a house, rather at the back, and he especially wouldn't let a child be out the front of a holiday home. But Dawn and Louie's back garden isn't as nice as the front, because there's too much shade from the large fig trees for the grass to grow, and there are large roots everywhere. The council would never let them cut down the trees, so perhaps that's why the child is in the front. Gilmore is a safe enough place, but still, you never knew really. The strangest things happen. Flora was always afraid of something happening to Malcolm when he was small. Gordon had to keep encouraging her to let go a bit, to allow the boy to climb trees and swim in the ocean.

'I wouldn't be able to survive losing him,' she told him.

'We're not going to lose him, Flora,' Gordon comforted her. He understood, though, and he knew that she was made more careful by the lack of siblings for Malcolm. One was all they got, and they were grateful for him.

Gordon realises the boy is studying him intensely, his lips moving as though he is whispering to himself. Perhaps he's trying to decide whether or not to trust him, and Gordon knows this is not the time to pester the child with questions. If he wants to tell him, he will.

'I had a bad dream in the night and I cried and woke everyone up so I had to come outside to sleep,' says Joe.

Gordon feels his mouth drop open a little. What on earth is he meant to say to that?

'Now I have to stay out here until Howard comes to get me, and I need to pee and I'm thirsty.' The boy's little face falls with the dilemma, and Gordon feels his hands ball into fists.

'Who is Howard?' he asks.

'He's my... he's my foster dad, but I'm not allowed to call him Dad, and Elizabeth is my foster mum, and do you want to know a secret?' Joe steps right up to the front gate of the house and pushes his little arm through the bars of the slatted metal, gesturing for Gordon to come closer.

Gordon steps towards the gate, bending slightly so that his ear is closer to Joe's mouth. 'What's your secret?' he whispers, even though there's no one else in the road. The calls and chirps of the birds at the feeder are the only things he can hear.

'Sometimes,' says Joe in a loud stage whisper, 'when Howard is at work, Elizabeth lets me call her Mum.'

Gordon stands up straight. 'Well, that's nice,' he says lamely, an immediate opinion of Howard forming. He sounds like a dreadful man.

'Joe – get in here,' a man – the man who is obviously Howard – bellows from the front door. Gordon hadn't realised that anyone was standing there.

Joe's face pales and he whips around and darts to the door, dragging his blanket behind him.

The boy is inside the house and gone in a moment and Gordon is left staring at Howard. He raises his hand and tries for a smile. 'Hello, welcome. I was just chatting to your... to Joe. He's a lovely chap. I'm Gordon, I live across the road.' He turns slightly to indicate his house, but when he turns back, the front door is closed. The man is gone and the house is silent once more.

CHAPTER EIGHT

ELIZABETH

Ten days ago

'Get in here.' The words jolt Elizabeth out of her light doze. Her eyes are gritty with lack of sleep. She has been awake since 2 a.m., when Joe cried out in his sleep and woke them. She tried to get up quicker than Howard, but he beat her to Joe's room, switching on the light and blinding them all for a moment before hauling the boy bodily out of bed and dragging him to the front door, throwing him out. 'If you need to make noise at night, you're an animal,' he hissed, 'and animals sleep outside.' He slammed the front door behind him, then held his hand up before Elizabeth could say anything. 'You know where he comes from. You know what he could grow up to become. I'm doing the best for him so that he breaks the cycle he was born into. He needs discipline and boundaries. Don't you dare go near him.'

He moved towards Elizabeth, forcing her to step back and to keep stepping back until she reached the bedroom they were sleeping in, then he gave her a light push. 'Get into bed,' he said, and she obeyed. 'Go to sleep,' he told her as he climbed in next to her, and she shut her eyes.

And then she waited as fury bubbled inside her and her skin grew clammy with horror.

Howard is getting worse. Again. Her twenty-year marriage has contained the cycles of violence for as long as she can remember. The cycle is a theory, developed by a doctor, that Elizabeth has come to know well. First there is the tension phase: weeks or months when she is walking on eggshells, when she tries to get everything right, when she agrees with everything he says and ignores his snide remarks and criticisms. And then there is the acute phase – the explosion – and she knows she will end up hurt in some way. But then there is the honeymoon phase, where he begs for forgiveness, where he buys her gifts, where he is kind and loving and giving and everything she married him for. It sounds simple enough when she thinks about it, but nothing is ever that simple. Sometimes the honeymoon phase lasts months and months and the tension phase lasts even longer. The blow-ups are intense and difficult but usually over quickly. Howard has not been this angry, this aggressive for nearly a year now, but she has still been careful, still done everything she can to keep him happy, aware that at any moment he could ramp things up. That is the point, she understands – exactly the point. But now Joe is in their lives and everything is different.

Last night, her heart was racing so fast she felt she couldn't breathe properly, but she waited, not moving, until eventually Howard emitted the light snore that she knew meant deep sleep, and only then did she creep out of bed, one limb at a time, and go to grab a blanket for Joe.

She couldn't bring him in, she knew that, but it was chilly at night, and in the morning she would accept what came when Howard realised she had given the boy a blanket.

She crept down the passage to the front door, feeling the

rough brown carpet underneath her feet, one tiny step at a time, her heart hammering in her chest, her ears straining to hear anything.

As she got to the door and began twisting the lock to open it, she felt him behind her, felt his breath on her neck, and she froze, a woman in a horror movie, hoping the monster would pass her by.

They stood there like that for at least a minute, Elizabeth's heart bursting out of her chest, her stomach churning, and then, without a word, he turned and went back to bed. He wanted Joe to have a blanket, which meant he regretted his reaction. He wouldn't say it, wouldn't tell her or apologise to Joe, but she knew him well enough to know that his return to bed without saying anything meant just that.

She found Joe hiding by the side of the house, and she took him in her arms and wrapped him in the blanket, rocked him until his tears ceased. 'I'm sorry, I'm sorry,' she kept whispering, until she felt the heaviness of sleep in his small body. She was overjoyed in the strangest way to remember that there was a bench at the front of the house, cream metal rusting in the sea air. It was obviously there so the previous owners could watch the birds in the garden across the street, the same way she had been doing from the kitchen window.

The bench was covered in an outdoor cushion, green and musty-smelling with age, but comfortable enough. It wasn't made for a small child to sleep on, especially not at night, but at least it was there when there was no other choice. She placed Joe on the bench and crept back inside.

When she returned to bed, Howard was awake, but he said nothing to her. After that, she got out of bed every twenty minutes to check on Joe, as Howard had known she would. When the sun finally rose, she felt she could rest a little at last. But Howard's yelling woke her.

She is beyond exhausted. She climbs out of bed and throws

on a pair of shorts and a T-shirt, trying not to look in the mirror when she brushes her hair. Her face is pale and her blue eyes sunken, dark rings underneath. She quickly applies light make-up. Howard hates to see any evidence of her distress. The last time she looked like this was... She can't think about that, or the time before, or the time before that. She needs to make this work. Joe is their chance to get things right, to really be a family, and that is all she has ever wanted. A real family.

Growing up, she assumed it would be easily done. Her parents were happily married and they'd built a life together, sharing the raising of their two daughters. Many years ago, Elizabeth's sister, Natalie, moved to the US to spend a semester studying physiotherapy. She fell in love with the country and a wonderful man and never returned. Their parents were happy to divide their time between Australia and Philadelphia, spending the American summer months with Natalie and her large family: a husband and four sons. If Elizabeth was honest with herself, she understood that they were extending their time in the US more and more. This year her mother packed winter clothes as well, saying, 'Sean and the boys say we've never really had a winter with snow, and it would be so lovely to spend a real white Christmas with them. It will only be this year, but I'm really looking forward to it.' She glanced up from her suitcase, catching Elizabeth's gaze, and then shrugged her shoulders apologetically. Her mother looks more like Natalie, who has brown hair and blue eyes, instead of the black hair that Elizabeth inherited from her father. Her face is as easy to read as Natalie's, too, and Elizabeth saw the pity her mother felt for her as the words hit home. She would be alone for Christmas, just her and Howard.

It was only March, and Elizabeth wanted to protest, wanted to tell her mother that they needed to be here for her, but she's forty-two years old and she has shared many quiet, childless Christmases with her parents. She can't begrudge them the noise and chaos and joy of a Christmas with Natalie. Her parents like Howard, but they are not fond of him the way they are fond of Sean, Natalie's husband. Howard always makes an effort when they come over, but their relationship has only ever felt forced, and the longer Elizabeth is married, the worse it gets. Howard wasn't always this man, that's how she comforts herself. He wasn't always like this.

If they had been able to have children, if their attempts at adoption hadn't fallen through, if they hadn't had to become foster parents, then perhaps everything would be different. If he never had a bad day at work, if she was smarter, if it never rained... She feels silly when she begins her justifications in her head. But she can't help herself. Wrapped up in all of it is her real love for Howard and her dependence on him.

Joe is their last chance. And because of this, she is acutely conscious that he must never see them argue, lest he inform his social worker without meaning to. That's why she holds back so much, although she has always held back when it comes to Howard. It's easier than confronting him. Projecting a perfect marriage is tiring and leads to headaches. The strain of being watched and judged by their case manager is also taking its toll on Howard. It must be, or he wouldn't be behaving like this.

Elizabeth is waiting for him to relax. She is praying that he will relax, that he will learn to just be with Joe and accept him for the boy he is, instead of worrying about where he came from. As foster parents, they haven't been given all the information, but they were given some. They know there was terrible neglect when Joe was a baby, and they know that he had a wonderful foster family for the first three years of his life. They know that his mother managed to get herself off drugs and that she then demanded him back, only to slip again. And now he is here with them, and he is sweet and kind and just wants to be loved, but any time he shows a hint of unacceptable behaviour, Howard panics. 'We can't let him turn out like his parents. It's our duty to make him a better person,' he says. Joe's biological mother, his real mother, was very young when she had him, a child of the foster system herself. After what happened the last time, she knows she will never get him back. But she wants him back, very much so. Jenny is manipulative and sly, will do anything to get what she wants.

Elizabeth shudders as she remembers seeing the news item, watching the story unfold. *Young child advertised for sale on the internet.* The story was everywhere for a few days. A young woman had tried to sell her four-year-old son for fifty thousand dollars. When she was caught, she protested that it was a joke, told the police that she would never have given him up even if she had been offered the money. But no one believed her.

Elizabeth felt the burning anger she always felt when she heard about child abuse cases, the fiery fury at the injustice that prevented her from having a child and yet allowed those who would discard their own children to have as many as they liked.

When Peter, their social worker – or case manager, as he was known – called her a few months later, he said, 'Look, I'm going to be upfront with this. This kid has come from a very hard place, and you will have read about it. We can't get it wrong again.' She connected the dots when she read Joe's file, goosebumps of shock appearing on her skin as deep despair for the child flowed through her.

Sometimes she finds herself shaking and sweating at the thought of the kind of person who would actually buy a child, and what that might have meant for Joe. It sounds like the stuff of movies, but Elizabeth has been involved with the foster system for long enough to know that however terrible her imagination is, what people are willing to do to children is worse.

Joe was instantly and forever removed from his mother despite her protests that she loved her boy and her promises to give up her drug of choice for good. The department had given her many chances to do just that. She'd even managed to get herself a university degree while she was sober. Elizabeth cannot help her hatred of Jenny, who seems to be smarter than her doctors and social workers. Just last week she sent Elizabeth an email begging for the chance to speak to her son. She told her that she had gotten herself straight and that she was ready to be a mother. *I'm going to put my degree to use. I'm going to be someone my son can count on. You need to let me see him*, she wrote.

Howard was furious and Elizabeth terrified. Jenny was not supposed to have their email address or to know where her son was. Howard called their case worker and threatened to involve the police. Peter calmed him down and Elizabeth had to change her email address, but the fear that Jenny will emerge from rehab and come and find Joe clings and leads to terrible nightmares. No one knows who his father is except Jenny, and she has chosen not to share that information. Elizabeth fears him turning up one day as well, just turning up and demanding his son. It's so incredibly complicated and she feels she has to be vigilant all the time. And at the same time, she has to be vigilant about what Joe sees of her and Howard, and how Howard treats Joe. Will Joe tell Peter about last night? Will he remember it in a few weeks' time? The tension headache that has been simmering for a day pulls tighter, and she rubs her forehead, grabbing some tablets from her bag and swallowing them down with water from the bathroom tap.

She heads to the kitchen to find Joe eating a big bowl of cereal as Howard makes pancakes. 'Someone has an appetite this morning,' Howard says cheerfully. Joe's legs swing happily back and forth as he spoons the chocolate cereal into his mouth. 'We don't need to feed him rubbish food,' Howard tells Elizabeth whenever he sees her giving him a cookie or some chocolate, but the chocolate cereal that is basically a dessert was his idea. 'It's a holiday,' he said as they walked around the store buying things for the trip. Joe jumped up and down, his excitement at fever pitch.

'I'm getting pancakes,' he says now, his green eyes shining, and Elizabeth touches his cheek gently, holding back the hug she wants to give him, because Howard hates it when she is overly emotional and touchy-feely with the child.

'You deserve pancakes because you are a brave boy,' she says.

'I am,' he agrees. 'I slept all night by myself.' A story changed instantly; a memory that will sound exciting when related to Peter. Joe is doing exactly what Elizabeth does; he is creating a better way of seeing the situation. He is too young to know what he's doing, but perhaps his early years have forced him to develop this skill already. *You poor baby.*

'Yes, you did, buddy and we're proud of you,' says Howard. He hands her a cup of coffee as the smell of pancakes catches in her throat. 'Looks like you need this,' he tells her. 'It's always hard to sleep well in a new place.'

Elizabeth takes the coffee with a weak smile. It is made just the way she likes it, with almond milk and one spoon of sugar.

'Sit down, you can have the second pancake,' he says, and she obeys him. He places a pancake in front of Joe, who has finished his cereal. 'Can you pour the syrup yourself, or do you need help?' he asks.

'I can do it,' says Joe, a huge smile on his face.

Elizabeth sips her coffee and watches him as he concentrates hard so as not to spill even a single drop of syrup.

What the hell is wrong with you? she hears her sister say. Natalie would never put up with Howard's hot-and-cold treatment. She would call him out every time he did it and then she would leave him if he didn't change. But Natalie has been married to Sean for eighteen years. Sean used to play professional football in some minor team in the US but now he coaches at university. He's six foot five and all muscle, but Natalie runs their lives. She makes all the decisions, she's in charge of discipline for their four boys, and she deals with the house – that's in addition to treating patients from home. Sean is more than happy to let her do it. Elizabeth has watched the two of them together, has seen how Sean's eyes still follow his wife around a room and tried not to let envy cloud her thinking. She is happy that her sister has such a good marriage.

Elizabeth's phone is in her pocket with messages from both her sister and her mother asking how things are going. She needs to reply to them, but that requires a summoning of energy so that she only relates something positive, only says that things are wonderful. She needs to be rested and in control of her emotions when she does that, and right now, she's exhausted. Howard is the one in control of everything.

Compared to her younger sister, Elizabeth feels like a dried-up shell of a person. She has failed to be a mother, failed to be what Howard wanted her to be, failed to be happy. She wishes she was one of those women who are dedicated to their careers, but she's not. She studied to be a pharmacist because she couldn't get into medicine; it was supposed to be something she did while she kept trying to find a way into her degree of choice. Instead, she found herself working for years in a profession that she had no real love for.

Once she met Howard and got married, she imagined that pregnancy would put an end to her career, but it never happened. Now she works part-time in a pharmacy close to home, which means that she was easily able to change her hours to take care of Joe when Peter contacted them. She works while Joe is at school, spending her days dispensing medicine and answering the same questions from elderly customers she answered the day before. If she and Howard are allowed to adopt Joe, allowed to keep him in their lives forever, she will give up her job entirely and not miss it at all. If she can make this work, if she can just get through the first few months, which she knows are going to be difficult, then maybe, just maybe, she and Howard will be approved to adopt Joe and they can finally be the picture-perfect family they have always wanted to be. He's been with them for a couple of months now and she's waiting for things to get better between him and Howard, waiting and hoping that the longed-for family will become a reality.

But in order to do that, she has to pretend, the same way that Joe has somehow understood that he has to pretend. She has to pretend that Howard did not fling Joe outside last night for waking him up. That Howard does not load the child up with so many rules and regulations it would make an adult's head spin. That Howard is not capable of hurting him.

He slides a plate in front of her. 'Eat up,' he says jovially.

And so she does.

CHAPTER NINE

GORDON

Today, 10.00 a.m.

He holds the small box of salted almonds in his hand, eating each one separately, making sure to chew properly so he doesn't accidentally choke on one of them. Almonds are very good for you and he likes them. As he eats, he watches what's going on through the kitchen window, the white net curtains giving him privacy. He worries about choking a lot nowadays. Choking, slipping, tripping. It's no fun getting old, but better than the alternative.

Things have gotten crazy over the road. He didn't even know Gilmore had so many people, although a whole lot of them are probably summer visitors, here to enjoy the beach. It's the school holidays after all. There are so many faces he doesn't recognise. This morning, he was in the garden watching everyone arrive and a woman waved to him, calling out, 'Hello, Gordon,' as she made her way to a group of volunteers handing out the orange vests the searchers would wear. He has no idea who she was or how she knew his name. He waved back anyway.

The school holidays mean it's nearly Christmas. 'Del will be here soon,' he tells himself. He pops another almond into his mouth, noticing that his hands are trembling a little.

Outside the house across the street, one police car has grown to two and then three, and the SES people are everywhere now. A constable, a woman with short grey hair, seems to be in charge, although he knows there are more police inside the house.

After his walk this morning, he made himself some tea and was just about to drink it when the bell rang.

He went quickly to open the front door, hoping that he would be able to see what was going on across the road. A young woman was standing there.

'Hiya,' she said, a big smile on her face, a bright pink cap on her head. 'We're looking for the little boy from across the road. He's gone missing.'

'Missing,' Gordon said, as he felt his heart flutter inside him. 'Joe?'

'That's it. We've just started. He's been gone for about an hour. Do you know him? Have you seen him? Have you seen anything?' She fired the questions at him, causing him to rub his head as he tried to make sense of them.

'No... no,' he murmured. 'I haven't. Not today. Not at all.' Had he seen him? He didn't want to tell the young woman he wasn't sure. He wasn't sure at all.

'Okay, well, he's only little, so his parents are quite worried. If you see anything or remember anything, just pop across the road and tell one of the volunteers, okay?' Her voice got louder and louder, and Gordon realised that he was standing and staring at her, so she assumed he wasn't quite understanding her.

'I will,' he said, and she turned and left.

Standing behind the closed front door, his whole body was hot, and he felt in desperate need of a shower and fresh clothes.

He hurried to his bathroom and stood under the water for at least fifteen minutes. He thought he heard the bell ring, but he wasn't sure, so he didn't move until his heart had slowed and he was feeling better. Joe was missing. Little Joe. When had he last seen him?

He is still hungry. The almonds haven't done much. 'Did I have breakfast?' he wonders aloud. He decides to make himself another snack, cutting up some nice Brie to put on the special crackers Malcolm sends him from Sydney, made with seeds and bits of fig so they go well with the cheese. He's only just finished preparing his plate when the bell rings, and he drops the knife he is using, cursing the clanging noise it makes as it lands on the floor. He bends down slowly to pick it up, and the bell rings again. Gordon throws the dirty knife in the sink and goes to the door, his knees aching from bending too quickly. He is flustered and sweating again.

Two policemen are standing at the door.

'Hi, I'm Constable Brown and this is Constable Fair-weather. We were wondering if we could have a chat with you, Mr Perry,' one of them says.

'Yes,' Gordon replies, knowing he has no option but to agree. He steps back. 'Yes, of course. Come in, come in.'

'Have you been here the whole morning, Mr Perry?' one of the policemen asks as they follow him into the living room.

'I went for a walk,' he says, 'and then I had a shower. Please sit.' He indicates the pale leather sofas, slightly embarrassed by how worn they are. He doesn't want to give them up. When he and Flora bought them, twenty years ago, it was the most they'd ever spent on a sofa set. Flora giggled, calling him a 'big spender', and then started singing the song while he laughed. He sees her now, walking across the furniture store, kicking out her legs and turning her head left and right as she sang, her hands on her hips and her brown eyes filled with laughter.

'Ah, that would explain it,' says one of the constables, and

Flora disappears. Gordon has already forgotten his name, and he hopes it doesn't matter. 'Someone came over to see if they could chat to you a while ago, but there was no answer.' He can't remember talking to anyone today at all.

'I had... had a shower. Perhaps I was in the shower?' he says to the constables.

'That might be it,' says the man with brown hair.

Gordon sits down so that the constables will sit as well. His legs feel a bit weak.

'Are you aware that the little boy from across the road has gone missing?' asks one of the constables as he takes a notebook out of his pocket.

'Yes, yes... I saw you there when I got back from my walk. I mean, I didn't know why you were... there, but I did see you, and then while I was having my tea, a young woman...' He closes his eyes as an image of a pink cap appears. He spoke to someone this morning – the woman with the pink cap. 'A young woman,' he continues, more certain now, 'came over and asked if I'd seen him, but I hadn't... I hadn't... not... not... not for a bit. Would you like something to drink?' he asks.

'No, thank you,' says the shorter of the two policemen, his reply curt, so Gordon doesn't offer again.

'Of course I would have helped look for him, but then... I needed a shower and...' Gordon stops speaking, disliking the way the constables are looking at him.

'Mr Ealy, that's Joe's father – foster father – told us this morning that you like to spend time with Joe,' says the brown-haired constable. He has dark eyes and a square jaw.

'I do,' says Gordon. 'He's a lovely little chap.'

'Do you often encourage children you don't know to come over here?' asks the constable, his words deliberate.

Gordon feels worry creeping along his skin. Why would they ask him something like that?

'Well... they like the birds, you see,' he says, gesturing

towards the front garden, an uneasy feeling flickering inside him. 'Joe likes the birds, but he... that man...' he shakes his head, 'Howard doesn't like him to spend time with me. I think, well, I think he doesn't like me.' He feels like he's babbling, and he should probably stop.

'Right, right...' says the constable. 'And you live here alone, do you?' He glances at his colleague quickly, and Gordon feels himself flush. His memory may be playing up, but he can still see when someone is trying to communicate something about him.

'My grandad keeps finches,' says the blonde constable kindly.

'Does he?' asks Gordon, intrigued.

'Yeah, he breeds them and sells them to pet shops. I used to love going over when I was a kid. I helped him feed them.' The man smiles at the memory.

'Joe liked the birds,' says Gordon.

'Liked?' asks the constable with brown eyes. 'As in past tense?'

'What?' asks Gordon, confused, and the man sighs.

'I asked you if you live alone, Mr Perry. Does anyone else live here?' He gestures around the room as though Gordon is an idiot. Gordon doesn't like him at all. He's unnecessarily rude, though the blonde one is nice enough.

'I do live alone,' he says. 'Malcolm is coming... he's coming soon. Malcolm is my son.'

'Yeah, okay,' says the constable. 'And you're sure you haven't seen Joe this morning?'

Gordon has never been questioned by the police, but this doesn't feel like simple questioning. This feels like an interrogation. He clasps his hands together tightly, hoping to keep himself focused. He doesn't want to say the wrong thing.

'That woman who came to the door asked me, and I told her I hadn't seen him,' he says, his head starting to hurt.

'Yes, but we just wanted to make sure. Do you mind if we take a quick look around?' asks the tall, thin one with the light hair. Was his name Fair... something?

'I don't mind,' says Gordon. He stands, hearing his knees click in protest.

'No, you sit,' says the dark-haired constable rudely. Gordon sits.

The policemen take only a few minutes to go through the house. Gordon hears them opening and closing doors and cupboards. He doesn't like to think of them looking through his things, but he knows better than to say anything. Why would Howard have told them something like that? Does he believe Gordon had something to do with Joe going missing? Howard doesn't deserve Joe, that's for sure. Poor Joe. Gordon would like to tell the police this, but decides to keep it to himself.

He waits on the sofa, wondering if he should call Malcolm. He knows Malcolm is coming soon, but not when he is coming, not exactly when. He feels like he has been waiting for a long time.

'Your shed is locked,' says the blonde policeman, coming back into the room. 'Do you have a key?'

'Yes, yes,' Gordon replies, standing up. He goes over to the timber buffet, painted in a light wash to match the sofas, and pulls at one of the drawers.

'The drawer sticks,' he says to the constable. 'Maybe you can open it?'

The constable gives the tarnished metal handle a couple of quick pulls, and the drawer springs open to reveal that the entire thing is full of keys.

'Shit,' mutters the constable. 'Do you know which one it is?'

Gordon looks down. There must be at least fifty keys in the drawer, collected over a lifetime and never thrown away – just in case. 'I used to. Malcolm is coming soon and he's going to label them all. That's what he's going to do, but you can try them. Go ahead.'

The other constable has come back into the living room, and he too stares down into the drawer. 'Easier to get a locksmith,' he says, 'but probably not worth it.' He looks at Gordon. 'We might be back,' he says, and it almost sounds like a threat.

'Thanks for your help,' says the blonde one. Gordon nods and smiles, because he's become aware that nodding and smiling old men aren't worthy of much attention.

The constables walk towards the front door, opening it as Gordon stands behind them.

The constable with the dark hair turns to him. 'A lot of press have arrived to report on the story. They might come and ask you about the people over the road.'

'I don't know them very well,' says Gordon. 'I mean, I've met Joe and Elizabeth, but... not well.'

'Yes,' agrees the constable. 'But if they do come and ask you questions, or anything like that, we'd ask you not to speak to them. We don't want things to be said that might hinder the search.'

Gordon has no idea what he could say that would prevent Joe being found, but he says, 'All right.'

He waits for them to leave, hoping they can't see how rattled he is by their visit. What else has that man across the road said about him? What else?

As they walk down the front path to the gate, the birds leap off the feeder and settle on branches higher up in the tree. The blonde policeman stops to watch them for a moment, then he turns back to wave at Gordon. He's a nice young man, but still a policeman who thinks he may have something to do with Joe going missing. When did he last see Joe?

Feeling exhausted, he returns to the kitchen and picks up a cracker loaded with Brie. He puts it in his mouth and chews, swallowing mechanically.

They'll definitely be back. Especially when they find out about the phone call he made. They'll be back soon enough then.

CHAPTER TEN

ELIZABETH

Today, 11.00 a.m.

Elizabeth stands in the shower, letting the water cascade over her body. She has run it as hot as she can tolerate. She has been allowed to go for a shower while the constables walk over the road and try to talk to Gordon. *Allowed.* Even under the hot water, she shivers momentarily at the thought of being in a situation where she has to ask permission to shower. Like prison.

She needed to change her clothes, because even though the morning air hadn't reached the high temperatures she knew were coming, the first police interview had left her sweaty and uncomfortable.

Even before the interview, she had felt the sweat beading on her face and her back.

'We looked up and down the street and through the house,' she has repeated, but she has not said, 'And we flung accusations at each other.'

'Where the hell were you?' Howard said.

'In the... Putting on laundry. Where were you? You were

with him!' she spat, fear over Joe's disappearance making her braver with her words than she normally would have been.

'I was asleep, alone because you locked yourself away. I was asleep and you just left him.'

'I heard you come out of the bedroom, I heard you.'

Round and round they went, back and forth, and then she called the police. When had Joe left the garden?

She steps out of the shower and roughly towels herself dry. Where is Joe? Where could he be? She goes into the bedroom and finds a dress to put on, the blue one she likes. There is a constable standing outside her bedroom door. A woman. Elizabeth has been told that she will not be allowed to go and help look for Joe. Both she and Howard have to remain in the house. She doesn't blame the police. If she was them, she would want to keep an eye on Howard and Elizabeth Ealy as well. What do the police know about them? Do they have people making calls and asking about them? Will they call Peter? Obviously they will. Peter could be on his way here right now to represent the Department of Community Services. He's the one who placed Joe with her and Howard. He's the one who thought they would make good parents for the little boy, and now that little boy is missing. It's all gone so completely, disastrously wrong, and it was never supposed to go wrong again.

She picks up a brush and runs it quickly through her curls, letting it catch and pull so her scalp stings, using the movement and the pain to brush away her memories of the last time it went wrong. She catches the edge of a smell, something sweet, body wash that lingered on skin, and then presses her hand down over her heart. At the bottom of her bedside drawer at home she has hidden a slim silver bracelet, hidden it so well that sometimes she forgets it's there. But when she remembers, if she's alone, she will pull it out and stroke the letters engraved on its smooth surface. The bracelet is for a smaller hand than hers, a hand she cannot let her mind drift back to.

This cannot be like last time – she won't survive it again.

Dropping the brush onto the bed, she picks up her phone from the bedside table and looks down at the messages from her mother and sister. They text every day and, after she spoke to her sister yesterday, they are both worried about her. *Everything ok?* from Natalie. *Are you okay, darling? Is Joe enjoying his holiday?* from her mother. How will she reply? What can she possibly say? She needs to call them, but she doesn't know how she will keep herself from spilling her secrets, from confessing the truth to the two women in her life who know her best. They are too far away to help, so why involve them now?

'Oh God,' she moans as she sits down on the bed and covers her face with her hands, feeling the despair come up from her toes. 'Joe,' she whispers. 'Joe' she says again, sending his name into the air over and over, hoping that wherever he is, he will hear her.

How long was she in the bathroom this morning, rehearsing the things she was going to say to Howard? Five minutes? Ten minutes? It doesn't take very long for a child to disappear, she knows that. She would never have left Joe alone. She would never have left him alone with Howard for more than ten minutes. She's only ever done that once before – only once. Could Howard have hurt Joe, actually hurt Joe, and then concealed it? She shakes her head.

They have been together for twenty-odd years, and for at least fifteen of those years Elizabeth has thought about leaving him, but she has always been drawn back into her marriage. It's like Howard can sense when she is getting close to making a decision and finds ways to remind her of all the reasons she married him.

At the beginning of this year, months before Joe came into their lives, she had actually started packing, secretly, quietly, without any fuss, moving things to a suitcase that was stored in their wine cellar, tucked behind some boxes. Natalie had come to Australia for a visit, escaping the ice of Philadelphia in January for a rainy Sydney. 'At least it's not cold,' she said cheerfully. 'I'm here to visit you anyway, so that's all that matters.'

Howard had refused to have her stay in the house.

'But we have so much space,' Elizabeth argued.

'It's not about space, it's about me wanting to be able to come home and not feel judged. I know your sister doesn't like me.'

She couldn't argue with that. It was the truth.

Natalie stayed with their parents, but Elizabeth spent every day with her, and she noticed that as she walked into her parents' house, as soon as she was away from her pristine mansion overlooking the harbour, her shoulders relaxed, her jaw unclenched and her spirit lifted.

'Listen, Bethy,' Natalie told her after a few days of long talks and shared childhood memories, 'I know we don't usually go there, but I'm going back home in a couple of weeks and I just need to say... you're not happy. When I came for dinner the other night, it was like someone else was sitting in your chair. You're so careful, so worried, and completely stressed all the time. You look ten years younger the minute you walk through the door here. You're not happy. I know it, and Mum and Dad know it, and we're all just keeping quiet because we don't want to upset you.'

Elizabeth burst into tears, relieved that someone had finally said something. And then she began her secret packing. But Howard sensed something, even though she had not changed her routine or behaviour at all. Perhaps he could feel that a decision had been made; perhaps she didn't respond in quite the same way when he criticised her, or grabbed her arm to make a point, or hissed at her for leaving a cup on the kitchen counter. Whatever it was, he went into a full-on charm offensive.

He booked the restaurant where he had proposed, reminding her of their early life together. He brought home a gift every night, usually something small and meaningful like chocolates from her favourite store, or a single rose the same colour as the ones that had been in her wedding bouquet. He sat with her late into the night over a bottle of wine, talking about the things they would do once he retired, the places they would go. He deferred to her in conversation and he wooed – actually wooed – her sister, asking her about her life and the boys and for her opinion on plants he wanted to put in the garden, knowing that Natalie was a keen gardener in the US. He made them both laugh over expensive dinners in beautiful restaurants, and by the time Natalie was ready to leave, she said, 'Look, maybe he's not that bad. Maybe I just needed to spend more time with him. He and I had some time to talk when we went to the nursery the other day, and he loves you, Bethy, he really does.' And Elizabeth began to question if that were the truth. No one's life was perfect, and no man was perfect. Howard loved her and spoiled her and she had everything she wanted – except her own child. Perhaps she was the problem. Just as secretly, just as quietly, she unpacked.

She was thinking about leaving again when Joe came along. 'His mother is a habitual drug user,' Peter told her. 'He's been in the system since he was eighteen months old. He had a good foster family, but things went awry, and now he's back and he needs a permanent home.'

And now this child, who needed them so much, is missing, and Elizabeth knows they are both to blame; Howard for whatever he has done, and her for still being with this man after everything he has done before this terrible day.

CHAPTER ELEVEN

GORDON

One week ago

He has begun, without realising it, to watch the house across the street, hoping for signs of the little boy. When he does see him, he feels relief that he is fine, and then he can go about his day.

When he and Flora were raising Malcolm, it was the late seventies and there was a lot of different advice about parenting. Flora was a fan of Dr Spock, despite his book being decades old, and she never let the boy shed an unnecessary tear. Gordon had his doubts at first, especially when watching other little boys and their rough-and-tumble play, but he always found conversations with Malcolm interesting and he never tried to turn him into something he wasn't going to be. Malcolm was good at cricket but terrible at other sports. School was where he excelled. But more than that, he was a sweet child and he has grown up into a deeply caring man who has even managed a divorce with a level of dignity that Gordon didn't think was possible. Gordon hopes he can find someone to be with as he gets older, but Malcolm seems content to raise Del and do his work.

This morning, Gordon shuffles around his kitchen, his aching hip reminding him of his age more than usual, his gaze continually going to the window that looks out at the bird feeder. He has not had the courage to go over and say hello after the way the man looked at him, but he has seen Joe out with his mother, or foster mother, a few times, on their way to the beach, and she always waves. She is a pretty woman, but much too thin for Gordon's liking. Flora was always a bit round and soft and enjoyed every meal she ever made.

Now, as he pours some boiling water over a tea bag, he sees the mother and the little boy come out of their front door.

'Time to introduce myself, I think,' he says aloud, pushing himself to make the move. His kitchen window is open to let in the lovely summer breeze that will hopefully keep temperatures in the mid twenties today, and he hears the little boy laugh at something the woman has said.

The man is not with them. Moving quickly so he doesn't miss them, Gordon reaches his front gate as they stand for a moment on the pavement and watch the birds. As he walks past the feeder, there is an enormous fluttering of disturbed wings, the birds taking off into the blue sky before settling again.

'Wow,' says Joe. 'Look how many!'

'Hello,' Gordon calls, waving as he walks so they don't leave before they've had a chance to speak.

The woman looks at him and something crosses her face, a flicker of something strange, but Gordon keeps going until he is standing directly opposite them with only the quiet street between them.

'I wanted to introduce myself,' he says. 'I'm Gordon and I've met Joe. I just wanted to say hello and let you know that if you'd like to come into my yard to watch the birds, that's fine.'

'Oh,' says the woman, and she turns and looks back quickly at the house, where the front door remains closed. 'Thank you,' she says, facing him again with a smile. 'Joe would love that.'

'Now, now, now? Can we go now?' asks Joe, jumping up and down.

'If Gordon doesn't mind.' The woman smiles. 'I'm Elizabeth, by the way. It's nice to meet you. We're only here for a few weeks, but we're having a lovely time, aren't we, Joe? The weather has been amazing.' As she speaks, she looks left and then right, and then with one more glance back at the house, she crosses the street, Joe's hand tightly in hers.

Gordon steps back to allow them in, causing the birds to lift off again.

'Oh no,' says Joe.

'They'll come back, Joe. Come and sit down quietly, and as soon as we're away from the feeder, they'll all return for their breakfast.'

Gordon points at one of the metal chairs next to the small round black metal table and Joe obediently sits down. A flash of a memory of him and Flora sharing a morning cup of tea at the table hits Gordon, causing a pang of melancholy, but he dismisses it as he watches Joe's face light up when the birds return.

'So many kinds,' says Elizabeth, standing behind the boy with her hands on his shoulders. 'Look, Joe – the pink and grey ones are called rosellas, and you know the white ones are cockatoos.'

'The cockatoos are very bossy,' laughs Joe as one of the big birds seems to shove aside a much smaller multicoloured lorikeet.

'They are,' agrees Gordon with a laugh.

'What's that one?' Joe asks, pointing at a red bird with bright green wings.

'It's...' Gordon starts to say, and then he stops. He has seen a bird like this every day for decades. What is it? 'It's...' he starts again, and then the answer is there, right in front of him, 'It's a king parrot,' he almost shouts, triumphant at having found the missing word.

'Beautiful,' murmurs Elizabeth.

'Would you like a cup of tea?'

'Oh, please don't trouble yourself,' she says, shaking her head. She looks, he thinks, tired and pale, as though she hasn't slept, even under the light tan her skin now has from her days at the beach.

'It's no trouble at all. And what about you, young man? My granddaughter, Del, says that I make the best hot chocolate, but because it's so warm today, I can make it with ice.' As he makes the offer, he quickly runs through the steps needed to make the special drink. Does he remember how to do it? He sees his hands moving and is relieved that he knows what to do.

'Oh yes please,' says Joe, his little body bouncing in the chair with excitement.

'If you're sure you don't mind?' says Elizabeth, and for some reason Gordon reaches out and touches her gently on the shoulder.

'I don't mind,' he replies. She closes her eyes briefly, as though absorbing his touch, and as he makes his way to the kitchen, Gordon thinks that maybe she hasn't been touched kindly by anyone in a long time.

In the kitchen, he walks purposefully into the pantry to get... He stops. What is he here to get? Outside he hears the little boy... Joe, that's it, Joe... shouting, 'Come back, birdie,' and he remembers: the cold hot chocolate.

It takes him a few minutes to make the hot chocolate and then blend it with ice the way Del likes him to do, but he keeps looking out of his window to check that Joe is not getting restless. The little boy is delighted with the birds, pointing out the way the lorikeets waddle, and covering his ears while he laughs at the loud squawking of the cockatoos.

He is ready with a tray with the cold hot chocolate and the

tea for Elizabeth when he realises that he has forgotten the sugar sticks that are in the pantry. He finds them quickly enough and picks the tray up again, walking slowly out to the front garden. *Milk?* he hears Flora say – she liked her tea quite weak. He'll have to go back for that.

Outside, the garden is empty except for the birds. Joe and Elizabeth are gone, and he looks up from his tray to see them being pulled across the road by the man, his hand wrapped tightly around the top of Elizabeth's arm. Elizabeth is holding onto Joe and Joe is protesting, 'But I wanted the cold hot chocolate. Gordon is making it. I wanted to see the birds and get my chocolate.'

The man stops as the family get to their front door and lets go of Elizabeth, crouching down to Joe, both hands on the child's shoulders, shaking him back and forth, the boy's head jerking loosely like a rag doll. 'Shut up,' he screams in his face. 'Don't you dare say another word.'

The tray gets heavier and heavier in Gordon's hands as he stands frozen to the spot. The woman turns to look at him, and he can see she is crying, but before he can say anything, the family are inside the house and the front door slams, the smack of timber echoing through the air and sending the birds fluttering away from the feeder.

Gordon stands for another moment in the silence of the quiet street, wondering what he should do. Eventually his shoulders start to ache and he realises that he is still holding the tray. He turns and goes back to the kitchen, putting the tray down carefully and taking everything off it, tipping out the chocolate drink into the sink and returning the sugar sticks to the pantry. He didn't need the milk after all.

'What a thing,' he mutters while he tidies up, his hands shaking and his mouth dry. 'What kind of a man does that to a little boy?' He picks up the cup of tea to pour it into the sink, cursing as it slips out of his trembling fingers and bounces against the metal. It's a pale blue cup that comes with a matching saucer. Flora used it every day and now he does the same. His heart races as he peers down at it, and he is suffused with relief that it's not broken. He leaves it there, not wanting to pick it up again until he can get control of himself.

It's not that Gordon has never seen terrible parenting. As a teacher for nearly fifty years, he has come across every kind of parent. He has seen parents who are wonderful and involved and who enjoy knowing exactly what their children are up to at school, and he has seen parents who don't care, seeing school as a place to give them some space from their kids. He's met parents who are fair disciplinarians and those who are harsh, even cruel. He's even met the very worst kind of parent, but he hates to think of that particular situation. It amazes him that he still feels such anger and impotence when he sees terrible parenting. He never could do much about it when he was a teacher, and he can do nothing now, and the awful thing is that this man is a foster parent. Joe has obviously been removed from a very much worse situation.

Elizabeth seemed scared as well. A wife should never be afraid of her husband. And there's nothing he can do about any of it. Is there?

He realises that he is pacing, and he calls Malcolm, interrupting his day at work, which he usually tries not to do. 'Is everything okay?' is Malcolm's panicked answer.

'Yes, yes, fine. I mean, I'm fine, but I just… I don't know how to explain it.'

He hears Malcolm take a deep breath in and release it slowly, and immediately regrets calling him. He hates to be a bother.

'Just take your time, Dad,' says Malcolm softly. 'What happened?'

Gordon copies his son's deep breath and then he explains, the image of the man holding the little boy clear in his head.

'Oh,' says Malcolm when he's done. 'Well, there's not much... I mean, it's not good – he sounds like a real dick – but they're only there for a bit and then they'll go home, and anyway, you never know what families are dealing with.'

'Maybe I should call the police? Do you think I should call the police?'

'No, Dad. Please don't do that. If they come, and the guy realises it was you, you're all alone there. Maybe wait until I'm there and just... I don't know. I think you should stay away from them. Maybe they don't like the kid talking to strangers.'

'Who's a stranger?' asks Gordon, confused.

'You are to them, Dad. Look, I really have to go. I have ten people on a Zoom call waiting for me. I'll be there soon and we can figure out what to do together.'

'But do you think I should call the police?'

'No,' says Malcolm, his impatience obvious, 'I told you no.'

'Did you?' Gordon feels a headache coming on, but he knows he needs to let Malcolm get back to work. 'I'll see you soon then,' he says, and ends the call.

He shouldn't call the police. Malcolm said so. But Malcolm isn't here and he didn't see what Gordon saw.

He looks down at the sink, at the blue cup lying on its side, and then he picks it up, still warm from the tea. 'You didn't see what I saw,' he says aloud. 'You didn't.'

CHAPTER TWELVE

ELIZABETH

One week ago

Elizabeth cuts her piece of toast into smaller and smaller pieces.

'I made breakfast, so eat it,' says Howard, and she gathers some bright yellow scrambled egg onto a piece of toast and puts it in her mouth, chewing in an industrious, exaggerated way. Howard has already finished his food, and now he is watching her as he turns a mug of coffee around and around in his hands, the slow spin of the cup making Elizabeth feel nauseous. She would have preferred to take Joe to the beach and eat later, but she made the mistake of taking him into Gordon's yard. Or at least she made the mistake of letting Howard catch her doing it.

Her arm aches. There will be a bruise. She is struggling to control her fury, her fear. They mingle like the egg and toast in her mouth, and she is not sure which she is feeling.

Howard sighs. 'I'm sorry,' he says.

Elizabeth pushes more food onto her fork with her knife. 'For what?' she asks, concentrating on her plate. Joe is eating his toast in small bites, his body stiff with fear.

'I shouldn't have done that, okay?' says Howard. 'It was

wrong of me and I'm sorry. I overreacted. Joe? I'm sorry, okay. I overreacted and I am really upset with myself because I did the wrong thing. Do you forgive me? Can you forgive me?' he pleads, his voice higher than normal, his despair obvious.

Elizabeth looks at Joe, willing the child to say no – to do what she cannot do. She wants Joe to burst into tears, to shout and cry, but he's only five, and he has learned in his short life that he needs to be careful, always careful. That was one of the notes in his file. *Joe is a cautious child and he will rarely express any emotion other than gratitude.* He nods, granting Howard a small smile. 'Okay,' he says.

'Thanks, buddy,' says Howard. 'I am really sorry. I just woke up and the two of you were gone and I got so worried.'

'We were talking to Gordon,' says Joe, as though this needs to be explained. His voice is just above a whisper, in case he is saying something wrong.

'Yeah, I know you were, but I don't know Gordon and he could be a bad man. He could be a really bad man and he could do something—'

'Howard, stop, you're scaring him,' says Elizabeth, her tone flat. She knows that if she raises her voice, it will give him an excuse to get angry at her, to turn this around on her.

Howard pushes his empty plate away and looks down at his hands. 'I can't get this right. I shouldn't have said anything. Please forgive me, please,' he says, and he puts his hand on her arm, gently, softly, so she is forced to look at him, to see the anguish in his eyes.

'I wanted to let you sleep, and we were only having something to drink with him and watching the birds,' she says. 'We were going to walk to the beach afterwards.'

'You wanted to get away from me,' he says, wounded.

She puts her knife and fork down on her plate and lifts her cup of coffee, swallowing down a mouthful so she can avoid saying anything else. She did want to avoid Howard for an hour or two. For the past few days, she and Joe have gotten up early and gone down to the beach for a paddle in the cool water. He only goes up to his knees, but he is going a little further every day, getting braver in his own time. It is the most blissful time of her day.

Joe keeps eating, swinging his legs and humming to himself. Elizabeth has noticed that it's something he does when he can sense tension in the air. He takes himself away with the sound, puts himself somewhere else so that he doesn't have to worry. She wishes she could do the same.

'You could have just asked us to come inside,' she says, tackling her plate again, cutting her toast into even smaller pieces so she has something to do with her hands.

'I know. You're absolutely right. I was incredibly wrong and I behaved badly. Do you forgive me?'

She has no choice but to offer him a tight smile and a quick nod of her head.

She is beginning to realise that the idea of the break is not just to get them away from the city, but also to remove her from her friends and family. She will sometimes spend the night with her friend Alisha; she calls it a girls' night, but really it's a way to have some time away from Howard. Alisha has two boys of seven and nine, so she has no worries about having Joe along for a sleepover as well. Joe loves every minute of it.

In the last couple of days, when Elizabeth has tried to call her sister or her parents, Howard always seems to walk into the room just as she starts dialling. 'Can't live without them, eh?' he will say, smiling as he cracks his knuckles, one finger at a time. Another woman, a different woman – her sister, for instance – would say, 'Yup, that's right,' and just carry on. But Elizabeth is not that kind of woman. Elizabeth ends the call instead and says, 'I'll speak to them later.' She would like to think that Howard has brought this out in her, that he is the one who has made her unsure of every move she makes, but she knows that she was always like this. She has been timid and shy her whole life, always afraid of saying the wrong thing, of doing the wrong thing. Perhaps that's why he picked her; perhaps he saw something in her that meant he would be able to control and manipulate her with just a few well-chosen words and the occasional dash of violence.

Just over twenty years ago, he walked into a pharmacy in the city where she was covering for a pharmacist on maternity leave and asked her advice about some cold and flu medication for his grandfather. 'Don't want the old boy taking something that won't agree with him,' he said, his smile wide and sincerity in his grey eyes. She was instantly charmed by him, by his taking care of his grandfather, and she took her time going through ingredients with him to make sure they wouldn't affect any other drugs his grandfather was taking. Once he had found a medication that was acceptable, he paid her and, handing over his card, said, 'I don't suppose I could entice you to join me for lunch today, could I?'

'Oh... I... I'm...' she stammered, blushing.

'We can eat at that café right across the road. We can sit outside and you will be perfectly safe, I assure you.'

She laughed then, and agreed to join him.

They had been dating for three weeks when he confessed that he didn't have a grandfather, that he had seen her in the window every day as he walked to the café for a cup of coffee and couldn't think of how to ask her out. He was so charming when he confessed, blushing at his own need to meet her, that she found this sweet instead of alarming.

'Now,' says Howard, happy to have dealt with the horrible morning so he doesn't have to think about it again, 'I think Joe and I are going to buy boogie boards and ride the waves today.'

Elizabeth drops her knife and fork onto her plate with a clatter. 'Joe can't swim yet, he can't swim,' she protests, unable to hide her panic.

'Sweetheart,' he says – again a gentle touch, a slight squeeze, 'relax. I know that. He can wear his special vest. I wouldn't let anything happen to my boy. Do you want to be a surfer dude, Joe? What do you say?'

'Yay,' shouts Joe, and Elizabeth gets up to clear the table.

'We can all go,' she says.

'Good idea,' says Howard. 'I'll get this young man covered in sunscreen and pack our bags and you can clear up.'

Elizabeth nods, knowing that she has no choice but to go along. Boogie-boarding will be fun for Joe, and as long as he has the inflatable vest, he'll be fine. She scrapes her plate into the garbage and then rinses it, placing it in the dishwasher. The screech of the fork against the plate, the clatter of the dishes and the running of water are the only things she thinks about. She does exactly what Howard needs her to do. She simply wipes the morning from her mind. It is easier to deal with it that way.

Soon they will have another check-in with Peter, who always seems to be running late and needing to dash off to his next client. There is no doubt that Department of Community Services workers are overloaded. Elizabeth wonders what Joe will tell him, what he will say it is like living with them. She thinks he will tell Peter that he is happy, that everything is wonderful, because as long as he obeys Howard's rules, his many, many rules, then everything *is* wonderful. Joe needs to hold his knife and fork properly, he needs to say please and thank you, he needs to ask Howard how his day was, he needs to tidy his toys before bed every night, he needs to tidy the cupboard that contains his plates and cups every night, he needs to wait to eat until Howard picks up his knife and fork... The list is long. If she and Howard had raised Joe from an infant, most of the things on the list would come naturally to him, but because they haven't, it feels as though the child has to think before he makes a single move. The same way Elizabeth has learned to do in her marriage. Exactly the same way.

And maybe Howard is right about Joe needing all these rules; maybe with work they can fight his genetic inheritance of addiction and whatever other terrible learned behaviours may be lurking in him. Are monsters made or born, or both? Howard is worried about Joe turning bad at sixteen, becoming violent and needing drugs to feel he is experiencing life. He worries that the boy could one day be a monster. Elizabeth is worried that she is already living with one. *Stop it, stop it. Don't think like this. He said sorry. What more do you want?*

By the time she is done with the kitchen, Joe is ready, his little face generously covered in sunscreen and his red and blue Spider-Man bucket hat on his head. He is already wearing his inflatable vest.

'I saw a store just near the beach. I'll dash in and get us a couple of boards,' says Howard.

They head down to the beach. The sun is hot but the ocean breeze makes it easy for Elizabeth to sit on the sand and watch as Howard patiently teaches Joe how to boogie-board, explaining again and again and supporting him when he feels scared. By the time they are ready to leave, Joe has caught a couple of waves, lying on his stomach on the board, and he is hooked.

Back at home, Howard pours them each a glass of wine and she assembles a cheese plate for them to share before she makes a late lunch. Joe is in front of the television eating his lunch, and she has a feeling that he will drift off for a nap after the long morning of sun and activity. It has been the perfect family beach day, like something out of a brochure.

There is a garden at the back of the house, a square of green lawn boarded by the timber fence that surrounds the property. It's not a particularly nice place for Joe to play, because of the large fig trees and their snaking roots that are everywhere, but it's cool. They sit on the balcony and sip their wine, Elizabeth relieved that the morning has gone well. If it weren't for the obvious bruise on her arm, she would be able to pretend that nothing had happened but boogie-boarding and sunshine.

'I think,' says Howard, 'that it would be better if Joe stayed away from that old man across the road. He's really overly interested in talking to him, and that gives me the creeps.'

'There's nothing weird about him,' Elizabeth protests. 'He's just a nice man who's happy for everyone to look at his birds.' Anxiety taps at her.

'I would prefer it if he doesn't speak to him again,' says Howard, staring at the trees. 'I mean, he's in our care. Imagine if something were to happen to him. I would never be able to forgive myself.'

'I don't think there's anything wrong with Gordon,' she says.

'But you don't know... not for sure. Do you want to take that chance with our boy? Do you?' He sounds like he is genuinely asking her a question, but she knows better. He is giving her a chance to tell him what he wants to hear.

'I don't... That's not... I just don't think Gordon is a problem,' she says firmly.

'Maybe I should go over there and speak to him, let him know that we're a little concerned,' says Howard. He puts his glass of wine down and cracks his knuckles.

'No,' she says, standing up. 'No, we won't speak to him again.'

Two years ago, Elizabeth started yoga classes and she grew fond of her instructor. She found the peace he exuded fascinating, and they began having coffee after class every now and again. She took to quoting him to Howard, hoping that perhaps some of the things Brent said about finding inner peace and breathing before reacting would strike a chord with her husband. But Howard didn't like her spending time with the man. 'He's just a friend,' she told him, 'and he's not interested in me. He has a lovely boyfriend.'

'I don't care,' Howard said. 'I can't stand you coming back

from every coffee date with your head filled with ridiculous ideas. It's just rubbish, spouted by people who don't know what it takes to be in the real world.'

'Well, I'm not going to stop having coffee with him. We get along really well,' she replied, unable to understand what he had against the man.

'Maybe I should have a word with him,' Howard said, and Elizabeth laughed.

'Go ahead,' she said. In her mind, she imagined Brent having some sort of breakthrough with Howard. She even played out a scenario whereby Howard joined the class and the two of them found a new way to relate without fear or anger.

But at the next class, Brent barely looked at her, and when she went up to him afterwards, he said, 'Your husband has some real issues, you know. He threatened me... not in so many words, but he said he would speak to my boss about my friend-ships with clients, and he went on about things being inappro-priate. It's just embarrassing, Elizabeth. I love my job and I really hate to have people complain about me. Best if we cool it on the coffee dates for now.'

Elizabeth was mortified, and she never returned to class, cancelling her membership that day.

'Well, that's an over-the-top reaction,' Howard said when she told him. 'I thought the guy was okay, a bit weird, but okay. I never asked you to quit the class. Still, you obviously felt some-thing was a bit off about him as well.'

She hates to think what a chat with Gordon would be like. Gordon is an old man, and he doesn't need to get embroiled in her family drama.

'Good,' smiles Howard now. 'Good,' he repeats.

Elizabeth takes her glass into the kitchen. 'Just making lunch,' she calls as she walks away, hoping that Howard will stay outside. She hates that he has made her question Gordon's motives. He's just a nice, probably lonely old man, and she knows she would have sensed if something was off about him. But she's not one hundred per cent sure, because she is never one hundred per cent sure about anything.

She goes through the pantry, finding the dry pasta she will use to make lunch, opens the fridge and gets out vegetables to make a sauce.

They have been fostering for many years now. It hasn't always been easy, but for the most part she likes to feel that she is contributing something, changing something. Once she learned she couldn't have children, they investigated all sorts of options, from surrogacy to adoption, but it was Howard who suggested they become foster carers. 'We have so much to give a kid, especially one who's had a rough time. It makes sense.'

It did make sense, and while they were waiting to be approved, Elizabeth felt excited and nervous at the same time. 'Just how I felt when I was pregnant with Jay,' Natalie said when Elizabeth described it to her. Elizabeth has heard other foster parents say that they learned a lot about themselves and their relationship during the approval process, but what she learned most was how brilliant Howard was at his facade. She would listen to him sometimes, speaking to a psychologist or a case worker, and think, 'He's such an amazing man.' And then she'd be baffled by her own thoughts.

When the case manager asked Howard what his childhood was like, he said, 'Filled with creativity and imagination. I was encouraged to read and I was also encouraged to do things on my own if I chose to.' She listened to him talk and wondered if she had missed something when he told her about his upbringing.

When the case manager asked him if he got along with his parents now, he said, 'Absolutely. I believe that when you get older, your parents can be your best friends.' She knew this was completely untrue.

Throughout the interviews and home visits, she listened

and nodded and smiled but remained silent on the real truth about the mercurial man she found herself married to. Mostly because on interview days she found it hard to see him as anything other than wonderful. In the lead-up to them meeting with someone from the system, he would become the man she fell in love with, kind and compassionate, suggesting spontaneous dinners out and bringing her flowers, asking her about her day and providing thoughtful answers and suggestions when she discussed her work. But also because more than anything, she wanted a child in her life, wanted to help a child who needed her. She had watched her sister with her four beautiful boys and could see the wonderful men they would become. She wanted to be able to turn a child's life around so that they too could become a wonderful adult.

If she ever felt the need to tell the truth, she would inevitably talk herself out of it, questioning her own thoughts. Howard was so sure of himself, and she never had been. The only thing she was completely sure of was her need to take care of a child. A small voice inside her occasionally pointed out that Howard's nature was not suited to being a father of any child, especially a child who had come from trauma, but she always managed to silence that voice. 'Maybe a child will change him,' she would think. 'I'll always be here,' she would tell herself. 'It's unfair of me to prejudge what kind of a father he will be.'

Once they had been approved, it took only a couple of weeks before they were called, and all of a sudden they had two children, a little boy of seven and a little girl of nine, to take care of. Their single mother was in hospital and the children were clearly well looked after. 'We're not supposed to be babysitters,' Howard said, but Elizabeth didn't mind. What she did start to mind was the regularity with which the children came and went. She never knew how long each placement would be for, and she was afraid to get too attached to any of the children – but she always got attached anyway.

The hardest placement was a six-month-old baby named Oscar, who was with them for five months. That was when Howard's need for rules and regulations became apparent. She had always understood that there was a particular way he liked her to behave, but they had not had any children in their home long enough for him to begin dictating how he wanted *them* to behave. But with Oscar, he began to make plans for how the child would grow up, for what would be expected of him. He pushed her to sleep-train him, but she was steadfast and refused, and while he gave in on that, there were times when she could see him planning all the rules he would institute as the child grew up.

'He shouldn't interrupt us when we're talking. He won't be able to get out of his bed after bedtime. He needs to learn to look an adult in the eye and speak to them. He needs to have good manners. He has to tidy up after himself.'

'He's a baby, Howard,' she reminded him. 'He needs to learn to walk and talk first. Caught up in a bubble of love for the child, she didn't take Howard as seriously as she should have. She was engaged in Oscar's smile, his laugh, in watching him learn to navigate his world. Only the visits from the case manager marred her joy, reminding her that the baby did not belong to her.

And then Oscar's father, who had been overseas and had not known of his existence, returned and wanted custody of his son.

Having been cautioned over and again by the case manager to be aware that this was a foster situation and to be ready to let go if she had to, she knew she should have been prepared. But she wasn't. Instead, she was utterly despondent. Packing up Oscar's things to hand over left her in a flood of tears that she thought would never end. The first morning without him in her home was devastating in its silence.

'He wasn't our child,' Howard reminded her, but she would

not be comforted. Winded by her despair, she refused place-ments for a year while she tried to move forward.

When she was ready to foster again, she made sure she kept some distance, trained herself to let go, to actually be able to say goodbye and not collapse in a heap. But then the idea of adoption came up. There were older children who needed homes. She agreed to it without even consulting Howard, and that was probably her first mistake. *Don't go there, don't go there,* she reminds herself now as a beautiful face appears in her mind and tears prick at her eyes. *This won't be like that. It won't. We have Joe and nothing is going to happen to him.*

She fills a pot with water and puts it on to boil.

That child was older than Joe, so it was different. Every-thing had been going so well and then... She pushes the thought away, because this is not like last time. This is different. She has to believe that. According to Barry, the case manager they were dealing with, it was 'not their fault' and 'could have happened to anyone'.

'You have no idea what these children have been through, no one really does,' he told her, but Elizabeth was convinced that they would never be approved for another placement. They took a break from fostering again. They took a break for a long time.

Last year, Howard agreed to try again, and now they have Joe, and Joe's mother will never be allowed to have custody of him again even if she wants to. Everyone is hoping that things work out with Elizabeth and Howard, and that the adoption can go ahead and Elizabeth will finally, finally have a child to call her own.

But Howard believes that Joe needs to be the perfect child. He needs to be clever and polite and good at sport, funny and able to make Howard proud every day. Appearances mean a lot to Howard.

Her mind goes back to the afternoon Joe arrived with his

little suitcase and a stuffed teddy bear that really needed a wash.

Howard couldn't bring himself to touch the toy. 'How about you let Elizabeth give Teddy a bath and you and I go to the store and pick out some friends for him,' he said, and Joe's eyes widened as he nodded his head.

Elizabeth would have preferred to settle the little boy in, but he took Howard's hand, and when they returned, Howard had to make three trips to bring all the things he had bought for Joe in from the car. Joe was stunned into happy silence. He didn't know what to play with first, and Howard helped him arrange all the new soft toys on his bed and then build the giant train set in the spare room. Watching her husband with the little boy, Elizabeth was reminded of everything that was good about Howard: his patience in explaining things, his ability to lose himself in the moment, his laugh.

'This one's going to work, I can feel it,' he told her that night.

But Howard would always be Howard, and now – however much she has thought about it – she can't leave, because she has a foster child, and a woman going through a divorce is not a good candidate to be a foster parent. If she leaves, she'll lose Joe, and she cannot, simply cannot lose Joe.

In a fight she once had with Howard, a fight early on in their relationship over something silly like what restaurant to eat at, she said, 'Maybe I should just go and leave you alone.'

He laughed and replied, 'But Elizabeth, if you do go, you will be the one who'll be alone. I'll make sure of it.'

They were both a little drunk at the time, having stopped at a bar while they decided where to eat, and she didn't take his words seriously. She simply said something like, 'Fine, we'll have Chinese.' But sometimes when she is lying stiffly beside him, her mind whirling as she tries to find a way out, she re-examines that statement. What did he mean? She had people in her life and he couldn't take them away, could he? What would he do if she told him she was leaving? How would he make her pay for it?

'Nearly ready?' asks Howard now, coming into the kitchen, startling her out of her thoughts so that she drops the colander in the sink, where it tips over and the boiled pasta starts to slide out. Howard quickly grabs it and rights it. 'Nearly lost it there,' he laughs.

'Yes,' she smiles. 'Nearly.'

CHAPTER THIRTEEN

One day the man returns home from work and finds the girl dressed, with a small backpack at her feet. He has bought her clothes over the last few weeks, ducked into department stores and estimated what will fit, walked out holding a bag close to his chest, hoping that he sees no one he knows. How would he explain what he's doing? How would he evade all the questions he has no answers to? He bought her the backpack, and even a cheap mobile phone. 'You don't have to do this,' she said each time, before thanking him for the gifts. But he needs to do it, needs to do something.

She had Christmas alone while he was with his parents. 'Come with me,' he said, but she refused. He keeps waiting for her to open up to him, to tell him everything, but today, when he finds her ready to leave, he knows that will never happen. She is taking her secrets with her.

'I'm going,' she tells him. Her face and body have healed, and when she speaks, she sounds confident, sure of herself, if a little jaded.

'You don't have to,' he says. 'You're better now and we can

get you some government help, get you into housing. There's all sorts of stuff for kids. I wish you would let me help you.'

'I turned sixteen today.' She smiles.

The man is shocked. 'Why didn't you tell me. I would have—'

'I know. But you've bought me so much, and you gave me the best gift I've ever received.'

'What's that?' he asks.

'You kept my secret and you made me feel safe. So I suppose it's two gifts. The two best gifts I've ever received. But you have a life, and you really need to get back out there. You should start dating. You're thirty-five, remember.'

The man laughs. 'Don't go,' he says. 'Stay here and you can find a job, save up until you can get a place.'

'Thanks, but I need to go. I just do. Maybe we'll see each other again.'

The man takes out his wallet and gives her everything he has. 'Don't argue, just take it, and you can come back any time you want. I'll be here for at least another year or so, and you have my number.'

'Okay,' she says.

At the door, they hug, the girl holding on tight.

'Can I ask you just one question?' he says.

'That's a question,' she laughs.

'Ha, ha... What's your name?'

The girl locks eyes with him, then takes a deep breath and tells him. And then she's gone.

CHAPTER FOURTEEN

GORDON

Today, 11.30 a.m.

He eats another cracker even though he's not really hungry any more, listening absent-mindedly to the radio as he chews. He takes his plate into the living room and turns on the television, watches as he eats the rest of his crackers. The woman on the news is talking about Joe being missing. He turns off the television, not wanting to see it, and returns to the kitchen.

There are so many people milling about outside. Gordon rinses his plate carefully and places it in the dishwasher before he goes back to the window.

There is a young woman standing right outside his front gate, standing apart from everyone and watching. She keeps rubbing her hands over her forehead and her short light brown hair, making parts of it stick up. She looks like she is sweating in the heat but also like she is afraid to go any closer to where all the people are. She could get a bottle of water if she did. The SES people are handing them out to everyone.

He studies the young woman, who is dressed in a black sundress covered in white printed birds. Her arms and shoulders are exposed to the sun and she's probably burning out there in the heat. Gordon feels sorry for her – she's a pretty little thing. 'No harm in being nice,' he hears Flora say, and he agrees. He jams his floppy blue hat on his head and makes his way out to the front garden, sending the birds fluttering to safety as he passes them. The young woman turns to look, drawn by the noise, and then she turns back to watch the house where everyone is.

'It's become a right circus, hasn't it?' he says, and she nods and then faces him, offering him a smile as she sizes him up, probably trying to guess his age.

'It has,' she says.

'Are you here to help with the search?'

'No... I'm just...' she begins, and Gordon hears her hesitation. He looks up and down the street, trying to see if she is with anyone.

'Did you come by car?' he asks.

'I did,' she says. 'I parked down the street. I didn't want...' and then she stops again.

Gordon knows someone struggling with something when he sees it. It's the teacher in him. He still looks at young people as though they are in his class and need to be nurtured and protected. He stands silently as he repeats the cloud formations in his head, reminding himself of something he used to know without even thinking about it. *Cirrus, altocumulus, cumulus.* There are more, he's sure of it, but they don't come to mind right now.

'Perhaps you're a reporter?' he suggests. 'I'm afraid the police did ask me to try and limit my interaction with the press. If you stay here much longer, one of those constables, the one with the short grey hair, will come over and ask you what you're doing here. She's not the one in charge, the other two are in charge, I forgot their names, but she does seem to be in charge of asking people who they are. She doesn't much like the press, see.' He gestures at the female constable with the short hair, who is gesticulating angrily at a cameraman, stepping forward so he keeps stepping back.

'I'm not a journalist,' the young woman says. 'I mean, I don't work for anyone specific. I work for myself, freelance, you know?'

Gordon rubs his head. 'Hot, isn't it?' Then, because he's not sure what to say, he says, 'That's turned into a right circus, hasn't it?'

The woman nods her head. 'It is hot,' she agrees. 'My name is Ruby.'

'Ruby, that's pretty. My wife's name was Flora. Do you want something to drink? A cup of tea or something else? It's very hot.' He doesn't want to be out here in this heat, and from the look of the young woman, neither does she.

She opens her mouth, and Gordon can see she is going to say no thank you, but then she thinks about it and says, 'Yes, thanks, that would be lovely, it really would.' She smiles, a beautiful wide smile that lights up her green eyes, and Gordon finds himself smiling back.

Across the road, the front door opens and Howard comes storming out.

'You can all get the hell off my lawn,' he yells at everyone standing there. 'What exactly are you here to do? Judge, gossip? Just leave, just get out of here.'

Gordon takes an involuntary step backwards, even though he is nowhere near the man. The female constable turns from dealing with the cameraman and moves quickly to Howard's side, her hands up as she tries to get him to calm down. She keeps speaking until he drops his head and nods. The people outside the house who have begun to move away stop and gather in groups again. A low hum of conversation drifts across the road as they resume speaking to each other. There is a lot of shaking of heads. Everyone is only there to help, and Howard has been very rude, but from the little Gordon knows about him, rude is his default setting – more than rude, actually.

'I'd love a drink, thanks, maybe inside. It's very hot,' says the young woman, reminding Gordon of his offer.

'It is, isn't it,' he agrees, and he turns around, gesturing for... for Ruby to follow him inside. As they pass the bird feeder, there is a flutter of wings, and a rush of churned air hits his face, cooling his skin.

'Oh,' says the young woman, looking up at the birds. 'How lovely.'

'They're foster parents, you know,' says Gordon as he walks. 'Foster parents,' he repeats.

'Yes,' acknowledges Ruby. *Ruby, her name is Ruby, remember a ruby is red. Her shoulders are red from the sun. Ruby red.*

He feels bad about mentioning that Elizabeth is Joe's foster mother, but it's been on the news already – he heard it on the radio – so he's not telling her anything she wouldn't have heard. A missing child is a big deal in Australia, especially a child missing while on a summer holiday – it's the kind of thing that keeps parents awake at night. He and Flora once spent a week in a caravan park with Malcolm when he was about eight, and Malcolm found himself a group of friends the moment he arrived. Flora spent every day of the holiday looking for him, and every time she found him, he would reassure her that he was having fun, and then disappear again.

'He's just exploring,' Gordon told her, 'he's fine.'

'But what if...' Flora would begin, and he knew she was running through a long list in her head – *but what if he drowns, or falls, or feels sick...?*

'He's safe in the park and the kids he's spending time with are nice enough. Try to relax, love,' he told her, but Flora was fond of a good panic.

When Malcolm was younger, if a child went missing the

news took a long time to filter through to the press, only neighbours and the police getting involved at first. But Joe has only
been gone for a few hours and the whole of Australia is already
involved in the story. Something popped up on the screen of
Gordon's phone as well. He tapped on it to read it, but he did
something wrong and it disappeared. His phone is being troublesome lately.

He walks into the house first and Ruby lets the screen
door clatter closed behind her. They are both instantly
enveloped in the cool, dim hallway. Gordon turns left to go
into the kitchen.

'This was built long before air conditioning, you know,' he
says. 'Designed to withstand the Australian summer. I have air
conditioning now, but I don't need it in here.'

The news has started on the radio again, and as he and the
young woman walk into the kitchen, the announcer he likes
says: 'The parents of the missing child are Howard and Elizabeth Ealy. They have been foster carers for a number of years.
The Department of Community services would not comment
on the case of the missing child.

'Police have interviewed neighbours in the street. All have
reported seeing the family out enjoying the town. The house
they are renting has only just been listed as a holiday rental
home.

'A source within the Department of Community Services
has indicated that the biological mother of the child is seeking to
regain custody. Police would not comment except to say, "Children within the foster care system and their families have a right
to privacy."'

Gordon hasn't heard that last part before. 'Well, imagine
that,' he says to the young woman, who looks down at her shoes
as though she doesn't want to be seen. Gordon taught a few
young girls like her in his time, girls who wanted to disappear.
He wonders what her story is. Everyone has a story.

She lifts her gaze from her shoes and looks around the kitchen as Gordon flicks the radio off.

'It's new,' he explains. 'Sit down, sit down.' He indicates a tall stool next to the tiny breakfast bar in cream stone.

'It's very nice,' she says.

'What would you like? To drink, I mean?'

'Water would be great, thank you,' she says.

'Yes, good idea, water and ice.'

It takes him a minute or two to fill two glasses with water and ice, but finally he is settled opposite Ruby on the other side of the bar. 'Malcolm did the kitchen last year,' he tells her, indicating the soft-close cupboards and smooth-sliding drawers. 'I mean, not him – he hired someone, a builder... I can't remember his name at the minute, but Malcolm paid.'

'Is Malcolm your son?' she asks.

'Yes, he lives in Sydney. Does well for himself... something in computers. Where are you from?'

'Sydney,' she laughs.

'Do you know him? Malcolm? I mean, it's a big city but maybe you know him.'

Ruby picks up her glass of water and takes a long drink. 'I don't think so,' she replies. She has a way of speaking as though she is rehearsing everything before she says it. Gordon thinks this is because she's so uncomfortable. He finds himself doing the same thing nowadays, but for an entirely different reason.

'Are you married?' he asks, before he remembers that young women are not supposed to be asked this question any more.

'No, not married,' she says, 'but I have a boyfriend called Lucas. He's a coder for computer games – he designs them. He's very clever.' She smiles.

He likes it when she smiles. 'Ah,' he says, enjoying how her face lights up when she talks about her young man.

'We've been together for six months,' she says. 'We live together and he's just... asked me to marry him.'

'Lovely! Did you say yes?' asks Gordon.

'I will, but... I need to sort some things out first.' Her gaze moves around the room. 'We have a cat named Felix,' she says, looking back at him. 'She's a girl, but Lucas decided on a name before we got her and he wouldn't be swayed, so we just call her Felix.'

Gordon lets the young woman babble on, pleased that she's opening up a little, though he can't quite keep track of what she's saying. Is Lucas the cat or the boyfriend?

'Lucas is kind,' she says, 'the kindest man I know. He'll be a good... dad, a very good dad.' The words seem to be more for herself than for Gordon, but he's glad to confirm who Lucas is.

'That's always important,' he says, and he gets up and finds some crackers in the cupboard, placing them on the bench top and taking one out, enjoying the salt and the crunch. 'Have one,' he says, and the young woman obliges, taking small, neat bites.

'Have you met them? The family across the road?' she asks as she brushes her hand across the counter as though getting rid of cracker crumbs, although there aren't any. 'I know it's a holiday rental, but have you met them?' He can hear the eagerness in her voice, the desire to know. She's not a journalist – didn't she say that? Yes, she said she's not a journalist. She works for herself. He doesn't think it matters if he speaks to someone who works for herself. Freelance, they call it, and Gordon is happy that he has remembered the word.

'Gordon,' she asks again, 'have you met them?'

Gordon takes a sip of his water, looks at the counter and then uses his hand to wipe off tiny drops of condensation from his glass. 'I have, yes. I haven't spoken much to the man, the father, not him, but I have spent time with Elizabeth and Joe. Poor little Joe.' His voice drops and his shoulders slump as he thinks about the boy and everything he has been through. He wants to say more about Howard, about how terrible the man really is, but he needs to keep that to himself. All the things that have happened in the last week or so are becoming jumbled in his mind. It's best if he keeps quiet in case he gets it wrong.

Ruby picks up her glass to take another sip of water. 'Joe,' she whispers, and Gordon is not sure if she's talking to him or not. 'Would it be okay if I recorded our chat?' she asks. 'Just in case I can write something about it later. I won't if you don't want me to.'

Gordon shifts a little in his seat. 'Will I get in trouble, do you think? If I say something, if I tell you anything?'

'No,' she says, and she seems so sure of herself, Gordon wants to believe her. 'You can talk to whoever you want. The police can ask you not to, but they can't really force you, and anyway, I'm not a journalist. By the time I write something, I'm sure the little boy will be home again with people who love him, and it will be just something interesting to read. I'm sure he will be home.' She nods her head. 'I want to find out what you know about the family and what it's like to watch something like this happen, from an outsider's perspective,' she adds quickly.

Gordon wouldn't mind the company. It's not often that anyone except Malcolm wants to listen to him talk. 'You'll need to be a bit patient with me. Sometimes I repeat things and I... well, I realise it afterwards. Malcolm tries not to tell me, but I know I do,' he sighs.

Ruby leans across the bench top and pats his hand. 'We can go slowly, and I don't mind if you say something more than once. It helps me with my writing.'

'Have you always been a writer?' Gordon asks her.

'No. I had some... trouble when I was younger. I didn't really manage to get myself together until a few years ago. I've had a few slip-ups, but I'm on track now, properly on track. I missed some school and I had to go back and finish, but I have a communications degree now. I've been a waitress and a dog walker and,' she shakes her head, a small laugh escaping, 'so many other things, but this is what I really want to be. It's hard, though, because journalism has changed, everything has changed, so I write for a few websites and I'm hoping to get a good story, a big story one day that leads to a permanent job.' She shrugs her shoulders, and Gordon nods at this idea, but he feels terribly sad for the little boy and his mother who have become a story for the whole world to judge.

'Maybe I should call Malcolm first, my son... He lives in Sydney, but he's coming... soon. He's coming to visit soon. Maybe I should call him and ask... about talking to you,' he says.

'You can if you want,' replies Ruby lightly, and she takes another sip of water, not meeting Gordon's eyes.

He thinks for a moment. He doesn't want to bother Malcolm at work. 'It's fine,' he sighs. 'I would like to tell someone. I mean, I tried to tell the police last week. I called them and I tried to explain what was going on, but they wouldn't listen. They just wouldn't listen.'

Ruby sits up straighter, then she reaches down and taps her phone. 'What did you tell the police, Gordon?' she says softly. 'You can tell me. You can tell me and I'll listen, I promise. What did you tell the police?'

'Well, I...' starts Gordon.

Ruby waits patiently as he gathers his thoughts. 'It's okay if you've forgotten,' she says eventually. 'We can talk about something else. You can tell me about the little boy, about Joe. What's he like?' She leans forward, eager to hear what he has to say, eager to hear about Joe.

'He's a nice little chap... likes the birds, but he wasn't...' Gordon stops speaking. Did she ask him a question? The police, they were talking about what he told the police. 'I haven't forgotten... Well, I have forgotten a lot of it, but I recorded it, you see. I recorded my conversation with the police.'

'You did? Why?'

He smiles sadly and looks down at his hands, which are clasped together. 'I started doing it a few months ago. I wanted to... Well, sometimes I can tell, you see, that I've been repeating myself. I thought that if I recorded things, then I could listen back and try to figure out when it's happening and why. You have to do your best to help yourself, don't you,' he adds, looking up.

'Oh Gordon,' she says softly, and then she doesn't say 'I'm sure you're fine' or something else like that; she just says, 'I'm so sorry.'

'It's all right, lass,' he says, and he pats her on the arm. 'Now let me get my phone... My phone is... Let me get it and you can listen, and you'll see that I tried to tell the police that the little boy needed help, because he did. He really did. I called them... I don't know what day it was, but I definitely...' He closes his eyes, because sometimes that helps him focus, and he sees himself holding his phone. He was wearing his blue and green striped shirt... Yes, that's it. 'I definitely recorded it,' he says. 'Shirl down at the bowling club... Do you know Shirl? She taught me how to do it in between serving drinks. She thought it was so I could record things Del says, but it's for me... for me.'

The young woman looks at him, and he can read the concern he's used to seeing on people's faces these days. It's meant kindly, but he hates that he is now the subject of other people's compassion.

'You recorded the conversation with the police on your phone,' she says.

'My phone,' he agrees. 'I'll go and get my phone.'

'Is it okay if I use the bathroom?' she asks.

'Yes, yes,' he says eagerly. 'I may be a while... I'm not sure where... Take your time.' He gestures to the hall, and Ruby follows where he has pointed.

Gordon goes to his bedroom to find his phone, but it's not there, and then he goes to the kitchen, but it's not there, and then finally he remembers leaving it in the en suite bathroom.

He carries it everywhere with him, afraid to set it down in case he loses it, but he loses it anyway.

He finds Ruby in the living room, looking at the picture of him and Flora on their wedding day. The black-and-white photo has pride of place on the timber console. It's in a glass frame with a white crocheted doily underneath. He makes sure to clean it every week, and he even carefully washes the doily by hand once a month, imagining Flora's hands crocheting it. He looks at himself, tall and handsome in a tuxedo. Flora is almost comically short next to him in a lace dress with long sleeves, but so beautiful. Her light brown hair is a stiffly curled helmet, flipped up at the ends, and he can still remember the sticky feel of it from all the hairspray she used. He feels the slight pain that always catches him whenever he thinks about losing Flora. She believed she had a bad case of indigestion, but it was her heart. By the time they went to see the doctor, they were told she'd had a series of small heart attacks. She was immediately booked in for an operation, but she didn't survive it. 'Her heart was too weak. I'm so sorry,' the lovely young doctor told him and Malcolm, tears in her own eyes.

'She's very pretty,' says Ruby, pulling Gordon away from the waiting room where the heater was turned up too high but he still found himself shivering at the terrible reality of what the doctor was saying.

'She was,' he agrees, 'and a lovely person, so kind.'

'That's what matters, isn't it,' replies Ruby. 'Kindness. Lucas is the kindest person I know.' *Who is Lucas?*

'Lucas is my boyfriend,' she says, as if she's heard his thoughts. Her phone buzzes and she looks down. 'Ha,' she says.

'Everything okay?' he asks.

'Oh yes. I left Sydney really quickly and I didn't think about where I would stay, but he's booked me a motel room.'

'He sounds like a nice young man,' says Gordon, and he makes his way back to the kitchen.

They sit down together and Gordon goes through his recordings until he finds what he needs. It took Shirl a bit of time to teach him how to record a conversation, then how to find it on his phone once it was done, but he was determined to learn and she was so patient. So far, he's listened to himself speaking to Malcolm and to his friend Bill, who he meets for a game of bowls every Friday. The conversation between him and Bill is almost comical, with the two of them repeating themselves and Bill struggling to hear because he only turns on his hearing aids sometimes.

'Here we go,' says Gordon, and he touches the phone screen to play the recording.

He watches the young woman's face as she listens, occasionally writing something down. It feels so strange to hear his tinny, warbling voice. In his head, his voice is still strong enough to carry across the school hall, loud enough to silence even the most boisterous class. Before the little lapses in memory, only the mirror told him he was old. Only the sparse white hairs left on his head and the skinny legs underneath his paunch let him know that he no longer looked the way he saw himself. He was upset after the call, hating the idea of being dismissed, but now, as he listens to his voice, he can see why the policewoman he spoke to was more concerned about him than about what he was trying to tell her.

'She didn't take me seriously,' he explains to Ruby when they have finished listening. 'So when the other thing happened, only a few days ago now, I didn't even bother calling them, but now I wonder if I should have. I really should have.'

CHAPTER FIFTEEN

ELIZABETH

Today, 11.30 a.m.

She is in the kitchen, making herself a cup of coffee, in need of a caffeine hit because her eyes are burning. She was up all night, unable to rest, unable to stop the terrible thoughts that trampled through her mind, and then... She sighs. Joe. He deserves better. Every child deserves better than what happened last night. And she can't say anything, not right now. She can't. She is sick at the thought of telling the police everything, because the result can only be awful. What she is hoping for – praying for – is that Joe has taken himself off for a walk and gotten lost. In her head she keeps seeing one of the volunteers arriving with him in her arms, saying, 'He just got a little lost.' She is holding tightly to this image. But if she says anything to the police, anything at all, the image changes. Joe is still found, but he is taken from the SES volunteer's arms and given to someone else, to Peter, their case manager, or to the police. If she says anything, he will not be returned to her. She is absolutely certain of that. She has to believe that he is just lost, because anything else, anything more, is unthinkable. Joe is lost and he will be back and that is all. *One lost child could have happened to anyone, but two? Foster parents are supposed to be better than the alternative for a child, not worse.*

'Excuse me, Mrs Ealy,' Constable Brown calls now from the living room, where he is sitting with Howard. She abandons her coffee and returns to the sofa, making sure to leave some space between her and her husband. His touch is making her skin crawl right now.

Constable Brown is sitting in the fabric recliner that reminds Elizabeth of the one her father has at home, although his is blue and this one is a strange paisley pattern. He says, 'We're still looking into this, but we feel we need to address a call made by Mr Perry to the police.'

'A call,' Elizabeth repeats, because the constable has stopped speaking. *Oh Gordon, what have you said? What have you told them?* A light sweat instantly covers her body. She has told the old man too much, thinking him harmless, dismissing him because of his failing memory, but he has gone to the police. The walls of the small living room seem to be closing in, and Elizabeth touches her chest where she is struggling to take a deep breath.

The constable clears his throat and crosses his legs. 'Yes. It seems there was an incident about a week ago, and he was concerned enough to call the police.' Elizabeth risks a glance at Howard, who clenches his fists. She hears the slight scrape-squeak of him grinding his jaw. When was her first visit to Gordon's home? It must have been a week ago and what happened then was bad, but not as bad as it got.

'I think it would be best if we listen to it together, and then you can explain what happened,' says Constable Brown, his voice firm so that Howard and Elizabeth can do little except nod their agreement.

He places his phone down on a square coaster on the coffee

table with a picture of the beach on it and the words *Gilmore Beach* in blue cursive writing.

'Ready?' he says.

'Whenever you are, Constable,' says Howard, his voice lubricated with condescension.

The constable nods and touches his phone, then rests his arms on his knees as he twirls a slim gold wedding ring on his finger.

The recording starts playing. 'Gilmore Police, Constable Trent speaking.' The constable is a woman, cheerful and ready to assist.

'Yes, hello, my name is Gordon, Gordon Perry, and I live on Warren Road.'

'Hello, Mr Perry, what can I help you with?'

'Well, I live on Warren Road... Oh, I said that already. Yes, and there's a house across the street. It's a holiday rental now. Dawn used to live there, but she's gone, and her children have decided to rent it out. It's on Warren Road.'

'I see, Mr Perry. I understand. And is there a problem at the house, the one across the road?' The constable speaks slowly and carefully, having instantly made an assessment, and Elizabeth feels her heart break for Gordon. He is clearly suffering from some form of dementia. The small amount of interaction she's had with him has made that obvious, and she wonders at the terrible feeling of knowing that there is something wrong with you, and then forgetting and knowing all over again.

'There's, um... there's a little boy.' His voice is hesitant, unsure.

'Is he alone? Is that the problem?' The constable's tone rises, slight panic in her voice.

'What? No, no, his parents are there, but I don't think... I don't think they're very nice to him.'

Elizabeth's shoulders rise as her jaw tenses. *Not very nice to him.*

'Right...' The constable takes a deep, patient breath. 'And when you say they're not nice to him, what do you mean?'

'Well, it's not... I mean, I think the mother is nice, but the father sent him outside and he doesn't want him to look at the birds in my garden. He won't let him look at the birds and he's only a little boy.' Gordon's voice is low and heavy, the words filled with sadness.

'Right, Mr Perry, but I still don't understand what you mean. Have you seen them hit him or hurt him in any way?'

'Well, no, but the father did grab him by the arm and shook him a bit and it looked quite hard. It's the house on Warren Road. I live on Warren Road, and my son Malcolm will be here soon, and he's going to... I don't know if I told him about the back fence...' Gordon's voice fades; he's still speaking, but he has obviously moved the phone away from his mouth.

'Mr Perry, Mr Perry... are you there?' the constable calls.

'Oh, sorry. Yes, yes, I'm here.'

'Okay, good, stay with me. I don't think there's anything you need to worry about there. I'm sure they're fine. Sometimes kids need a bit of discipline, don't they?' The policewoman's tone is firm, and Elizabeth can hear that she has immediately dismissed what Gordon has said. A fleeting thought hits her. What if they hadn't ignored him? What if they had listened and come out to the house after Gordon called. Where would they be now? Where would Joe be? She wraps her arms around herself, pressing down hard on the bruise that is still there, not quite faded.

'But he won't... I think the little boy is scared of his father. It's not his real father, you see. He won't let him call him Dad, and if you're taking care of a child, how could that hurt? I mean, if he was in my care, he could call me... He likes the birds, you see.'

'Yes, okay, I understand. Mr Perry, is anyone with you now? Do you live alone?'

'I do, but Malcolm is coming with Del soon. They're coming for a visit and Del and I are going to the beach.'

'That's good, do you know exactly when?'

'Um... I have it written down somewhere. Malcolm always says I should write things down.'

'I tell you what, Mr Perry. I'm going to get someone over to have a little chat with you in the next few days. Don't worry about anything at all. Someone will come over and just chat and we can figure all this out. Can you give me your exact address? And can you also give me your son's name and maybe his number if you can remember it?'

Constable Brown leans forward and picks up his phone. Elizabeth doesn't need to look at Howard to know he is furious. His jaw is tensed and his shoulders squared. In contrast to his anger, all she feels is relief that Gordon has only called the police once. If he had called them after Howard's last interaction with him, they would have been at their door immediately, and Joe would have been taken from them. She silently thanks God that Gordon kept his counsel after his first call. But Joe is gone anyway.

'Can you explain the incident Mr Perry is talking about?' the constable asks, and he sits back in the recliner, relaxed and willing to wait, still twirling the wedding ring.

Howard shifts forward on the sofa and puts his hands flat on his knees. Howard's wedding ring is thick and heavy, the right size for a man with big hands.

'What exactly are you asking us here?' he says, enunciating each word crisply. 'It's quite obvious that the old man is losing it. He's got some sort of agenda, something against me and my family, and he's trying to turn your attention away from him. I told you I was concerned about him.' He raises his voice a little, warming up to a tirade. 'Anyone listening to that would understand exactly what he's trying to do. He's just... a weird pervert, and he probably has my son. He has him, and instead of tearing his house apart like you should be doing, you're asking me to listen to this crap.' He stabs his finger on the coffee table.

'Please, Mr Ealy, if you could just calm down.' The constable lifts a hand, showing Howard his palm. 'All we are trying to do is establish exactly what has happened to your foster son. Can you tell me if it's true that he's not allowed to call you Dad? He is a very young child, and from what I gather, you were hoping to adopt him.'

Howard stands up, his jaw jutting. 'He's not my son yet, Constable, not yet, and I didn't want him to get attached if he was only going to be moved on. I am not prepared to stand here and listen to this bullshit. Come, Elizabeth.'

He gestures at her, and she stands as well, but the constable says, 'I think I need a word with Mrs Ealy alone, if you don't mind.'

Elizabeth looks at Howard, and then the constable, unsure, wishing she could just run from this house. She sinks to the sofa again. She would rather be with the constable than with Howard, but defying him is risky. He glares down at her, heat in his gaze. Closing her eyes, she tries to still her shaking body. *Go away, go away.* If she looks at him, she will stand up and go with him. If she looks at him, he will have won. *One, two, don't look, three, four, five...*

'Fine,' he hisses.

When she feels him stomp off, making enough noise to demonstrate his displeasure, she takes a breath, deep and long. She will pay for this, although what more can he take?

The memory of the last time they were close to adopting a child returns, the last terrible time, and the way that ended. *Oh sweetheart, I am so sorry*, she sends to a child she will never see again. But she will see Joe again, she will, she has to.

'Mrs Ealy,' says the constable gently, 'is there anything you need to tell me, anything at all? You're safe with me, I promise,

and you can tell me anything. All we want is to find Joe, safe
and sound.'

Elizabeth lifts her head and opens her eyes. The constable
has a son – maybe he has more than one child – so he understands what it means to take care of a child, to love a child. And
because he does, he may understand everything she is holding
back. He may understand it, and if she tells him the truth, he
will help her and guide her and bring Joe back to her.

He watches her, his mouth a firm line, the wedding ring
going around and around.

'Nothing,' she says. 'I have nothing to tell you.'

CHAPTER SIXTEEN

GORDON

Two Days Ago

It's another perfect summer's day, only a few slips of white cloud drifting across the blue sky in the breeze. Gordon is drinking his morning coffee at the little table in the front yard. 'No fighting now,' he says with a smile as a pair of lorikeets gang up on a cockatoo to get the bigger bird away from the seeds. The birds always bicker, but mostly seem to like being near each other. Gordon thinks it's a pity that people aren't more like birds.

He looks over at the house across the road. All is quiet. He is trying not to be too worried about the little boy. The police didn't seem interested in what he had to say. A day after his call, a lovely young woman holding a small iPad appeared at his door. 'Gordon Perry?' she asked when he opened up to see her there.

'Yes,' he said, offering her a smile that she returned. She had long dark hair, woven into an intricate plait.

'My name is Benita, and I'm from Ageing, Disability and Home Care.'

'Yes?' Gordon said, a little confused.

'I work with the Department of Community Services, and I just wanted to check that you're doing well and have people who can care for you.'

Gordon understood instantly that this was because of his call to the police. He knew that the constable he had spoken to wasn't listening to what he had to say about Joe. It was all very clear in his head as he looked at the young woman, as it was some days. There were days when he woke up and the whole world seemed brighter, and he could feel the comfort of his thoughts whizzing through his brain. But then there were other days... days that made him feel angry and sad. Only last night he had spent half an hour looking for the remote, only to find it in the fridge. He had taken himself off to bed then, horrified at the lapse and hoping for a better morning. As he looked at the young woman, he knew he couldn't tell her about that. She probably couldn't imagine a time in her future when thoughts would slip away, wispy things that couldn't be caught, and ordinary things would seem impossible.

He asked her in and made her a cup of tea, his hands trembling slightly at having someone from the government in his home.

'We just want to make sure that you're okay living alone,' she said. 'I have a couple of questions to ask. Is that okay?'

'No,' he said, his fear morphing into anger. He was in his own home, and he had a right to say no. 'No,' he repeated firmly. 'I understand your concern, and I know I shouldn't have called the police, but I'm not going to answer any questions now. My son will be here soon, and then you can talk to him. You can wait and talk to him.' He found himself getting agitated.

'That's fine.' She smiled, a warm smile that immediately calmed him. 'Do you have his number?'

He gave it to her, and she seemed happy enough to leave armed with that. He knew she would be back. Even though he felt well, he had been a little afraid of the questions she might have for him. He'd only been trying to help little Joe.

Malcolm has said he wants Gordon to have some home help. His son is worried about him, and that makes Gordon worry about himself.

The slam of a door echoes through the air, and he looks at where it has come from, seeing the woman and the little boy running from the house opposite. He puts down his coffee and stands up. The woman pauses at the gate, looking around her wildly, and then back at the house.

Gordon hurries to his own gate. 'Come over here,' he says, knowing that they are both scared. It is obvious. Joe's face is red, his eyes bright with tears, and the woman has a flower of hurt on her cheek.

'We...' she begins, her voice clogged with fear. She opens the gate and crosses the road, Joe's hand clutched in hers. 'We need to hide,' she says, panicked, her head swinging back to the house again and again. She is wearing a pair of shorts and a bright red T-shirt, and Joe is dressed in blue and green. Both are barefoot. She pulls the little boy across the road, wincing as her feet hit the hot asphalt.

'Ow,' says Joe, and she picks him up, moving quickly.

'I'm sorry, Elizabeth,' Joe wails.

'Don't worry, sweetheart. It was an accident,' she says.

'Come on,' says Gordon, and he steps back to allow them into his garden, turning around to lead them into the house. But before they even make it to the front door, there is another echoing slam, and the man appears. He too is dressed in a T-shirt and shorts, but somehow he still manages to look smart, even though he is also barefoot. He runs across the road, not noticing anything but what he is focused on: Elizabeth and Joe.

'Quickly,' says Gordon, but the woman has frozen in place, terror on her face.

The man barges through the gate and grabs her arm. 'Don't

you dare,' he hisses, then he crouches down and grabs the child by the shoulders. 'What did I tell you about touching my stuff, what did I tell you? Now you've broken it.'

He pulls his arm back, and it seems like he will slap the boy, but Gordon shouts, 'No!' and the man stops himself.

Joe's body wilts, as though he is having trouble standing up. The man holds him tightly by the shoulders again, shakes him some more. 'Why did you touch it?' he shouts, his voice strangled with fury.

'No,' screams Elizabeth. 'No, stop!' She pushes at the man, and Gordon stands helplessly, not knowing if he should get his phone and call the police or try to grab the man. He wrings his hands, terrified.

The man looks very strong. He utters a sound like a growl and lets go of Joe. Standing up, he grabs Elizabeth by her hair and pulls. 'Don't you start that shit with me. He has to learn.'

'Stop it,' shouts Gordon. 'Stop that. It's disgusting.' He tries to make his voice loud and strong, but he can hear that it is croaky and filled with fear.

The man lets go of Elizabeth and storms towards Gordon, who takes a few tottering steps backwards. He seizes him by the shoulder, squeezing just hard enough to frighten him, but not hard enough to bruise, holding him tight so Gordon cannot move away. Gordon knows that the man is being very careful about what he is doing – that he knows what he is doing, that he has done this before – and the fear that runs through his veins is not for himself, but for Joe – for little Joe. What kind of a man is this?

'And why,' asks the man, speaking carefully and slowly, 'are you interfering in my family's life? What exactly is it you want, old man, because I am beginning to think there is something about you that I should be worried about.'

Gordon risks a quick glance at Joe, whose eyes are wide with shock as he wraps his little arms around himself.

The man's grip tightens on Gordon's shoulder, and Gordon works hard not to let him see the pain he is causing. 'Old men aren't supposed to be this interested in young boys, but you seem to always be looking at Joe, always watching him. What do you want with him? Do you want to touch him in a way that's not very nice? Is that what you want? I think the police need to know that a pervert is living in this respectable neighbourhood close to the beach. I really think they need to know that.' The words come out in a threatening hiss, filled with venom.

'I don't... don't... You're... you're...' Gordon stutters, his mind racing along with his heart.

The man lets go of his shoulder. He slaps Gordon's back a few times in what seems to be a friendly fashion, but it's very hard and nearly knocks Gordon off his feet. 'I don't... don't,' he imitates, and then he laughs. 'Go home, Elizabeth, and take Joe with you. I need to order myself a new iPad, since mine is broken. Just go now.' His voice has turned soft and menacing.

Gordon watches as Elizabeth grabs Joe's hand. With a stricken look at him, she mouths, 'I'm sorry.' Then she sets off back across the road, pulling Joe behind her, his small feet tripping over themselves as he looks back at Gordon, both of them flinching as their feet touch the baking road.

'Stay out of it, old-timer,' the man spits.

Gordon stands up straighter, pushing his shoulders back, but when he catches the man's gaze, he is appalled by what he sees there. Absolute control and a lack of empathy are obvious in his grey eyes, in the set of his jaw. This man will hurt him and feel nothing, and Gordon feels his shoulders round, his body sag.

A quick nod, a small smile, and then the man too leaves the garden.

Gordon rubs his head as he watches the birds settle back around the feeder, peace returning. The street is empty, the house across the road silent again.

The whole thing has taken no more than a few minutes, although to Gordon it feels as though a lot of time has passed. He cannot believe what has just happened, that someone has been so violent towards him – towards a woman, towards a child, for God's sake. What is the world coming to? He thinks for a moment about calling the police, but immediately dismisses the idea. They won't believe him, and he won't be able to explain it correctly. Malcolm will receive another call. For a moment he is overwhelmed with helpless anger at his failing brain and body, at his frailty and his inability to help the woman and child. As a younger man he found himself in a few scrapes, and he could deliver a punch with the best of them. To be this weak is humiliating, and as he shuffles back inside his house, he allows himself a few quiet tears at his own impotence.

Only when he has stumbled to the kitchen and poured himself a stiff whisky, and is sitting down in the air-conditioned cool of the living room, does he remember that Malcolm will be here soon. It is way too early in the morning for a drink, but he has no idea what else to do to settle his nerves. He sips slowly at the whisky, feeling acid rise in his throat in protest. He hasn't even eaten breakfast. 'Malcolm will be here soon,' he mumbles, to comfort himself. His son, who is six foot four and who works out at the gym in his building every day, is fit and strong. He will be able to talk to the man from across the street. Do more than talk if necessary.

An hour later, the whole thing feels unreal, as though it might not have happened at all. Gordon goes out into the front garden and looks at the house opposite, which is shuttered in the late-morning heat. As he watches, a curtain in the front room twitches.

He turns and goes back inside. He is afraid for himself now, actually afraid for himself.

CHAPTER SEVENTEEN

ELIZABETH

Two Days Ago

Panting, she dashes into the house, a sharp pain in her foot from where she stepped on a stone in the road. 'Wait,' says Joe, crying, but she pulls him along, rushing into the bathroom, and locking the door. Sliding onto the floor, her heart thuds, her eyes filled with tears as her chest heaves with panic. Joe stands looking down at her for a moment, and then he sits down next to her, his own cheeks wet, but quiet in the way he becomes when he is afraid.

She has no idea what to do. She touches her pocket and is nearly sick with relief to find that she has her phone. She doesn't remember picking it up. Taking it out, she starts to dial the police and her parents and sister over and again, but always stops short of pressing the call button. Her finger hovers over the screen as she tries to think about what she's going to say, how she's going to explain it. Taking deep breaths in and out, she tries to calm herself so she can think properly, and she wants to weep when she hears Joe imitating her. She puts an arm around him, pulls him close, but she has no idea what to say to him, no idea what to say to anyone.

There is so much she has kept from her family, so many things she has not told them as the years have gone by and she has talked herself out of leaving again and again. Joe sits quietly next to her, stunned and sad. His little lips tremble every now and again, but she can see him stopping himself from shedding tears. 'Big boys don't cry,' Howard said to him yesterday when he fell at the beach. *Big boys don't cry.*

She hears Howard come back into the house, slam the front door, and then there is silence except for his footsteps as he walks around looking for them.

She waits, holding her breath, safe but not safe behind the locked bathroom door.

And then the footsteps stop in front of the door, and she sits up, grabs Joe's hand, braces herself for the sound of Howard throwing his body against the wood, forcing the door open. She has never seen him this angry before, this vicious. He has hurt her over the years, but he uses his words more than anything else. Bruises fade quickly, but his hissing anger stays with her. And he has never grabbed her hair like that. He has never done that. On her phone, she dials triple zero once more, her thumb hovering over the call button. If he throws himself against the door, if he tries to get in, she will call them. What has happened to set him off like this? It cannot simply be the broken iPad – he can easily replace that. There seems to be something more simmering beneath the surface now, something darker, blacker.

Last night, she and Joe were playing the Hungry Hippos board game together before she started on dinner. Both of them were giggling as they pushed the levers to help the hippos collect the balls, and Howard came in and said, 'Aren't you two making a lot of noise.'

'We're playing,' she said jovially, 'and when you play, you have to make lots of noise, don't you, Joe?'

'Lots and lots,' Joe giggled.

'Look at you, the perfect couple,' Howard said, and he turned and left, somehow taking all the fun out of the game so that she and Joe finished quickly and packed up. It was such an odd thing to say, but as she thinks about it now, Joe leaning up against her, she realises that her husband is jealous. He is actually jealous of her relationship with Joe. He has been happy to be a foster parent because the children have come and gone, because – except for the one placement that ended so badly – when the children have left, her attention has always returned to him. But now Joe is here and he will, hopefully, be here forever, and no matter what Howard has said about wanting a child, about adopting a child, he really wants to be the only focus of Elizabeth's attention. She takes a deep, shaky breath, tears pricking at her eyes as she tries to prevent herself from crying. She needs to be brave in front of Joe. What on earth is she going to do now?

She realises that Howard is still standing outside the bathroom door; she can feel him there, a looming presence. He is waiting for her to say something, to do something, but she remains frozen, except for the arm she wraps around Joe again as she lets go of his hand. She shuffles further away from the door, pulling him with her, her back against one wall of the bathroom, her thumb ready to press the number. If he tries to get in, she will call the police.

But that's not what happens. Instead, she hears the sound of Howard slumping against the wall and then sliding down to sit on the floor. She waits, staring at the door. Her leg begins to cramp because she is sitting on it, and she changes position.

And then she hears a guttural choke, a wail, and she realises that Howard is crying. She's never heard him cry before, and the sound is disconcerting, frightening even. She starts to stand up, her body yearning to comfort him. His terrible pain is obvious, even through the door. She half stands, and then Joe moves beside her and she sits back down. If she opens the door now, if she comforts Howard, he will have won something from her. She knows this. Finally he stops crying and he says, 'I'm sorry, Beth. I'm so sorry. I have no idea what just happened.'

'You hurt me,' says Elizabeth, raising her voice a little so that he can hear her through the locked door. Her eyes move up and down the white-tiled wall, finding a crack where the top of the door meets the tile. 'You hurt us,' she says.

'I know, I know I did. It happens, you know it happens. I don't know... I just kind of blacked out and I don't know what I did. I was so angry, but I'm sorry. Do you hear me? Joe, I'm sorry, I'm really sorry, buddy. Sometimes grown-ups do bad things and they need to know to say sorry, so that's what I'm saying to you. My father never said sorry to me, Joe, he never said sorry after he was mean to me and I don't want to be like him, I can't. I'm sorry, Joe, do you forgive me?'

Joe stares at the door, his green eyes wide with incomprehension. He's only five and he has no idea what to say or do here. He has forgiven Howard once in the last couple of weeks and now he needs to do it again. He cannot understand how the word 'sorry' can be repeated over and again until it loses all meaning. Elizabeth has been listening to 'sorry' for years. She has been forgiving Howard for years and she can feel that this child, this little boy, is now complicit in the terrible dance she and Howard take part in. How can she allow this to go on? Joe cannot be made to dance along with her – it is too cruel.

If she calls the police, they will come and arrest Howard, and she will be able to go home to her parents and then to leave him, just leave him and never look back, but – and this 'but' is so huge, so enormous that she cannot even contemplate it – they will take Joe from her. Perhaps she would be able to foster a child as a divorced woman, but the Department of Community Services will not allow Joe to be with her as she deals with the trauma of divorce from a violent partner. Howard is in control of their money, in control of her whole life.

Outside the bathroom door, he is whispering the same phrase again and again, 'I'm sorry, I'm sorry, I'm sorry,' his own pain in each repetition.

Her thumb hovers over the call button and she knows that if she dials, she will lose everything. The decision has already been made.

She puts the phone down and takes a deep, shaky breath, preparing herself to betray this child so that she can keep him in her life. Her own weakness sickens her. She should not have allowed this to happen. But she has, and the only good thing she has is this little boy, and the potential to have him forever.

'Howard is saying that he wants you to forgive him for being mean, Joe,' she whispers to him, her hand stroking the dark hair off his face. 'He wants to know if you forgive him. If you do, you can tell him. You can say, "I forgive you, Howard." She keeps stroking his head and he looks up at her with so much love, so much trust in his eyes that her heart cracks open for him. He has not had it easy in his little life. When he was taken from his mother, the social worker said he hadn't yet begun walking because he was mostly confined to his cot. He was eighteen months old but underweight and had no words yet. He barely smiled and he didn't laugh. He was nursed back to health by his first foster family, but then his mother returned and turned his life upside down again. Now he is with her and Howard. And she wants him to be hers with every fibre of her being. He should not have been on the iPad, because he's not allowed to use it without one of them sitting next to him, but she had left him alone to have a shower and he had grown bored. It would have been fine if Howard had not seen him and yelled, frightening him so that he dropped it.

She should tell Howard to leave, she should tell him to go and leave them alone, and then she should call Peter and confess what has happened. She owes that to this little boy, to herself, but she cannot move. Outside the bathroom door, Howard waits in silence now, and finally Joe says, 'I forgive you, Howard, it's okay,' his small voice clear and strong.

Elizabeth wraps her arms around him and hugs him, holding on tight, and he does the same. 'You're a brave boy,' she says.

'And you, Bethy?' calls Howard. 'Do I have your forgiveness as well? I need you to forgive me because I don't think I could survive without you. You're my life, Elizabeth, you know that, my life and my love. Please say you forgive me.'

'I forgive you,' she says. As she says it, there is a rumble of thunder through the air, a summer storm suddenly announcing itself.

'It's going to rain,' says Howard. 'Maybe we can do something inside together, like a real family.'

Elizabeth stands up, stretching her legs and pushing against her back. 'We can bake a cake,' she says, as the sound of rain hitting the roof and the windows drowns out her words. Picking up Joe, she opens the door, and Howard is there, his shoulders hunched, his face tear-stained. He holds out his arms to her and she lets herself be hugged as he murmurs, 'Sorry, sorry, sorry,' into her hair, his arms surrounding them both. He has a broad chest and his arms are strong and she is enveloped in the smoky wood smell of his cologne, and for just a moment, as Joe wraps his arms tighter around her, she wants to stay right here forever.

It's not like she doesn't understand where Howard comes from. After they had been dating for six months and he was a regular at their family dinners, always charming, always equipped with an expensive bottle of wine, she stopped accepting his excuses for not meeting his parents. *They're travelling... They still work, so they're tired at night, they go to bed early... They have friends they want to see.*

'Do you not want me to meet them? Is there something

about me that embarrasses you?' she asked him one night, confronting him when she usually wouldn't, buoyed by Natalie's entreaties to 'put your foot down. Either he wants to be with you forever or he doesn't. And if he wants to be with you, he will want you to meet his parents.'

'No... no, God no, you're amazing,' he said. They were lying in bed, the television on in the corner of the room, neither of them in the mood for getting up on a cold Sunday morning. 'It's just,' he sighed, running his hands through his hair, 'they're not the nicest people.'

Elizabeth laughed, thinking he was making a joke. 'Oh, come on,' she said. 'You're nice, so they must be nice.'

'You don't know,' he replied, shaking his head, and in his eyes she could see a deep pain, shadowed and large.

'It's fine,' she said. 'I don't have to meet them.'

'No, I want you to. They need to meet my future wife.'

She laughed, delighted. 'Your future wife?'

'If you'll have me. I didn't want to do it like this. I wanted it to be special. I've booked a cruise, a harbour cruise for the first week of spring. It's just us and a chef and I—'

'I don't need that,' she said. 'I would love to be your wife.' She kissed him and then lost herself in the moment.

They went on the cruise two weeks later to celebrate, the spring weather making it easier to be inside the boat as the wind roared off the water. They feasted on prawns and lobster and champagne, and he presented her with a diamond ring surrounded by tiny sapphires over the caramel cheesecake dessert. She thought herself the luckiest woman in the world.

She met his parents for the first time on the night of their engagement party. Howard's father looked like him; tall, with the same grey eyes. His mother was a small woman; overweight, her hands covered in cheap rings. It was a small party, just family and a few friends at a dinner catered by a friend of Natalie's. Howard's parents sat at one end of the table and said very little to anyone. Elizabeth watched them closely all night, wanting them to feel comfortable, but she'd already been humiliated by Howard's mother stepping back from her when she went forward to give her a hug when they were introduced.

'Elizabeth was thinking about a summer wedding,' Jean said, looking at Howard's mother. 'Do you think that would work for everyone in your family, Margaret?'

Margaret started to open her mouth, but Howard's father, Jerry, put his hand on her arm. 'I'll tell you what she thinks: whatever works. She doesn't like to be difficult, do you, Margaret? Just nod your head.' Howard's mother obediently nodded her head, and the situation was so absurd that Natalie couldn't help a spluttered laugh.

And from down the table, Howard's father looked at her and uttered the words, 'Uppity bitch,' spitting them out with such venom that Natalie was immediately subdued.

The whole table descended into a moment of embarrassed silence before Howard said, 'This fish is delicious, Natalie. Maybe your friend can cater the wedding as well.' And that allowed conversation to resume, as most of the people at the table discussed menus for the wedding.

Both Jerry and Margaret sat in silence for the rest of the meal, refusing to be drawn into conversation with anyone. When she saw they were leaving, Elizabeth followed them to the door, wanting to say goodbye, but Howard was with them, and as she got there, she heard his father say, 'Stupid boy. On your own head be it.'

His mother said, 'But Jerry—' and his father grabbed her hand and pulled her out of the door, leaving Howard staring after them.

'They didn't like me,' Elizabeth said softly.

'They don't like anyone, even each other,' Howard replied.

Elizabeth wanted to discuss it, to try again with his parents, but even though they came to the wedding, she and Howard saw very little of them after that. Once they knew there would be no grandchildren, they pretty much ceased contact with their son.

Sometimes Elizabeth thought about what it must have been like for Howard, growing up in a house where silence and fear reigned, and because she thought about it, she understood some of Howard's behaviour and she forgave it more often than she should.

Today has been frightening, but as she steps away from Howard, she has a terrifying realisation that some line was crossed today that should never have been crossed. And because of that, it will be easier for him to cross it next time. She immediately dismisses the thought. If she holds on to that thought, she will need to take action, and any action she takes will lead to consequences she cannot bear.

'Yes, let's bake a cake,' says Howard now. 'What kind of cake should we bake?' he asks Joe, who has his head on Elizabeth's chest.

'Chocolate,' shouts Joe, lifting his head, his voice loud with joyful anticipation.

'Yay, chocolate,' says Howard, and he holds out his arms to the boy, who leans away from Elizabeth so Howard can take him. He swings him easily onto his shoulders as he walks to the kitchen. Joe giggles and reaches up to try and touch the ceiling. Elizabeth follows, exhausted but determined to create a new memory, to paper over what has happened. The drumming rain soothes her thoughts as a wet, fresh smell drifts in through an open window. Summer rain.

She is not sure she has the ingredients for a cake, but she is happy to discover that the owners of the house have left everything she needs, including chocolate chips and icing sugar.

The rain comes down for twenty minutes, hard and fast, cooling the air. Elizabeth takes care of creaming the butter and sugar, enjoying, as she always does, the feel of the slick butter combining with the granules of sugar, and leaves Howard and Joe to mix the cocoa and flour together. Howard is patience itself, letting Joe handle the wooden spoon and wiping up spills without comment when they add the eggs. 'Good job, buddy,' he keeps saying, and then when the cake is in the tin and Elizabeth slides it into the oven, he takes two teaspoons so that he and Joe can eat the tiny bits of remaining batter.

'You shouldn't really be eating raw eggs,' says Elizabeth with a smile.

'Ah, come on, Mum,' laughs Howard. 'It's the best part.' Elizabeth's heart warms and Joe giggles. All she can feel is joy at the lovely afternoon.

'How about a movie?' says Howard once they have finished with the mixing bowl.

'Good idea,' says Elizabeth. 'Why don't you two go and watch one while I clean up and get lunch ready.'

'Okay, sounds good to me. Come on, buddy,' says Howard, lifting Joe off the chair he has been standing on. Elizabeth hums as she cleans the kitchen.

The rest of the day is perfect. Howard plays with Joe all afternoon, constructing a house out of empty carboard boxes for Joe's superheroes to live in. They eat dinner as a family, and then Howard says it's his turn to clean the kitchen so Elizabeth can get Joe bathed and ready for bed.

Once Joe is asleep, she sits next to Howard on the grey sofa as they share a bottle of wine and watch the news. She takes small sips of the heavy red wine, holding it in her mouth to feel the sting of alcohol before swallowing as she seeks the courage to say what she wants to say.

'Perhaps...' she begins, and then she stops herself, unsure if she should say anything.

'Perhaps?' Howard prompts her.

'Perhaps you should go and apologise to Gordon. He's an old man and I think... I think you scared him.' As she says the words, her hand trembles a little and she puts her wine down on the timber coffee table, afraid of spilling it. She has no idea how Howard will react to the suggestion, but the thought of the old man across the road has been bothering her all afternoon, the idea of what he must think of Howard and of her.

Howard sighs, and Elizabeth feels her body stiffen. 'You're right,' he says. 'I should. But Beth... I'm so... ashamed, I guess. I'm just so ashamed.'

Elizabeth is stunned by these words. In all their years of marriage, Howard has never said something like this. 'I... I don't know what to say,' she says, touching his hand. 'Thank you for saying that, thank you. We were scared and I don't want to feel like that again. I hate feeling like that.' A rush of relief as the words *thank you, God* run through her mind. Maybe he has scared himself. Maybe Howard understands that a line was crossed, and he will never cross it again.

'I know,' he says. 'And I am really trying here. I want us to be a family with Joe, a real family. I don't want what happened last time—'

'Let's not talk about last time,' she says quickly, wanting to hold onto the good feeling of something changing forever. Thinking about last time breaks her heart and leads her down a dark path. 'Joe is a different child, he's younger and he's... wonderful and it's going to be fine.'

An image appears of a smile, and she hears a voice, 'Come on, Beth, you love ice cream.' *Oh sweetheart, I am so sorry.* Picking up her wine, she finishes the glass, swallowing down the memory and dismissing it. 'It's going to be fine,' she assures Howard, reassures herself.

He leans towards her and kisses her on the lips. 'It is,' he says. 'I should tell the old guy that I'm sorry, but...' He shrugs.

'Why don't I take him a piece of cake?' she suggests. 'I'll tell him you're sorry and he can accept the apology or not.'

'That's a great idea, thanks, Beth,' he says, and he turns back to the television.

Elizabeth gets up and goes to the kitchen, where there is still half a chocolate cake left. She cuts a large slice and selects a pretty side plate bordered by pink roses to put it on.

'Listen for Joe,' she calls as she leaves.

She walks quickly across the road, enjoying the kiss of the cooler air on her skin, deliberately not thinking about her bare feet running across this morning. She is nervous when she knocks on Gordon's door, but she pushes her shoulders back and readies a smile on her face. Howard is sorry and all he can do is apologise. People need to be given a second chance. She quickly pushes away the thought that she has, over twenty-odd years of marriage, given Howard many, many second chances. She just wants to be happy, to be a mother and have a family. That shouldn't be too much to ask.

The door opens and Gordon is there, the light from his hallway behind him, glasses balanced on the end of his nose.

'Elizabeth,' he says, wary. Then he smiles when he sees she is holding a plate with a piece of cake. 'I was so worried about you, about both of you. Is Joe okay? Is he all right? I was going to call the police, you know; I was, but then...' He takes his glasses off and waves them around, and then he folds them up and puts them in the top pocket of his shirt. 'Come in,' he says, stepping back. 'Come in,' he repeats.

'Oh no,' says Elizabeth, 'I can't stay,' as a small wave of fear crests inside her at the idea that Gordon could have called the police, and what would have happened then. She has been so involved with Joe and Howard in the last few hours that this hasn't even occurred to her, and now she wonders at herself for not thinking about the possibility. 'Thank you for not calling them,' she says gratefully. 'It's... Howard wasn't himself this afternoon. He's under a lot of stress with work,' she lies. 'I just wanted to give this to you and tell you that he is deeply sorry.

We are both deeply sorry. There is no way that should have happened and it's unacceptable. I hope you can accept our apology.' She holds the plate out to him.

For a second it looks like he might not take it, but then he smiles. 'You don't have to worry about me, Elizabeth. But I do worry about you and that little boy. I know that sometimes, especially today... the world seems so different now, so fast... but I know that we all have bad days. He scared me, your husband. He really did.'

'I know,' she says, still holding the plate out to him. 'And I can promise you that it was totally out of character for him. He has never done anything like that before and he has assured me that he never will again.' She bites down on the lie because she can see that Gordon doesn't believe her. She just wants this to be over so she can go back home and sit on the sofa with Howard and forget this day ever happened. 'Please accept our apology,' she almost begs. 'Please, Gordon.'

Gordon studies her intently, and then he smiles. 'I've always been partial to a piece of chocolate cake,' he says, reaching out and taking the plate. 'We'll say no more about it.'

Elizabeth returns his smile, utter relief flowing through her. 'Thank you, Gordon.'

'All right then,' he says, and then he steps back to close the front door.

She turns to go, but he says her name again. 'Elizabeth.'

'Yes,' she says, turning around.

'You can come over here any time you like, you know. Any time at all. If you need help or anything. My son Malcolm will be here in a few days and my granddaughter will be with him. Joe and Del can play and you can just... rest.'

'Oh,' she says. 'Thank you... thank you,' and she wants to tell him again that Howard is never like he was this morning, that they are all fine, but she leaves it. 'Thank you,' she repeats sincerely, and she walks back across the road.

An hour later, she is ready for bed, relaxed from the wine and exhausted from the day. 'I might have a shower,' she says, standing up from the sofa.

'I might join you,' Howard smiles. She returns his smile, wanting, hoping to hold on to the feeling of this perfect day.

Just before she is ready to turn off her light, her sister calls from America.

'How's the holiday?' she asks.

'Blissful,' says Elizabeth, and she means it.

CHAPTER EIGHTEEN

GORDON

Today, 12.45 p.m.

'What other thing, Gordon?' asks Ruby. 'What other thing should you have told the police?'

'Well,' says Gordon. 'It was like this...'

Gordon likes talking to Ruby, likes her pretty green eyes and the way she listens. He takes his time with the terrible story, remembering the fear he felt when Howard put his hand on his shoulder and squeezed, when Howard clapped him on the back so hard it stung and nearly knocked him off his feet. Ruby nods her head and sometimes writes things down in a little notebook she has pulled out of her bag.

He tries to remember everything, even mentioning the apology slice of chocolate cake. It was a very nice piece of cake, but each bite felt heavy in his mouth, as though the eating of it meant he was forgiving the man and what he had done. Howard didn't deserve to be forgiven.

It occurs to him that he really shouldn't be telling her all this. If she writes her story and Howard sees it, he will say Gordon is lying, that Gordon is strange. 'I was only being friendly,' he imagines Howard saying. 'There is something wrong with that old man.' The things Howard was saying about him, implying about him and his friendship with Joe, were sickening, sickening and cruel. Agitation rises inside him. How dare Howard accuse him of being so vile?

'If you see something, say something' is a phrase Gordon has heard a lot over the last couple of decades. It's meant to concern people who are planning nefarious things, but Gordon thinks it could apply to anything. He saw something. He saw a child being hurt, a woman being abused, and because he is old and frail and not terribly sure of himself, he can do nothing about it. The one thing he can do is to say what he saw.

'What should I do, do you think?' he asks Ruby, because she is young and seems clever and she is sure to know. He wishes once again that Malcolm was here, but he's not because... He can't seem to remember why. 'I mean, he's missing now – Joe is missing – so what should I do?'

'I think you should tell the police,' Ruby says emphatically. 'They do need to know. I understand that they didn't believe you after the phone call, but they will believe this, they have to.' She sounds completely certain of this. 'He can't just be allowed to get away with hurting Joe... with hurting the little boy. He shouldn't have had him in the first place,' she says, her eyes dark with anger.

Gordon wants to say something, and if she is by his side, then the police are sure to listen and believe him, instead of just dismissing him as an addled old man. But even as he thinks about this, he can feel bits of the story drifting away. How hard did Howard squeeze his shoulder? Did he grab Elizabeth by the hair? What kind of cake did Elizabeth bring him? What did he say to her in reply when she asked for his forgiveness?

He wrings his hands and then smooths down his hair. 'But what if I forget some of it and they think I'm lying?'

'I'll come... I can come with you,' says Ruby, and Gordon is not sure if she really wants to, but he needs someone there with him, he knows it.

'I appreciate it, lass, I do,' he says.

He stands up, picking up his phone, and Ruby does the same, then together they go to the front door, but when they get there, the lawn of the house across the street is crowded, the press pushing past people who say, 'Hey, watch it.' They are trying to get to the door and it takes a moment for Gordon to see what's happening.

'They've definitely found something,' says Gordon.

'Not Joe,' says Ruby softly. 'They haven't found him or they would be...'

'They would be celebrating if they found him and he's okay. I imagine they would be celebrating,' says Gordon.

'I'll go and check. You stay here, Gordon, stay here,' Ruby tells him, and she walks quickly across the road.

Gordon watches carefully as she looks around for a moment, trying to determine who the best person to speak to is. He would ask one of the volunteers if it was him.

There is a portable gazebo set up on the front lawn of the house, and a familiar-looking woman is standing behind a trestle table filled with bottles of water that she is handing out to whoever asks. She is wearing one of the orange vests of the SES, but she looks quite old, so perhaps she wasn't able to walk around in the heat of the day. Gordon squints, trying to determine who it is, and then he realises that it's Orla from the bowling club. Orla is only a year younger than he is, but she could be a decade younger. She refuses to give in to old age and spends all day, every day, involved in charity work and running clubs and visiting people who can't leave their homes. Flora used to find Orla somewhat irritating, as the woman always wanted to know what charities they were involved in, and would offer a smug smile when Flora confessed that she mostly donated to good causes. But Orla was very kind when Flora died, filling Gordon's fridge and checking up on him almost daily for a few weeks. Ruby should speak to her, because Orla knows everything and is always happy to share what she knows.

Ruby obviously comes to the same conclusion, because she walks purposefully to the table and then waits patiently while Orla opens a new bunch of plastic-wrapped water bottles, handing one to a man standing next to her.

Orla is delighted to be asked what has happened, and Gordon watches her gesture widely as she explains. But as she does, Ruby seems to shrink a little, her shoulders rounding, her head dropping, and Gordon feels sick at what she might be hearing. He wants to go over there himself and listen, but he won't be quick enough and Orla won't want to explain again. He wills Ruby to return quickly.

Finally Orla stops speaking and turns her attention back to handing out water, and Ruby turns around, giving a small shake of her head that lets him know the news is not good. She walks back across the road.

As she comes into the yard, the birds scatter from the feeder and a lorikeet nearly flies into her face. She stifles a scream.

'What is it?' asks Gordon, panic rising in his chest. 'What did they tell you?'

'They found...' Ruby touches her chest. 'They found... Oh Gordon,' she says, tears on her cheeks.

CHAPTER NINETEEN

ELIZABETH

Today, 12.45 p.m.

'I don't think that's the truth,' says Constable Brown to Elizabeth's statement that she has nothing more to tell him. He stops moving his wedding ring, sits forward a little more.

'You're saying I'm lying?' snaps Elizabeth.

'Not at all, but I am a little concerned that there is something more you want to say. And anything you do say could help us find Joe. That's all we want – to find Joe. I know that sometimes it can be hard to tell people what you're going through. I want to let you know that I'm here to listen without judgement.'

He sits back and steeples his hands, his piece said, and Elizabeth wants to reiterate that she has nothing to say. But Joe is missing, her little boy is missing, and if she doesn't say something... then perhaps she is partly to blame. Mostly to blame? Entirely to blame?

'I can bring in someone else for you to talk to if that would be easier. Constable Williamson is outside; she's... someone who would understand. Would you like me to get her?'

Elizabeth shakes her head. The thought of explaining things to yet another person feels like too much. 'I...' she says, and then she leans forward, buries her head in her hands. She will be making a grave mistake if she says anything. Howard will never forgive her. But perhaps, just perhaps, as the hours pass, she is moving towards never forgiving *him*. *What has happened to Joe? What does Howard know about what has happened to Joe?* She can't confront him, can't ask the question of him and demand an answer of her husband of twenty years. But maybe this man can, this young man who has a seven-year-old son and who only wants to find Joe. Maybe he can.

She sits up and takes a deep breath.

She can feel the constable waiting for her to speak. He is sitting forward again in the recliner, his hands clasped together as he waits. In her mind, sentences run together as she mentally deletes and rewrites what she is going to say.

'Mrs Ealy, it's okay to tell me what happened, it really is,' says the constable.

She sits straight on the sofa, wishing that her parents and her sister were here. But they are all together in the USA, far away.

She touches her chest, steeling herself to take this leap, this terrifying leap into the unknown realm of telling the absolute truth. She takes a breath, and then says, 'He doesn't let Joe call him Dad, but I let him call me Mum. I want you to know that.'

The constable nods. 'I understand.'

'And...' she begins, but hesitates. In her mind she can see her own line in the sand, and once she has stepped over it, she will not be able to step back again. It will be obliterated. Everything will change. Her marriage will be over, she is certain, and she will lose Joe. But hasn't she lost him already? All her decisions until now have cost her the little boy she loves, though it has all been to protect him, to keep him safe. His little heart is more important than her broken heart, than her broken life. He needs to be saved now, protected now – wherever he is, if it's not too late. She has been praying for the last few hours, the words running through her head, praying that he is still alive to be protected, and it occurs to her that if she is capable of a thought like this, then she is capable of believing that he has been hurt – capable of believing that someone may have hurt him. That Howard may have hurt him. That's the truth, and she needs to tell the police so that he can be saved. *Please God, let him be saved.*

'Howard is violent,' she says, and then she touches the short sleeve of the blue dress she is wearing. She likes the dress because it is cool in summer, likes the way it feels as it swishes around her calves and likes the fact that the sleeves are short but a little longer than normal. They cover up a lot. Her fingers move the material of the sleeve up, and the bruise, a ring of black and yellow, is visible.

'I see,' says the constable. His face remains carefully neutral, scrupulously non-judgemental, but behind his brown eyes she knows that connections are being made... frightening, life-changing connections. 'And is he violent... with Joe?' The words come out slowly, a father unable to bear the thought of a child so young being hurt. Oh, how she wants to say no. Her hand goes to her mouth, covering her lips.

And then she nods her head just a fraction, not enough so that if she is accused of lying, she couldn't say, 'I never said that.'

'And can you tell me what has happened to Joe?' he asks softly, quietly, as though asking at too high a volume might make what has happened to the boy a reality.

She shakes her head and covers her face with her hands.

The constable waits in silence for one minute, two minutes, but she doesn't have anything else to say. She will not explain last night. What would be the point?

'Okay, I think I might need to have a word with Mr Ealy.' He gets up and goes to the kitchen and summons Constable

Fairweather, who comes to sit in the recliner. 'Just in case you get worried,' says the constable, and Elizabeth tries for a word of gratitude, but terror keeps her silent. What is Howard going to do now? What are the police going to do?

Around her, the sounds coming in from outside disappear as she strains to hear Constable Brown moving towards the bedroom where Howard has gone, where he has taken himself away from her, from what is happening and what he may have done. She laces her fingers together, squeezing hard so that the sides of her ring push into her skin, the sapphires bright blue in the early-afternoon light. She hears the knock on the bedroom door, the loud rap of knuckles on wood, the policeman announcing himself, 'Excuse me, Mr Ealy,' his voice raised.

The bedroom door opens and then closes with a soft click. Elizabeth's heart thumps inside her as she feels a chill run through her body. She has made a mistake, a terrible mistake. Rising from the sofa, she looks towards the short passage that leads to the bedroom. 'If you could wait here,' says Constable Fairweather gently. 'You don't need to worry, we're here,' he says as she sinks back onto the sofa, her mouth dry. *What have I done? What have I done?*

And then she hears Howard scream, 'What?!' The word reverberates through the house, and Elizabeth clutches her stomach, where she feels a cramp of anxiety. *Oh God. Oh God.* She drops her head to her knees, covers her ears with her hands, blocks it all out.

But she cannot miss the sound of the bedroom door opening, so she sits up, chewing her lip, waiting for the blow to come.

Constable Brown is alone.

He tilts his head slightly at Constable Fairweather, who gets up and follows him to a corner of the room. Elizabeth watches as the two of them have a whispered conversation.

'I'll make a call,' says Constable Fairweather, and he leaves the room.

Constable Brown takes his place on the recliner. 'Mr Ealy... um, your husband has denied your allegations. He has claimed... that he has never harmed you in any way. He has claimed that you have done something to Joe and are trying to point the finger in his direction, to distract us so that we do not question you about it. He says you hurt Joe, Elizabeth. You hurt him.' There is steel behind his words, and something else, something like disgust. *What kind of a mother hurts her child?*

He waits, letting the words sink in, letting Elizabeth feel the betrayal of them. 'No,' she whispers. 'No.' She cannot think what else to say. She looks down at her feet, at the carpet, which is a darker grey than the sofa. It is worn and threadbare in places, and she thinks that she should tell Petra, the owner, to replace it before the house is rented out again. And then she thinks that the room would benefit from a carpet with blue in it, or perhaps a nice sisal. The thoughts about the room go around and around in her head as she watches her feet in brown leather sandals move on the carpet. And behind those thoughts is the truth that Howard has turned on her, smoothly, easily, without even worrying about it. She has protected him for all these years, has kept the truth about him from the whole world – including what happened last time they were going to adopt, even though she is not completely certain about that truth. But she has still kept quiet so that they could stay married, so that the world would see him one way instead of another, and now, without a second thought, he has simply thrown her to the wolves, happy to watch them rip her to shreds in order to protect himself. 'No,' she says again, her voice cracking. 'No.' There is nothing else to say. Only this one simple word. 'No.'

The policeman sighs. 'A detective will be here soon, but Mr Ealy is refusing to speak to anyone without a lawyer present,' he says, his tone flat with disappointment. He stands up and moves closer to her so that she has to look up at him.

'Can he do that?' she asks, her heart jumping in her chest.

'He can, but I have to tell you that it doesn't look good.' He slides his hands into his pockets. 'Constable Fairweather is calling the station to ask them to send over a couple of detectives, because Mr Ealy's refusal has now elevated the situation and made us think that he is concealing something. That perhaps you are both concealing something. And I have to tell you that it will be better for you if you simply tell me what happened.' He crouches down, chin in his hands, and looks up at her, appealing to her to tell the truth.

'Oh God,' she whispers, looks away.

She should never have said anything, never have opened her mouth.

'Is there anything, anything at all, that you can tell me about this morning that you may have forgotten to mention? I can see that you love Joe and that you desperately want him home, but I am concerned that you're worried about mentioning something in case you get blamed. I want you to know that we both want the same thing. We both want Joe found, and anything at all that you can tell me would help.' His brown eyes are dark and intense, his brow furrowed with concern.

Elizabeth pays attention to the fact that he doesn't say she will not be blamed. He doesn't say that she will be safe from the law. He has been very careful not to say this, in fact. She shakes her head. If Howard can refuse to speak to the police, then so can she. Anything else she says will only get her into more trouble. She has taken the leap and crash-landed. Everything is rubble.

The constable holds her gaze for a few moments, giving her time in the silence to make a different decision. When she doesn't say anything else, he says, 'Okay then,' and stands, walking away.

Elizabeth leans forward and drops her head into her hands again, using her palms to push against her eyelids. Black spots appear, distracting her.

Outside the house there is a sudden rush of noise and movement, and she sits up, a thrum of excitement running through her. *They've found him – they must have found him.* The front door opens and she hears fragments of questions being shouted from the press. The two constables move quickly across the living room to see what's happening. *What? Where? Can you tell us... What have...?* She cannot hear what they are asking about.

She rises from the sofa, but before she's even stood up properly, the front door is closed again, the noise toned down, and Constable Brown is back in front of her. He raises one hand, and she can see he is holding something in the other.

'Best you sit down, Elizabeth,' he says softly, and she sinks back onto the sofa. It's the first time he has used her Christian name, and despair rushes up from the tips of her toes, immediately choking her so she feels the need to cough.

'What?' she croaks, and he shows her what he's holding.

It's a navy-blue sandal with two Velcro straps – perfect for small hands. It's decorated with yellow spots and black crocodiles. 'Snap, snap,' Joe likes to say as he puts them on. 'Don't bite my finger, Mr Crocodile.' He chose them himself from the selection the young woman at the shoe shop brought out to show him. 'I can put them on myself,' he said to her, delighted at this.

The constable lays the sandal flat on his palm, and she notes that it is not quite as big as his hand. She can see it has sand sticking to it, and she reaches for it.

'I'm sorry,' he says, pulling it away. 'Evidence.'

'Please,' she begs, 'please.'

'There's no way to get anything from it,' whispers Constable Fairweather, and she wonders why this is as Constable Brown opens his hand so she can pick it up. She reaches to touch it again, jerks her hand back, covers her mouth. It's wet... soaking wet. She feels sick, but she picks it up and holds it to her, not caring that sand now covers her hands and dress, that a damp patch immediately forms. She rocks back and forth as though it is Joe she is holding, Joe she is comforting.

'Where?' she manages to say.

'An SES volunteer found it floating in the part of the estuary that leads to the ocean. It was caught behind a bush growing in the water.'

'Joe, Joe... my little Joe,' she murmurs.

The constable sighs, a deep sadness in the small sound. 'We need to know if you know anything,' he says. 'It's imperative that you tell us where the child may be, even if you know there is no point to the search, even if you know something terrible has happened. You need to tell us, Elizabeth.' His tone is matter-of-fact, only the policeman there now.

'Nothing,' she gasps, the pain inside her so strong she cannot believe it. He didn't come from her body, but he is hers and now he is gone. 'I don't know where he is. I don't know, I don't know.'

He leans forward and touches her gently on the shoulder. 'We'll keep looking, Elizabeth. It could just be that he lost his shoe. We will keep looking until we find him.' But he doesn't sound as though he holds even the tiniest amount of hope that Joe will be returned safe and well. Constable Brown has made up his mind about what happened to him.

She keeps rocking, trapped in her own world where there is only sorrow and despair. She is not even aware of the policeman walking away.

'Joe,' she whispers. 'Joe.'

CHAPTER TWENTY

GORDON

Today, 1.00 p.m.

Ruby's head is bowed, unhappiness in every step.

'What is it?' he asks. 'What is it?' He finds he cannot stop moving from one foot to the other, as though he needs to run. His heart is racing – what have they found?

'His shoe, they found just one shoe, and it was in the water.' She looks down as she speaks, the words barely above a whisper.

'But where did they find it?' asks Gordon. 'He was just here a minute ago. I made him cold hot chocolate and he and his mum had to go home. He just walked across the road. I'll go look for his shoe, shall I?' That will help. He can find Joe's shoe easily enough. It must be somewhere in the house.

Ruby sighs, and Gordon knows that he's messed up again. He's said something twice or he's forgotten something. He knows that sigh. It's the sigh of someone trying to be kind. He should go look for the shoe, but maybe he's made a mistake. 'Tell me again,' he says, 'and explain it carefully.'

'Perhaps you need a rest,' she says.

Gordon wants to deny this, but he suddenly feels absolute

exhaustion settle over him like a blanket.

'All right, lass,' he agrees. He moves to go inside and feels himself shuffling, something he hates to do, so he lifts his feet purposefully.

In the living room, he sinks into his comfortable leather recliner, pushing it back with some effort.

Ruby follows him and picks up her bag. 'I should go,' she says. 'My boyfriend booked me a room at the Bluebird Motel. I can come back later.' But she doesn't sound like she wants to go, and Gordon doesn't want to be alone watching the horror of what happened to Joe unfold. Joe was here, but now he's gone. When was he here? Is the shoe somewhere in the house, and if he finds the shoe, will they find Joe? That doesn't make sense, but right now, nothing does. He's so tired, he's not sure what's right or wrong, but he knows that he doesn't want the pretty woman in the bird dress to leave.

'Please don't go,' he says. 'I just need a short nap and then we can continue working on your article.' He remembers the article. 'I want to help, I do.' He wants her to stay, because he likes her, likes talking to her, but also because when he feels like this, this terrible foggy tiredness, he is afraid that he will fall asleep and never wake up. He knows he's old, understands that death is closer than it ever was, but he would like to be able to say goodbye to those he loves. He doesn't want to go to sleep alone and never wake up. He hasn't told Malcolm he has this fear, but perhaps he is coming to a time when he needs to share it. For now, if Ruby is here, she will try to wake him if he doesn't wake up. Hopefully. Ruby – that's right, Ruby in the bird dress.

'Are you sure?' she asks. 'I can just work quietly while you nap.'

'I'm certain,' he says, even as his eyes close. 'Help yourself to...'

He feels like he is flying, and he looks down at his feet, sees that he is running fast. His feet are bare and running over the sand. He feels water lapping at the sides of his feet, cool in the heat. He knows it's hot. 'Dad,' calls Malcolm, and Gordon looks up, sees his son standing in the water. He is tall for fourteen and he loves the beach. 'Come in, Dad, it's magic,' says Malcolm, and Gordon wades in, feeling the delicious cool water eddy around his body.

When he opens his eyes, there is a young woman sitting on the sofa, working on a laptop.

'Who are you?' he asks.

'Gordon, I'm Ruby,' she says softly. She smiles, a pretty smile he thinks he recognises. He rubs his eyes and pats his shirt to find his glasses in the top pocket. He slips them onto his face. 'Ruby,' he says.

'I came here this morning to interview you about what's happening across the road, about the boy being missing. You fell asleep. You've had a little nap,' she says.

'A nap... Well, I'm not one for napping during the day – messes up my sleep at night – but I must have needed it. I know you, do I?' He doesn't think he knows the young woman, but she looks nice enough and he doesn't feel worried about her being in his home, so maybe he does know her.

'You did,' she agrees. 'You were upset because they found his shoe – Joe's shoe. They found it and...' Her voice catches in her throat. 'I should have...' she begins, and then she stops talking. Gordon wants to ask what she wants to say, but he's worried that she's already told him.

'Yes... Joe.' He nods, and then rubs his eyes. 'Poor Joe. Do you think they've found him by now?'

Ruby opens her phone and runs her finger along the screen. 'No... they haven't said anything, and I've been watching the house. It's quiet. People have left to get something to eat and drink. It's very hot outside.'

'Something to eat sounds good. What time is it?'

'It's after one.'

'I've missed lunch,' says Gordon, standing up, struggling a little to get to his feet. 'I need a sandwich. Do you want a sandwich... Ruby?'

Ruby gets up too, putting her laptop on the coffee table. 'I can help,' she says, and she follows him into the kitchen, where he points out the bread and motions her to the fridge. 'Take anything you want. I'm always happy with cheese and salad.' He leaves to use the bathroom.

When he returns, she has made him a lovely cheese and salad sandwich, even put some potato chips on the side. She is standing next to the kitchen counter, looking down at the plates she has prepared as though wondering what else she needs.

'You found your way around,' says Gordon.

'It's okay, isn't it?' she asks, uncertainty in her voice. She looks so worried he smiles widely to reassure her.

'Definitely,' he says. 'You make a nice sandwich.'

'I had a job in a sandwich shop for a bit,' she says, turning to the fridge and pulling out a jar of pickled cucumbers. Gordon enjoys a pickle with his sandwich, so that's a good idea. She grabs a fork from a drawer and places one on each plate as she speaks. 'I was twenty and I had two other jobs at the time. Rent was really expensive, even though I shared with two other girls. The owner used to let me take home the leftover sandwiches for dinner at the end of the day.'

'You must have been sick of sandwiches eventually,' says Gordon, manoeuvring himself onto one of the tall stools next to the kitchen counter. He picks up one neatly sliced half of his sandwich and takes a bite. It's the perfect ratio of cheese, lettuce and tomato, with a touch of mayonnaise. 'I can never get enough of them. Yours is better than what I can make.'

'I was always grateful for free food,' she says.

'Why?' he asks as he picks up a potato chip, shoving it into the sandwich for extra crunch. He takes a bite and realises that she is looking at him and that she hasn't answered his question.

'I grew up in the foster system,' she says finally, taking a quick bite of her own sandwich.

'You did?'

'Yes, I bounced around a bit when I was younger. I never felt comfortable, not ever. Even when I was too small to understand what I was experiencing, I knew that I had no real place to call home. I found myself in so many strange kitchens over the years. I learned pretty quickly where to find everything and what the rules were. When I was thirteen, I lived in a house where there were locks on the fridge to stop kids stealing food.'

'That sounds terrible,' says Gordon. He tries to imagine stopping a child who is hungry from eating, the steel resolve it must take, and why anyone would want to be that kind of person.

'It was,' she says. 'I never felt full. But I live with my boyfriend now and I have my own kitchen and there are no rules. Lucas likes a midnight snack and so do I.' Her face gets a slightly shy look as she says this, and Gordon understands that she loves her boyfriend very much. He remembers feeling like that about Flora after they'd been together for a few months.

'Were all your foster homes like that?' he asks. He has finished his sandwich, and Ruby stands up and takes his plate, rinsing it off in the sink and putting it in the dishwasher, which he notices is finally getting full. He never noticed how long it took for a dishwasher to fill up until he lost Flora. It takes a lot longer now that he is alone.

'Not all,' she says, sitting down again. 'When I was about seven, I lived in a home with another child who had originally been a foster kid but who had been adopted by the family. He had a lot of problems – uncontrollable anger, things like that – but his parents were patient, loving people. They fostered me for five years and they were going to adopt me too, but when I was twelve, my foster mother, Monica... her name was Monica... got sick and died.' Ruby sniffs, and Gordon can see that the hurt over that is still there. She looks away from him and around the kitchen until she spots the box of tissues he keeps on the counter. She hops off her stool and grabs one, dabbing at her eyes and nose. 'I really loved Monica,' she says.

'You poor thing,' says Gordon.

Ruby nods. 'Anyway, obviously the adoption didn't go through. Monica's husband, Leon, kind of fell apart, and he couldn't care for me or his adopted son. He returned me to foster care and I couldn't even be angry with him, because... well, because I knew it wouldn't help. I was sent back into the system and placed in one home and then another and another, and then a group home where I thought I would stay until I turned eighteen. I was actually okay with that. I preferred the group home over trying to settle into another family. Monica and Leon had taught me how to be a good person and they'd taught me about love and sacrifice. I never found people like them again.'

'It must have been very hard on you,' says Gordon, standing up and patting her hand. He fills the kettle and finds some biscuits. He has no idea why the young woman is telling him all this. He's pretty sure she was here to interview him, but then he wonders if perhaps she used to be a student of his.

'Did I teach you?' he asks. 'I retired twenty years ago, though, and you look really young. Maybe I taught your mother?'

The kettle clicks off and he pours water into two mugs. Does the young woman want tea? He's not sure he asked her.

She's looking at him intently. 'I'm Ruby, remember, Gordon? I'm here to interview you about the family across the road. Their little boy has gone missing.' She sounds very sad, and Gordon hopes he hasn't said anything to make her sad. But then he remembers Joe.

'Poor little Joe,' he says.

'I was telling you that I was in the foster system, that I

ended up in a group home and I thought I would stay there until I turned eighteen, but an opportunity came up for adoption again, and for a child of fourteen, that was an unusual thing. Most people want little kids so that they can mould them, but there was a couple who were willing to take an older child.'

'That's lucky, isn't it... I mean, that's good; you must have been... happy. Did you want some tea, love?'

'Yes, thanks... Sit down, Gordon. I can do it.'

Gordon returns gratefully to his stool. He doesn't know how she likes her tea. 'I just have milk in mine, thanks.' He opens the packet of lemon cream biscuits and bites into one. He seems to spend the whole day eating, because sometimes he thinks he's had lunch but he's not sure. He likes a lemon cream biscuit. Flora did as well.

The girl, Ruby, puts a mug in front of him, and he looks at her spiky brown hair and remembers. She's here to write an article about Joe going missing. He looks at his watch. It's after 1.30, and Joe has been missing since this morning. He remembers that she was telling him something. 'You were saying that you were getting the chance to be adopted by another family,' he says, the story returning. 'Do you think Elizabeth wants to adopt Joe? It will be good if she does, but not if Howard does, not him. I don't like him.'

'Yes, you said that,' says Ruby. 'I was going to be adopted, but then...' She falls silent and stares down into her tea. 'Oh Gordon,' she says, 'I've been keeping so many secrets and I think... I think I need to tell someone.'

Gordon knows about secrets, especially about young people with secrets. As a teacher, he often found himself talking to students who had something to say but didn't know how to say it. Gentle encouragement was needed then, that and letting them know you were willing to listen. 'You can tell me, lass. I can't promise to remember, but you can tell me.'

CHAPTER TWENTY-ONE

ELIZABETH

Today, 1.30 p.m.

'I need,' she says, standing up, 'I need to use the bathroom.' She is clutching the shoe tightly, unwilling to return it to the constable.

'Go ahead,' says Constable Brown. He stands as well and walks her to the bathroom, watching her go in. She wants to scream at him to leave her alone. She hasn't hurt her little boy, but she knows she can scream all she wants. No one will believe her, not now.

She takes the shoe with her to the bathroom, conscious that if she sets it down for even a moment, it may disappear. Joe did. She took her eye off him for a moment, only a moment. In the bathroom, she closes the lid of the toilet and sits down. She feels safer here, less scrutinised by everyone. She has her phone in the pocket of the sundress she is wearing. The constable is going to ask for it, of course, but there is nothing to see on it.

She has bought a couple of new sundresses since Joe arrived to live with them, and she has made sure they all have pockets. Joe is fond of picking up treasures when they go for a walk. She often returns home with her pockets stuffed with small rocks, flowers, coins. Joe likes to collect everything to store in his treasure box, a wooden box she found in a dollar store that is painted with a picture of a train. It's a curiously old-fashioned-looking thing, with its metal latch and carved wood, but Joe loves it.

She scrolls through her phone, looking at all the pictures she has taken of Joe. She only sends them to Natalie and her parents, or looks at them herself. And every time she sends one and Natalie responds with *So cute* and an emoji, she feels the balm of motherhood wash over her. Finally she has some pictures of her own to send after years and years of liking her sister's. But now... what now? What kind of a mother loses her child? What kind of a foster parent loses the child they are supposed to be taking care of? Joe has had enough bad parenting in his life. She allows herself some quiet tears. *Where are you, little boy? Please come back. I promise to do better, to be better.*

After a few minutes, she sniffs and blows her nose. She never shares the pictures she takes of Joe with Howard. Not after the first time she showed him one and he said, 'Getting ready to fill up your phone with your new great love, are you?'

It could have been a question asked with love and gratitude for the boy's presence in their lives, but his tone betrayed what it truly was: an expression of outright jealousy. He likes to be the centre of attention. She realises he was almost enjoying the desperate search taking place, the endless people smiling and nodding or patting him on the shoulder – the father with the missing child. Until the police started looking in his direction. Now he has pointed the finger at her, and then clammed up and asked for his lawyer. Should she just tell the police everything?

She wraps her arms around herself. What has Howard done to Joe? What will Howard tell the police she has done? And which one of them are they going to believe?

CHAPTER TWENTY-TWO

As the years go by, the man thinks about the girl often, searches crowds for her face, hopes she is well. When he meets someone and falls in love, he tells her about the girl, and then, because life is busy and he is busy, he forgets about her; the young woman who shared his apartment for a month while she healed. When he has his own child, he gazes down at his baby in the bassinet and tries to imagine what kind of a person could damage the body of a child the way the young girl's body was damaged. He thinks about all the children who are in homes where they are not safe, and he imagines becoming a foster parent, taking in those who need a safe place to stay. But it's just a passing thought. He is grateful he got to help someone the way he did, and he hopes that the girl finds love and a home and one day has a family of her own.

He still sees someone every now and again who reminds him of the young woman, with her brown hair and green eyes, but every time he gets closer, he realises it's not the same person. He understands he will never see her again.

CHAPTER TWENTY-THREE

GORDON

Yesterday, 3.00 p.m.

Gordon studies the calendar hanging from a small nail on the wall in the kitchen. It's a calendar made up of photographs. There are twelve different pictures, starting with one of him and Del in January, from a Christmas visit a couple of years ago. In it, they're both wearing large floppy blue hats. They're Gordon's hats, so Del's is way too big for her, something she found very funny. The picture has captured her mid-laugh, simple joy on her face. All the photos are of him and Del. Last month's was of them in the ocean, taken from behind. She is holding his hand as she jumps over the small waves that rolled in. He remembers her shrieking with delight in the cold water. Last Christmas was rainy and much cooler than normal, so the water was never very warm. Malcolm had the calendar made for him for Father's Day, and Gordon will treasure it forever. When the year is done, which is only a couple of weeks away, he will put it in a drawer with all the birthday cards from his son and granddaughter.

He studies the calendar, looking for today's date, and

compares it to the date showing on his phone. Malcolm is definitely supposed to be here by now. He likes to come early in the morning to beat the holiday traffic, and he should have arrived. The date is circled in red, because today is the day Malcolm is coming, but it's three in the afternoon and he's still not here.

He looks down at his phone, fretting over whether to call him. If he's stuck in traffic, he would have called, would have let him know. What Gordon is worried about is the possibility that he has already called him and Malcolm has explained why he's not there and he has simply forgotten.

'I'll give him another hour,' he mutters, and goes to the fridge to get himself some of the cherries he bought yesterday. Del loves cherries and they have been very good this season. Gordon pops one in his mouth, enjoying the sweet, dark juice, then he grabs a handful and goes to find a plate.

As he closes the fridge door, he sees a message on a piece of paper, written to himself.

Text from Malcolm, it says.

He dumps the cherries on a small white plate and looks down at his phone. Why would he have written *Text from Malcolm*? He opens his phone and looks at the last text message.

> *Hi Dad. We just got off the phone but I wanted you to have this in case you start to worry. Remember I won't be down now till Wednesday late afternoon because I have a last-minute meeting on Tuesday night. I'll be there before dinner. Don't worry.*

'Of course.' Gordon smiles, remembering the conversation with Malcolm last night.

'Write a note to yourself, just in case you forget,' Malcolm told him, and then he stayed on the call while Gordon did as he suggested.

Relieved that he doesn't have to worry any more, he picks up his plate of cherries to take back to the living room, where he's watching a cricket match.

Just as he gets himself settled on the sofa, the bell rings, and he grumbles a little at having to stand up again.

Elizabeth and Joe are standing at the open front door, and Gordon's first instinct is to close it, simply shut the door and not let them in, not after what happened last time. Yes, Elizabeth brought him a piece of cake and apologised, but *he* didn't – Howard didn't – and it really should have been him who came over. It's arrogance, Gordon thinks, having your wife apologise for your bad behaviour, arrogance and probably a belief that you've done nothing wrong. Flora would never have stood for such a thing from Gordon, not that he ever would have been in that position, but if he had been, she would have made sure that he was the one to apologise.

This morning he went out to fill the bird feeder and saw Howard standing in the front yard across the road, watching his house. His instinct was to raise a hand, to wave as he would to any other neighbour, but he didn't. Some part of him expected Howard to wave first, expected him to call out that he was sorry about everything, but the man just stood there watching him, his body completely still. Gordon filled the feeder quickly and hurried inside again, disconcerted by Howard's unwavering stare.

Where is Howard now?

'I'm so glad you're home,' says Elizabeth quickly, as though she has understood that he is worried about letting them in.

'I'm watching the cricket,' he explains.

'Howard has gone into town. He's gone to get his iPad changed because the new one has a problem, something... Well, I don't know, but he'll be gone for a while and we wondered... well, Joe wanted to know if he could just watch the birds for a bit.' She throws out the words, her tone breathless, as though she is in a hurry to get it said. They both know what she is saying. It's safe. That's what she's explaining to Gordon. It's safe.

'Please, Gordon,' says Joe, his big green eyes filled with hope. 'Please can I sit on the chair and watch them? I'll be really, really quiet. And maybe... maybe you could make me a cold hot chocolate?'

Gordon laughs at the boy's guile. 'Absolutely I can. We're losing the cricket anyway. I definitely can make it for you. Why don't you and your mum sit down and keep an eye on those cockatoos. They like to bully the others. I'll get some tea and cold hot chocolate sorted.'

'Yay,' says Joe, jumping up and down.

'Thank you... thank you,' says Elizabeth, leaning forward and touching Gordon lightly on the arm, and he has to hold himself back from offering a hug. She looks like she needs one. She and Joe turn around and make their way to the table and chairs in the garden. This morning's heat has let go a little, a sea breeze bringing relief, so it is pleasant in the garden under the shade of the large tree.

He busies himself in the kitchen, muttering the steps he needs to take to get everything made so he doesn't forget something. Today has been a good day and he feels more like his old self, except for forgetting that Malcolm was only coming tomorrow, but that could happen to anyone. 'Nothing wrong with me,' he mutters. Outside, Joe shouts, 'Share, birdies!' reminding him of what he is doing. He is not surprised to see his hand tremble a little as he takes the tray outside; the fear of what could happen if that man returns making itself known.

'He won't be back for ages,' says Elizabeth, helping him unload the tray.

In the garden, the rosellas and the lorikeets squabble while some little finches hop about, eating what they can get to. Gordon settles himself on a chair, as Joe laughs at the finches getting close to the cockatoos and then jumping back. For just a moment there is nothing but the birds, and the light breeze against his skin, and he feels real peace. He hopes that Joe and Elizabeth feel it as well. Flora loved this front garden. She had always dreamed of a little garden and her own space to watch birds come and go.

Joe sucks at the hot chocolate through a straw, his mouth comical as the straw gets blocked with crushed ice that is too big. 'Take a spoon,' laughs Elizabeth.

'It's the best thing I've ever tasted in my whole entire life,' says Joe, making Gordon smile. He and Elizabeth sit companionably, watching Joe and the birds, and not talking until she says, 'I hope you know how sorry we are about what happened.' Her voice is soft, as though she doesn't want Joe to hear what she's saying.

Gordon shrugs. 'It must be hard for you,' he replies, wanting her to open up if she needs to.

'It's... We're fine,' she says, shaking her head. 'Just fine.'

'He wouldn't want you to be here, I don't think,' says Gordon.

'No,' agrees Elizabeth. 'But perhaps I'm tired of thinking about what he wants.' And then she laughs in a self-conscious way. 'Look at me being silly – sorry, Gordon.'

'No need for sorry from you,' says Gordon, 'no need at all.'

They chat about other things in quiet voices as Joe points at birds and laughs.

'The town is really busy now,' she says.

'It's the summer holiday crowd,' he replies. 'Some people come back year after year. I have a few friends at the bowling club who come every summer and have done so for three decades.'

'How lovely to have a summer home.'

'Yes, but things are getting a bit crowded now. Soon the

small houses will all be gone. I hear they're wanting to put up a big hotel as well.'

'That will be a shame,' says Elizabeth. She sips her tea and takes a small bite of the lemon cream he put on her saucer.

'We went for a walk on the beach and then we crossed the river onto more beach,' says Joe, and Gordon immediately knows he is talking about the section at the end of the beach, where ocean and river meet and bush lines the edge.

'Yes, the estuary,' says Elizabeth. 'It's beautiful and we found some lovely shells, didn't we, Joe?'

'Mm-hmm,' nods Joe, 'and then we had to cross back and the water was high, high and Mum... Lizbeth had to carry me and I had to hold my sandals in my hand but I didn't mind.'

'The tide comes in really fast,' says Gordon. 'Malcolm used to love wading through to get to the section with bush and then swimming back when he was a kid. Flora always worried about him, but he was with friends. I was sure no harm would come to him.'

'We weren't as protected as kids then, were we?' says Elizabeth. 'I remember Natalie and I spending hours roaming the streets in summer. My mother would give us five dollars and that fed us for the whole day.'

'Times have changed,' he muses, 'and maybe not for the better.'

'Maybe.' She shrugs. 'I never knew there were so many children in need until I decided to become a foster parent.'

'I was a teacher and I saw some... some who suffered,' he sighs.

'Really, and what...' She glances down at her phone. 'He's on his way back. Say goodbye, Joe, come now.' Gordon cannot miss the slight panic in her voice.

'How do you know?' he asks.

'Tracking app,' she says, showing him the screen of the phone. 'It works both ways,' she adds. 'Come now, Joe, please.'

'Can we come again, please, please, please?' begs Joe.

'We'll see,' she says, looking down at the phone again. 'Thank you, Gordon, thank you so much. It's been lovely.'

'It's a pleasure – whenever you want. Malcolm will be here tomorrow with Del. I have a message from him. I thought it was today, but it's tomorrow, late afternoon.'

'Tomorrow,' she says, thoughtful, and he nods and smiles, pleased that she looks a little more relaxed. Although as she takes Joe's hand, she glances down at the phone again, and then hurries him across the street, and in moments they are gone, the door closed, the house silent.

Gordon stays in his garden for a little while, and then he becomes aware of the time and not wanting Howard to see him. He picks everything up and hurries inside, wondering at his fear and hating that he has to feel it.

'Malcolm will be coming tomorrow night,' he tells himself. 'Tomorrow night.'

CHAPTER TWENTY-FOUR

ELIZABETH

'And it's our secret,' says Elizabeth for the fourth time, 'a secret just for us.'

'I know,' sighs Joe, sounding irritated. She cannot explain to him how important it is that he keeps the secret of visiting Gordon. She also cannot explain to herself why she took him over to Gordon's house, why she did something that she knows will anger Howard if he finds out.

She spoke to her sister early this morning, creeping out of the house before Joe or Howard woke up to call her at the right time.

'Hello, stranger,' Natalie answered. 'I haven't heard from you for a few days. Still living it up in the sunshine?'

'Yes,' Elizabeth laughed. 'The weather has been amazing.'

'Lucky you,' sighed Natalie. 'We're expecting a million feet of snow tonight. I love a white Christmas, but there's a limit.'

'Maybe one December you can come here, celebrate with us. The boys will enjoy a summer Christmas, and they can meet Joe.'

'That would be incredible,' said Natalie. 'They can learn to surf. Have you heard anything new about the adoption? Do you know if it's going ahead?'

'No,' said Elizabeth. 'No, but we have a meeting with the case manager soon. I keep worrying that they're going to send him back to his mother. I don't know what she's up to, what she might do, but... Well, I didn't call to talk about that.'

'Oh Bethy, I know you're worried after what happened last time, but that was an older child. You couldn't have predicted that things would go so wrong.'

'I know, I know, but...' Elizabeth stopped speaking, wondering if enough time had passed that she could confess the truth of what had happened, even though she is not entirely sure what that is. 'How are Mum and Dad?' she asked, changing the subject.

'Cold,' laughed Natalie. 'Mum cannot believe how cold it is. She and Dad spend a lot of time in big shopping malls, having lunch and getting their exercise on the walking tracks. I'm loving having them here, but I know it's going to be a little lonely for you at Christmas. I wish we could all be together.'

'I know. Maybe one day...' Elizabeth tried to keep the wistful tone out of her voice, to disguise just how much she missed her parents and her sister. But Natalie has always been good at reading her.

'What's wrong, Bethy?' she asked softly.

'Oh, nothing,' Elizabeth began, 'nothing... Just, you know Howard...'

'No, I don't,' said Natalie firmly. 'I don't know because you never tell us. Not me, and not Mum and Dad. You never explain what's really going on. Last time I was over, I saw something I didn't like, but he must have realised, because he went into a full charm offensive, and it was only when I was on the plane home that I understood I'd been played. He's a clever man, Bethy, and I know you've been together for ages, but I've kept quiet for long enough. I don't think you're happy with him.' She took a deep, audible breath, and Elizabeth could feel her relief at having said what she had obviously wanted to say for years.

'If I leave him, they'll take Joe from me,' she said, instead of contradicting anything her sister had said.

'You wouldn't be the first woman to sacrifice her happiness for the sake of a child, but – and I don't want you to take this the wrong way – you have no idea if Joe is going to be yours or not. You know this isn't a sure thing. You have to protect yourself, Bethy – and maybe if you leave they'll let you keep Joe anyway, because you'll be happier and that will make you a better foster parent.'

Elizabeth felt the conversation getting too deep – the truth was too much to bear. 'Don't worry about me,' she said brightly. 'I'm just having a bad morning. I promise you I'm fine.'

Natalie sighed. 'Okay… okay, but I'm here if you need to talk. I don't care what the time is, just call me.'

'Thanks, Nat, I will. Give my love to Mum and Dad. I'll call them tomorrow.'

'Will do, kiss Joe for me,' said Natalie, and they ended the call.

She walked back into the house on silent feet, but Howard was up, and in the kitchen already, a cup of coffee in his hand.

'Sneaking in, eh? Did you have a little chat with your sister?' he asked, his tone mean and snarky.

And her heart sank, because she understood that he was back to being the usual Howard. Since the incident at Gordon's house, he'd been kind and gentle and easy to get along with. He'd been patient with Joe when he dropped something or made a mistake. She should have felt nothing but relief and happiness, but as the hours passed, she had realised that anxiety was mounting inside her in increments. It felt like it was coming up from her toes. She was waiting for him to change back, to return to being the Howard she knew all too well. The anxiety was somehow worse than anything else, because it wasn't as if she could accuse him of being nice to her. And now this morning the change had happened, probably because he knew she was talking to her sister and he hated her being close to anyone but him.

Something inside her reared up, a dark red anger at the way he made her watch what she was doing all the time. 'Yes,' she snapped. 'I was talking to my sister. I wasn't doing anything wrong and I'm not going to let you make me think I was. I can call my sister one hundred times a day if I choose to.' As the words left her, she suppressed an urge to slap her hand across her mouth, horrified that she had said anything.

'Whoa,' laughed Howard, 'where did that come from? There's no need for you to be rude. If you want to talk to her because you need to think about people aside from me and Joe, that's just fine, Elizabeth. Just fine.' Her stomach churned at the words, and she felt her face flame. He put his still full cup of coffee carefully on the counter and walked away, leaving her feeling like a bad wife and mother, and also like she had overreacted. She hated that he made her question herself all the time.

They spent most of the day at the house, Howard on his new iPad, occasionally muttering to himself when he couldn't get something to work, while she read a book and Joe played at her feet, building a complicated construction with his Lego, occasionally showing her something he had made. 'This is the big building and this is the truck and the truck is going to bash into the big building and it's going to crash down, down – watch, watch.'

'I'm watching, Joe. That's a big crash, you'd better build it up again.'

She was cleaning up from a late lunch when she heard Howard yell from the living room, 'Ow, bloody hell.'

Joe was sitting at the table drawing, and so she didn't worry about asking Howard what was wrong, knowing he would tell her soon enough, and then she wondered at herself, at her ambivalence towards him, because her only thought had been, *Oh for heaven's sake, what now?*

'What have I told you about clearing up the Lego properly?' Howard yelled, storming into the kitchen, a small red brick in his hand. 'I stood on this in my bare feet and it really hurt.' And then he threw the brick forcefully, not at Joe, but at the table, where it bounced up and hit Joe on the forehead.

'Ow, ow...' cried Joe, and he burst into tears.

'Howard!' Elizabeth yelled, shocked.

He looked at her with disgust. 'Oh God, the waterworks. Imagine if I cried whenever I needed your attention,' he sneered, as she crouched down and examined Joe's forehead, a tiny spot of blood forming where the brick had hit him.

'It's okay, love, it's okay,' she shushed, wetting some paper towel and dabbing gently at Joe's head. 'Let's get you a Band-Aid. Let's get you a special Band-Aid.' She stood up and grabbed the first-aid kit from the pantry. Joe's tears subsided as she took out a box of plasters with the Marvel Avengers logo. She ignored Howard, who was watching the two of them, pretended he wasn't even in the room.

'Now look here,' she said to Joe. 'Who's going to help Joe get better?' She pulled out a whole lot of the character Band-Aids and laid them out for him to choose from. 'Will the Hulk help you, or maybe Spider-Man?'

'Captain America, Captain America,' said Joe, all tears gone.

She carefully opened and peeled the plaster, sticking it onto the tiny nick. Then she placed a kiss on top of it, leaning her lips against his forehead briefly, inhaling the smell of the baby shampoo she used to wash his hair.

'How about a story?' she said. It was suddenly too hot in the kitchen with Howard glowering at them, his anger heating up the air.

'Yes, yes,' Joe said gleefully. 'I'll choose, I'll choose.'

'Okay, you get the book you want and I'll get some cookies, because brave boys need cookies.'

'Screw this,' spat Howard. 'I'm going into town to change the stupid iPad. Something's wrong with it. Have yourself a lovely afternoon.' He turned and stormed off, stamping his feet loudly like a child and slamming the bedroom door when he went to change.

Elizabeth didn't react.

She joined Joe in the living room, and they sat together on the sofa as she read *The Rainbow Fish* to him and he ran his fingers over the multicoloured scales on the fish and ate his cookies. When the front door banged and she heard Howard's car pull away, her whole body relaxed and she felt a rush of simple joy at his being away for a few hours, though this was quickly followed by a heavy sadness that this was the way she felt about the man she was married to. It wasn't right. She was too old to still be trapped here.

'Lizbeth,' said Joe. 'Mum, Mum, keep reading.' He patted the page, and she realised that she had stopped before the end of the book.

'"And he swam off to be with his friends",' she read. 'All finished, Joe, now what?'

'The birds,' he said, 'can we go and see the birds in the garden, in Gordon's garden? He can make me cold hot chocolate. Please, please.'

Elizabeth hesitated, and then she looked down at her phone. The store where Howard had purchased the iPad was a twenty-five-minute drive away in a bigger town. He would be gone for a while. She opened the tracking app and made sure that he was heading there, and then she got angry at herself for having to check.

'Yes,' she said, determined, 'let's go and see if Gordon is home. He may not want visitors today, but we can ask.'

Before they left the house, Joe carefully peeled off the Band-Aid. 'Why don't you leave it there?' she asked. His forehead held the tiniest of marks.

'I don't want Gordon to see,' he said, and Elizabeth stopped for a moment, the enormity of Joe concealing what had happened, protecting the secret of Howard's temper just as she had done for years, washed over her. He had only been with them for a few months, and yet he knew, he understood that this was how they did things.

'Okay,' she said lightly, when she had composed herself, and they walked across the road, Elizabeth only mildly worried about an unfriendly reception from Gordon. She was sure he wouldn't turn Joe away.

They had a lovely afternoon, only marred by her having to hurry Joe back to the house and set him up on the sofa with a movie so he looked like he had spent the afternoon there. She repeated that seeing Gordon was a secret, but she believed Joe wouldn't say anything, because he was good at keeping secrets. But he is a child, just a child, and so she can't be sure.

She makes an effort with dinner, spending an hour putting together the fish pie that Howard loves, hoping to distract him with the promise of a good meal.

'That smells good,' are his first words as he walks in.

'I thought it might be nice,' she says. 'It's five, do you want some wine? I've opened a bottle of red.' She smiles.

'Absolutely.'

'Did you change the iPad?'

'Yeah, no problem there, and I got our little man a gift. Hey, Joe,' he calls. 'Come see what I got you.'

Joe comes running into the kitchen, unable to resist the lure of a gift. 'What, what?' he asks, excitement radiating through his whole jumping body.

Howard takes a box out of the bag he is carrying.

'What is it?' asks Joe, trying to grab for the box.

'Now wait, wait a minute,' says Howard. 'Sit down and be patient. It's a Spider-Man watch, but it's a special watch because it means Elizabeth and I will always know where you are and that you're safe.'

He opens the box, taking out the red watch emblazoned with Spider-Man and making sure it's working before fitting it onto Joe's wrist.

Joe looks on in silent awe. 'Wow,' he says as he gazes at it, 'wow,' making Elizabeth laugh.

'Now you have to take really good care of it, okay, and never take it off unless you're going for a bath.'

Joe nods his head furiously. 'I love it. Thank you, Howard, thank you, thank you.'

'Good man,' says Howard, ruffling his hair. 'Now go and watch your movie until it's time for dinner.' Joe does as he's told, almost walking into the kitchen door because he is concentrating so hard on the watch.

'That must have been expensive,' says Elizabeth when they are alone.

Howard shrugs. 'Now we'll always know where he is. It's good for him to start getting used to wearing it. When he's a bit bigger, he can text you using it and a whole lot of other stuff. I haven't gone through all the instructions yet.'

'It's a lovely gift,' says Elizabeth, not wanting to acknowledge to herself that it's an apology gift, just like all the apology bracelets and bottles of perfume she has received over the years.

Howard yawns. 'I may just lie down for twenty minutes,' he says.

'Good idea,' she replies.

Dinner passes pleasantly enough. Joe and Howard enjoy the fish pie. It is only over dessert of ice cream with chocolate sauce that Joe slips up.

Later, she will think that they almost made it. That she and Joe almost made it to bedtime, after which the visit to Gordon would have probably never been mentioned.

Almost.

CHAPTER TWENTY-FIVE

GORDON

Yesterday, 7.30 p.m.

'So, I'll be there late in the afternoon tomorrow,' says Malcolm. 'I wish I could leave earlier, but I need to make sure the system is working properly. The company will close for a week over Christmas and that's when they're a bit vulnerable to hackers.'

'It's fine, son, no rush,' says Gordon. Malcolm told him the name of the company, but it has slipped his mind. 'Have a good night,' he says.

'I will. Love you, Dad. See you soon.'

Gordon puts his phone on charge in the kitchen, grabbing a couple of dark chocolate Tim Tam biscuits to have with his tea in the living room. He's waiting for the Christmas movie *Love Actually* to begin. They screen it every year, and every year he watches and has a bit of a cry because it was Flora's favourite movie and they used to watch it together. It makes him feel better, kind of lets out all the sorrow over Flora that is always there.

He sits himself down in front of the television, putting his

Tim Tams next to his tea, waiting to enjoy them with the opening credits.

It's only when a strange sound startles him that he realises he's drifted off. He is instantly awake, his heart racing. He's not entirely sure he heard anything. Maybe he simply dreamed it. It was a yelp, a swallowed scream – nothing like an animal would have made. He gets up and goes to the window in the front sunroom, looking out onto the still light street.

Across the road, Howard is getting into his car. He starts the engine and screeches away, smoke from his tyres filling the air. Gordon watches him go.

I wonder what that was about? he thinks. Should I go and check on Elizabeth and Joe? Mind your own business, old man. But what if something has happened?

He dithers for at least half an hour before finding his slip-on shoes and replacing his slippers on his feet. He can't concentrate on the movie anyway, since he's missed most of it. He can't stop thinking about Elizabeth and Joe. He may as well go over there.

He'll just ask if everything is okay, and if Howard comes back, he'll hustle himself home. He walks across the road slowly, checking left and right in case the black Mercedes returns.

The house is silent, so he rings the bell and waits, remembering all the times he and Flora came here for tea or drinks or dinner with Dawn and Louie. They were lucky to have them here, that's for sure.

It is warm in the evening air, the day's heat lingering but not oppressive. There hasn't been much rain, so the humidity is not here to bother anyone just yet. February will be thick with it, but Gordon has his air conditioning so he's not worried. It's just after eight, and the sun is setting, casting an orange glow over everything. He takes a breath, rings the bell again, and then, because he can hear that someone is inside, does it once more. What on earth is taking them so long?

CHAPTER TWENTY-SIX

ELIZABETH

Yesterday, 7.30 p.m.

She puts a spoonful of ice cream into her mouth. Howard and Joe both have vanilla, but she loves the combination of strawberry with the rich, thick chocolate sauce.

'Gordon makes the best cold hot chocolate,' Joe says conversationally, and she feels the ice cream stick in her throat, stick and refuse to go down, despite it melting. *Oh no, oh no, oh no.*

'And when did you see Gordon?' Howards asks, his tone mild, just asking a question. He scrapes his spoon around his bowl, the slight squeak loud as he waits.

Elizabeth looks up, catches the look of panic in Joe's eyes. He has been backed into a corner. He was okay keeping the secret, but now that he's let it slip, he's not sure how to lie about it. She wants to shake her head, to let him know not to say anything, but Howard looks from her to Joe and back again, preventing any silent communication.

'When did you see Gordon, Joe?' he repeats, his voice lower, more threat in his tone.

'I... I...' starts Joe.

'This afternoon,' she says quickly, not willing to let Joe suffer for her decision, not willing to force him to stay here for what's coming. 'Go and get ready for bath time, Joe,' she says.

'Stay right where you are, Joe,' says Howard, the words spoken slowly, his voice soft with fury. He leans across the table and pulls the child's bowl away from him. There is still ice cream left, and Joe eyes it hungrily.

'Didn't I tell you, Bethy,' Howard says, almost spitting on her sister's nickname for her, 'not to go and see him? There's something wrong with him, with his interest in Joe. You know what can happen, don't you, you've read all those terrible stories, and yet you're still intent on going over there. Imagine if Peter knew you were taking Joe to visit a man who might do something terrible to him.'

She can't bear his ugly, ugly words and the way he enjoys saying them, and she can hear his implied threat about Peter. 'Okay, that's enough,' she says, standing up. 'He's a nice man and we looked at the birds. Joe, go and get ready for your bath.' She barks the words, trying to conceal her fear, and Joe jumps up.

'Sit down!' shouts Howard, slapping his hand down on the table, and the little boy drops back into his seat, his eyes already filling with tears, his head swinging between the two of them, unsure who to obey. 'My mother would never – I would never – have disobeyed my father,' hisses Howard. 'Never.'

Elizabeth is stunned into shock for a moment. Then the enormity of the words he has just used makes her shake with fear, with rage, with the knowledge that everything Howard hates about his father he has simply and willingly become. Her body grows hot with fury at her own stupidity for believing that he wanted to be a different kind of man.

'And you don't really speak to your father, do you, Howard?' she says. She leans across the table and picks up his bowl. If Joe can't have any more ice cream, then neither can he.

But as she does this, he grabs her wrist and pulls her across the table, slamming her down with his other hand. Holding her by her hair, he delivers a mighty blow to her back, and instantly she can feel he's cracked a rib. Her breath leaves her body in a whoosh of air.

'No, no, don't,' screams Joe.

Howard lets go of her and rushes around the table, looming over Joe with his hand raised as the boy cowers in his chair. His hand comes down and Joe jumps off the chair, hitting his back on the table and dropping to the floor. Elizabeth screams. Howard steps towards her and shoves his hand across her face, turning it towards Joe, who is still and quiet on the floor. 'Look what you made me do,' he hisses. 'Look what you did.' He lets go of her and steps back.

'Monster,' she whispers. 'Monster... monster,' she spits.

He takes a step away from her, and she can see that she has frightened him. She can feel her nose running, tears on her cheeks and the sharp arrow of pain at her side. She bares her teeth at him. 'Monster,' she says again. She wishes her teeth were fangs. She would rip him into tiny pieces.

'Oh...' he says as she stares at him. 'Oh God, oh God,' he continues, looking at her with panic in his eyes. But she doesn't say anything, doesn't move. 'You,' he says, and he doesn't scare her, because his voice is weak now, and she can see he is breathless with fear over what he has done. 'You did this. You did it.'

He turns around, looks everywhere, and then locates his keys on the console. He darts for them, picking them up and slamming his way out of the house.

Elizabeth opens her mouth to let out her stifled scream as she looks down at Joe, but then she covers her mouth and yelps instead.

She kneels down next to Joe, touching him gently. 'Joe,' she moans, 'Joe, please.' Her rib is definitely broken. She is finding it hard to take a deep breath.

Joe rolls onto his back and opens his eyes. 'That hurt,' he says, tears appearing.

'Are you okay?' she asks. 'Are you okay?' Her own tears match his. She presses down on her side, pushing against the pain.

He stands up and puts his little arms around her. 'I'm okay,' he comforts her, even as he cries. 'I'm okay.'

She is on her knees, her back aching, but she holds onto him until he lets go.

'He was mad,' he says softly.

'Yes, but he shouldn't have hurt you.'

'He shouldn't have hurt *you*,' Joe says with the simple logic of a child.

She has no idea what to say to that. She stands up and looks around the dining room. Only an upended bowl of ice cream, strawberry pink pooling on the table, indicates that anything is amiss. The other two bowls are still upright.

'Bath time,' she says to Joe, her voice fractured with despair.

While he is in the bath, she inspects his whole body, noting the redness on his back that is already beginning to bruise. She listens for Howard's return, terrified, but also seething with rage at him, at what he has done to this little boy who is not his to hurt. No child is ever anyone's to hurt.

She allows Joe some more ice cream, locking herself in his room with him as he eats, and then they brush his teeth and she reads him a story until he falls asleep.

She moves a blanket and pillow into his room for herself. She needs a shower and she would like to inspect how bad her back looks, but she can't risk leaving Joe alone for a moment without her being able to hear if Howard returns.

She cleans up the kitchen, wipes down the dining room table, watching as the time heads towards eight. On the tracking app, she can see that Howard is in town at a pub. She hopes he stays there. She hopes he gets drunk and can't drive home, or that he drives home and kills himself in a car wreck. At this thought she swallows a sob. How has her life come to this, and what on earth does she do now?

She has to let go of this little boy so that someone better can take care of him. She wants to scream and howl and beat her fists against the wall. Instead, she sinks into a chair, drops her head into her hands. And then the doorbell rings. Her body stiffens and she waits. She doesn't want to see anyone. Has someone heard what happened? Have they called the police? It rings again and then again, and she gets up. The person is not going away.

She opens the door and Gordon is there, and she can see that he has heard something, that he has spent some time debating whether to come over. What has he heard? What does he know? The pounding of her heart pulses blood through her head, and she winces slightly. She should send him away, but he is here now and she feels some relief at seeing a friendly face, at knowing that there are men in the world like Gordon.

CHAPTER TWENTY-SEVEN

GORDON

Yesterday, 8.15 p.m.

Elizabeth opens the door, her eyes red-rimmed, her cheeks flushed. 'Oh, Gordon,' she says, and she offers him a weak smile.

'I heard a noise,' he says, feeling awkward now that he's here and interfering. 'And I just wanted to see you're okay. You and Joe. I just wanted to check,' he continues gamely.

'Just...' She swallows, shuts her eyes briefly as her face scrunches and she takes a long, shuddering breath. 'Just fine,' she says. 'I... There was... a spider, a huntsman. It startled me.'

'Yes,' says Gordon. He doesn't believe her, not for a moment, not a single moment. 'They can be scary. I've seen some that are bigger than my hand, but they're harmless, more scared of you than you are of them.'

Elizabeth nods her head.

'Is he gone?' asks Gordon, knowing without even a single doubt that the strange sound, the strange scream, was not about a spider.

'Um... under the fridge?' she suggests, and Gordon feels like he is in the middle of a dance to which he doesn't know the steps. If he moves the wrong way, does the wrong thing, he risks upsetting Elizabeth and causing her more trouble, but he cannot simply remove himself. She needs something – help, or just a friendly ear... something.

'Perhaps Howard was going to get some insect spray,' he says. 'I saw him leave. I'm quite handy with a glass and a piece of paper. Maybe I can get him out for you?'

Elizabeth nods and steps back and lets him in, leads him to the kitchen. Now they are in the dance together. There is obviously insect spray in the house. It's a home surrounded by bushland, and it's summer. Petra would have left plenty of spray.

'Would you like a cup of tea or a glass of wine?' she asks.

'I never turn down a cup of tea,' he says, letting her lead the dance as they twirl away from the lie of the spider. 'Where's Joe?'

'Sleeping,' she says quickly. 'Sleeping,' she repeats.

Gordon sits down at the familiar kitchen table. He runs his hand over the smooth timber, remembering helping Louie bring it in off the back of his ute at least thirty years ago. 'Good solid stuff this,' Louie said. 'Will last a lifetime.' The table has indeed lasted a lifetime, longer than Dawn and Louie anyway.

Elizabeth places a cup of tea in front of him, and brings over a small blue pot of sugar with a tiny silver teaspoon, and a matching blue jug filled with milk.

'Did I ever tell you what I did before I retired?' Gordon says, looking at his hands as he adds sugar and milk and stirs his tea. Elizabeth, he notices, has a glass of wine in front of her, and even though he's not looking at her, he sees the trembling of her hand as she lifts it to take a sip.

'Yes,' she says quietly. 'You mentioned that you were a teacher.'

'I was,' he says, looking at the floor next to the fridge as if waiting for the fictional spider to crawl out. 'I taught geography,' he says. 'You know, the environment, weather, cloud formations… cumulus, cirrus, nimbus.' He repeats the words that he used to call to mind as easily as his own name.

'That's nice,' says Elizabeth, taking another sip of wine. She is sitting strangely in her chair, in a kind of lopsided way, as though she has some pain in her side. He notices but cannot ask.

'Yes, I enjoyed it, and Flora, you see, was a nurse. She finished her work at the local hospital at five so every day, once Malcolm started school, he would walk across the road to the high school where I was and we would wait in my classroom together for Flora to be done so we could all drive home together. We only had the one car, you see.' He looks up at Elizabeth, meets her steady gaze. She nods for him to go on.

'Anyway,' he says, taking a quick sip of tea, 'because I was there late, sometimes students would come and spend time with me as they waited for their parents, or just for a chat. The girls liked to fuss over Malcolm, and he liked it too. There was one girl, named… Marybeth.'

'My sister calls me Bethy,' Elizabeth says.

'Ah – Natalie,' he says, 'you mentioned her.' He is amazed that he has instantly recalled the name. 'Anyway, Marybeth was a slip of a thing, only thirteen, and pretty, with white-blonde hair and blue eyes, and she used to stay in my classroom often, which I never quite understood, because she only lived a few minutes' walk from the school.' He talks quickly, because he is afraid of the story disappearing, although he's noticed that the past is always there – it's only the present that seems to vanish in an instant. 'She would do her homework and sometimes play with Malcolm while I did some marking, and I always let her know that she could talk to me if she wanted to, but she never said anything. Except for one time. Malcolm was bored, and he was picking up and putting down things on my desk, trying to get me to pay attention to him, as kids do, and I said, "Careful with my things, Malcolm. Please go and sit down, I'm nearly done." But he was in a bit of a mood, so he kept touching things, and then he picked up my mug, the mug I always used to drink my tea from, and he said, "Look, I'm a teacher, drinking tea," and he lifted it to his lips, but it slipped and fell on the floor, smashing into pieces.'

He hears an audible gasp from Elizabeth, but he keeps his gaze focused on the fridge. Most people would respond with a laugh. Most people who have no idea what could happen if tempers flare at the wrong time.

'I stood up,' he carries on, 'and I said, "Now you've done something that has upset me. Come along and help me clean it up. Perhaps you need some fresh air." And Malcolm said, "Sorry, Dad," and he helped me clear up. It was only when we were done that I realised that I couldn't see Marybeth. For a moment, I thought she had left, but then I heard her crying. I looked around and found that she was hiding under the desk. She must have been terrified of what my reaction would be. I coaxed her out and patted her until she stopped crying, and I told her again that she could talk to me, but she picked up her bag and said she had to go home. At the door, she stopped, and without turning around she lifted her top so I could see her back. "Last night I broke a plate," she said, and then she was gone. I will never forget the sight of that ugly black bruise. It covered the whole of her little back.'

He looks up to meet Elizabeth's horrified gaze, her face pale. 'Poor child,' she whispers. Her eyes dart to the kitchen door, and he knows she is thinking of Joe.

'Yes,' agrees Gordon. He stops to take another sip of his tea, feeling the sorrow and anguish of that moment from decades ago wash over him. 'I went and spoke to our principal, Mr Starling. I told him what I had seen and what she had said, and he told me... he told me to stay out of it. It was a family matter. Things were different then, different times.'

Elizabeth stands up from the table and gets her bottle of wine. Gordon watches in silence as she pours another glass for herself, tilting the bottle towards him, offering him the chance of a glass, but he shakes his head. He prefers a good whisky, and not this late at night. She sits down again. 'I think you're telling me this sad story for a reason, Gordon,' she says.

He nods. 'I could be... When I see something, I want to say that I've seen it. I'm losing parts of myself, bits and pieces fading away. Malcolm, my lovely son Malcolm, thinks I don't know, but I know it's happening. But some things – things that I might prefer to lose – hold fast. Two weeks later, Marybeth didn't turn up for school. The next day we heard she had drowned in the river that ran at the back of her parents' property. It was entirely possible, except for the fact that I remember her as a good swimmer. It was regarded as a tragedy, but I think it was something else, and I have always regretted not going to the police, not interfering, especially in my capacity as a teacher. Things are different now.'

'Yes,' agrees Elizabeth, her gaze dropping.

They sit in silence for a moment.

'But not so different,' says Gordon. 'There's no spider.'

'No,' says Elizabeth, tears slipping down her cheeks.

CHAPTER TWENTY-EIGHT

ELIZABETH

Yesterday, 8.15 p.m.

As Gordon speaks, she can picture him as a young man standing at the head of a class, looking out over a group of children and worrying about all of them. She realises that she has done to Gordon what a lot of society does to old people. She has dismissed him because of his failing memory and his frail body. She has looked at him and thought, 'You can do nothing to help me.'

But in the only way he can, he is trying to help her. The story of Marybeth may or may not be true, but either way she understands the message he is trying to give her. *Get out. Get out before you lose everything – including your own life.*

There was a moment in time when she could have changed things. It was over a decade ago, and she knows that she remembers it differently to how she experienced it. A decade ago, Howard walked out on her. It wasn't the first time he had done it, but it was the first time she didn't resort to begging and pleading for him to return. At first it was because she knew he would be back after a few days anyway. He usually was. He staged his walking-out when she bested him in an argument, when he couldn't twist her words so that she ended up believing she was in the wrong. The argument was over something so stupid she was embarrassed to tell her sister and mother about it. It was something to do with a train strike that was supposed to happen the next day. She knew it had been called off and he told her it was going ahead, and from that slight disagreement their whole marriage was laid bare. They flung accusations and insults at each other for an hour. When he read or saw something that confirmed what she had said – what she had refused to back down from – he packed his bags and left, telling her she was vindictive and sly. Over a train strike. Howard never caught the train.

Usually she would call him, apologise and ask him to return, and he would demand changes from her, and she would promise to be the person he wanted her to be. Sometimes she had to call for a few days in a row, but this time, this time she just left him to it.

And she went on with her life. She shopped and saw friends and her parents and called her sister. And she accepted a placement of an older child who was in a last-chance foster situation. She accepted it without asking Howard, without thinking about the consequences of doing something without him knowing. She just went on gut instinct and said yes.

'She's a runaway,' Barry, the case manager, told her. 'She will not stay in any home we have ever put her in. Do you think you might give it a go?'

If Howard had been there, she would have had to refuse. Howard preferred younger children. He liked feeling that he would be the one to mould and shape them, and he was increasingly frustrated by the fact that they were only with them for a short time. 'We need to look into fostering a much younger child,' he always said, 'a child we can one day adopt.' He was working his way up to introducing his rules, to becoming his father, although she didn't know it then.

When she thinks about what has kept her in her marriage all these years, Howard's acceptance of her need to foster is one very important thing. He has always claimed to understand that there are many needy children in the world and that he and Elizabeth are in a good position to help. But she knows that he has always liked the idea of one day adopting a child, of being able to tell the world that he has saved a child from a terrible life. He sees himself as a hero, and when he cannot play that role, he lashes out.

But over ten years ago, he was gone – off in a hotel or somewhere else – and Elizabeth accepted a young girl into her home, despite how troubled she was.

She thinks about all this as she listens to Gordon, and when he stops speaking, she knows at last that she can be honest with him.

Breathing in, she pictures a box in her mind where she keeps the truth about her marriage locked away. She visualises her hand holding a small gold key, and she uses it to open the box, and then she starts to speak. She tells Gordon some but not all of what she suffers – without mentioning the incident that brought him over the road in the first place. There is always the chance that he will go back home and call the police, and she can't risk that. She is not sure he will remember what she said in the morning, and that is perhaps why she does it. She can confess the truth and then take the steps she needs to take at her own pace. She knows what needs to happen now.

Gordon listens, sometimes shaking his head, sometimes taking a small sip of tea, and sometimes reaching across the table and holding her hand for a moment, his skin soft and warm.

'I can't let it go on,' she says when she is done, her head aching with the effort of telling the truth. Her eyes keep straying to her phone, her fingers moving quickly across the screen to check the app. Howard is still in the pub. I can't,' she repeats, 'but it means I lose Joe – they will take Joe from me.'

'Surely not,' he says, frowning. 'Don't they let everyone suitable foster, single and married alike?'

'They do,' she says, 'but I don't think they would want me to have him if I were going through a divorce. They would regard me as not quite stable. And if they found out about the violence...' She picks up her glass and takes another quick sip. She cannot contemplate what it would mean if they found out about the violence.

'You might be able to get him back later, I suppose,' he says. 'He loves you very much. I can see that. I would think that would be taken into account.'

'Perhaps,' she agrees, and she stands because she needs to sleep and she is sure Gordon does as well. 'But would I want him to have to go through it with me? I don't think so.'

'Sometimes there is no good choice,' says Gordon. 'Only a decision to be made between what you can and cannot tolerate.'

Elizabeth nods. She has been making one choice for years. She cannot do that any more.

At the door, as she sees him out, Gordon offers her a hug, quick and gentle so that she can relax against him a little.

'You just come to me if you need help,' he says. 'Malcolm will be here tomorrow, and he's a good lad, strong and good. You just come to us and we will help you.'

She watches him walk across the road to his house, where the front garden is quiet in the warm night, the birds hidden by the dark but probably resting in their tree. She knows that she has accepted the choice she didn't want, the one she has been fighting against since Joe arrived and the true extent of Howard's violence crept out day by day. She will choose her own life over being Joe's mother. The knowledge settles inside her, heavy with a dark sadness that she knows will stay with her forever.

She goes to sleep in Joe's room, lying on the floor, the door locked.

The blanket she has placed on the floor carries the slight smell of sunscreen because she had used it in the garden during the day. It is impossible to get comfortable, each position becoming agony after a few minutes because of the cracked rib. Staring at the ceiling, she feels the minutes pass in her bones as she listens to Joe's soft breath. Just once he moans aloud in his sleep, and she is instantly on her knees next to him, patting him until he is breathing deeply again. Her head pounds, her side aches, and her heart is broken as she listens to the little boy sleep. She would like to climb into bed with him, to curl up next to him, but she is conscious that she needs to begin creating some distance now – for him and for her. Tears slip down the sides of her face and she lets them. The only thing she can do as the night draws on is cry.

It is after 1 a.m. when Howard stumbles in. She hears him moving around, swearing and mumbling. He tries Joe's door, the handle twisting back and forth as she lies still in terror with her phone in her hand. But he gives up quickly enough, and she hears him in the bathroom and then closing their bedroom door. Her body finally relaxes into light sleep, relief that he has drunk himself into unconsciousness allowing her to rest, even as each breath in and out reminds her of what he has done.

In the morning, she and Joe get up quietly and eat breakfast. Her eyes are burning and her side is painful, but she smiles and talks about the beach and the sunshine and what the two of them are going to do today, even as she plans their escape.

Then she lets him into the front garden to play, sets him up with a red and blue checked picnic blanket and his collection of superheroes and the fruit set he likes to play pretend-chef with.

Wednesday morning has bloomed bright with sunshine and heat. It will be a beautiful day.

Joe is subdued and cannot be joked with. She allows him his silence. She takes a piece of toast and a carton of juice out to him because he hasn't finished his cereal.

'Do you want me to sit and play with you?' she asks him.

'No... No thank you,' he says, his tone and words familiar. It was how he spoke to them for the first week he was with them. Cautious, polite, ready for something to go wrong. And he was right to hold back. Everything has gone wrong.

She needs him to eat. She is worried about him. On his back, a blue bruise is spreading, telling of his little body being hurt. She wants to rub some arnica cream over his skin, but to do so would be to acknowledge what happened, and she can't do that with Howard in the house.

She feels like they need to keep up this facade for just a little longer. She is far from home and they only have one car. If she is to get away today, if she is to go now, then she has to be sure that Joe is somewhere safe. Howard will come after her, and she needs time to plan and think without worrying about the little boy and what might happen to him if Howard finds her, finds them.

It would be possible to take Joe to Gordon, but that would put Gordon in danger. A proper plan needs to be made, and what she would really like to do is talk things through with her sister. It will be safer to make this move when she is back in Sydney. But she will be making it. There is no doubt in her mind about that now.

'I'm going to make myself some coffee,' she says to Joe.

'Okay,' he says softly. She strokes his head briefly and he closes his eyes.

'You're not wearing your Spider-Man watch,' she says.

'No,' he agrees, and she wants to ask him why, but she understands. She has whole drawers filled with unopened bottles of perfume. Accepting the gift is one thing. Enjoying it is another.

Back in the kitchen, she makes herself a black coffee, hating the bitterness but needing the caffeine as she sips slowly, her thoughts going around and around, her stomach churning.

The bedroom door where Howard is sleeping remains closed.

CHAPTER TWENTY-NINE

GORDON

Today, 7.55 a.m.

He wakes later than usual, exhausted after a night dreaming of Joe running down the street being chased by Malcolm, who keeps shouting, 'Wait, wait.'

Hauling his body out of bed even though he would prefer to lie there for some time, he feels his muscles strain with the effort. Malcolm is coming tonight. Yes, tonight. He picks up his phone, where he has attached a sticky note in large shaky letters. *Malcolm coming tonight.* A visit to the grocery store is needed, because he wants to make sure that he at least has some food in for his son, but he can't remember what Malcolm likes. Del is easy; she likes anything to do with chocolate. He always buys too much and then Malcolm lectures him about... something.

Filled with purpose now, he does his stretches, his knees bending as he touches his toes. He's aware of his head thumping as he gets dressed, selecting a blue and red checked shirt that looks like all his other shirts, with large buttons so he can do them up, and two pockets so he can keep his glasses in a safe place. It will be warm today, and he wants a walk before it gets too hot. He pulls on shorts and then spends some time doing up the laces on his sneakers. Malcolm went with him to buy them, and they look very impressive and feel sturdy on his feet. He means to find that path between the two houses and make sure he remembers the way to the beach.

After drinking a glass of water, he eats a glorious purple plum in a few sweet, tart bites. He loves summer fruit, but he can't have too much these days.

Before he leaves through the back gate, he goes out to the front of the house to refill the bird feeder.

Joe is in the front garden across the road, sitting on a checked blanket, his toys around him, but he is not playing. Gordon doesn't want to cause any trouble, but he cannot imagine that saying hello could be a problem. He feels so sorry for the little boy. Last night Elizabeth told him... Did he see Elizabeth last night? He cannot remember, but there is something poking at him in his mind. Joe looks lost in his thoughts, his mouth a small frown. He does not look like a five-year-old child should look on a summer morning when the sky above is vivid blue.

Once Malcolm gets here and Gordon explains what Joe and Elizabeth are dealing with, he's sure his son will know what to do. It's a terrible thing to have to question yourself all the time, to feel inadequate. He remembers being the one other people came to for help and advice. 'Getting old is for the birds,' he mutters as he walks to his front gate, and the birds descend behind him, filling the morning air with squawks and song.

'Hello,' he calls to Joe, who is sitting cross-legged on the blanket, his chin resting on his hands as he gazes into the distance.

Joe waves at him and then resumes his position.

Gordon looks at him for a moment. 'Is everything okay?' he asks. A silly question. Everything is not okay. Everything he was told last night returns in a rush of images, and he remembers it all as though it has just happened. Last night Elizabeth told him that Howard hurts her... that's his name, Howard... but she said he doesn't hurt Joe. Gordon doesn't know if he believes her, but he knows that she means to leave, and he is sure he cannot do anything to help her until Malcolm is here. Even if the man has not physically hurt the child, seeing what happened between the two adults in his life hurts him more than enough. Children are changed when their parents fight in front of them. Their security and their belief in their world is changed. He would like to grab the boy and run with him, but that would only cause more trouble. Malcolm will sort it out for him, with him. They can go over there tonight, together, and tell Elizabeth to come and stay with him.

'I wish I didn't live here,' says Joe, and then he turns to look back at the house, obviously afraid of being heard.

'My son Malcolm is coming tonight,' says Gordon. 'I'm going to ask him to help you.' He looks at the kitchen window, worried that he will see Elizabeth there, or even worse, Howard.

'Is he a policeman?' asks Joe. He sits up straighter, interested now.

'No, he's...' There is a flutter of the blue curtains at the kitchen window, and Gordon feels his stomach turn. He cannot do anything here and he cannot put himself in danger. He waves at Joe. 'I'm going for a walk. I'm going to find the path that leads down to the beach. It's close to here,' he says.

'Yes,' agrees Joe. 'How will you get to the path?'

'Out the back... I go out the back gate,' says Gordon, and he remembers that he needs to latch the gate behind him when Del comes, lock the gate to make sure she is safe in the back garden.

'When will you come back?' asks Joe.

'Soon,' calls Gordon, and he hopes that this is the truth. He turns to go, walking down the side of the house to the back garden and out the back gate. He marches quickly, desperate to be far away from the little boy and the terrible guilt he feels at not helping him.

After a few minutes, he slows down. He's looking for the path. He needs to look for the path. But he needs to do something else as well. He just can't remember what.

CHAPTER THIRTY

ELIZABETH

Today, 7.55 a.m.

She listens as she mixes batter for pancakes, hoping that will tempt Joe to eat, and needing to do something with her hands. Her ears strain for sound as she cuts up fruit, her body tense, her stomach twisting. She lays the table and glances out of the window to check on Joe, then makes more coffee.

When she hears the door to the bedroom open, she finds she cannot face Howard just yet, not just yet, so she darts into the bathroom and takes a few minutes, the water in the basin running so that the gushing sound gives her something to concentrate on. They are supposed to leave to go back to Sydney the day before Christmas. She has a whole stack of presents waiting for Joe at home. Will he be allowed to keep them if he is taken away from her? Should she give him one lovely Christmas with her to remember – and will it be lovely? Will Howard be contrite enough about last night to allow them a couple of weeks of peace? 'Get your ducks in a row,' she hears Natalie say.

She emerges ten minutes later, her resolve in place, the

words in order. Howard is standing in the kitchen, his face slightly red as though he has been for a run. He is peering out of the window to the front garden.

'Listen—' she says to him.

'Where is Joe?' he asks urgently. 'He's not anywhere in the house. Where is he?'

CHAPTER THIRTY-ONE

GORDON

Today, 3.30 p.m.

Gordon watches the young woman, watches Ruby, who has abruptly stopped speaking, leaping up from her chair and picking up his still half-full mug of tea. She cleans quickly and efficiently, the way Flora used to, and he is grateful for her help, so he doesn't tell her he was still drinking the tea. She seems to need to clean.

He is looking forward to Malcolm being around to help him. The last few days have left him terribly tired. He wants to tell this young woman about Joe, about what he believes Joe experienced at the hands of that man and about how badly he felt for him and for Elizabeth, but she seems to need to tell him something first, to almost confess something first. She doesn't seem to be interviewing him at all – just telling him about her life. It seems strange that she has come all this way to tell him her story.

'Shall I make some more tea?' she asks, and Gordon nods. The girl is looking for something to do, some way to distract herself. Sometimes it's better to wait for a person to get their thoughts together. He thought that was what Elizabeth was doing after they had their little chat. He hoped to open the door this morning to see her and Joe standing there, asking for help. He would have let them in and kept them safe. He's an old man, but he would have kept them safe. Instead, Joe has gone missing. Last night when he went over to see Elizabeth, he knew she was hurt by the way she moved. What more was she hiding?

Anger against a child is so easy because it goes one way. Pick a fight with a man in the pub and you're likely to get a good smack yourself, but get angry with a woman or a child and you're in control. Howard looks like a man who enjoys being in control. Gordon sighs, tired of this sadness, tired of not knowing what to do. He wishes he hadn't interfered – or that he had figured out the right way to interfere – because who knows what's going to happen now.

Ruby puts another cup of tea down in front of him. She only has a glass of water for herself.

'You want to tell me something, Ruby,' he says, looking up at her. 'You can talk to me. I know you're supposed to be interviewing me, but there's something you want to say. I can feel it. You were talking about being adopted, weren't you? You said you were happy about the idea of being adopted. It would have been nice for you to finally have a family, I imagine...'

'It would have been,' she agrees, as she takes a seat opposite him at the kitchen counter. 'And so yes, I was happy at first, but then I moved in and everything was...'

Gordon is horrified to see her eyes fill with tears, and for a moment he thinks he may have done something to upset her. He tries to think back to what he has just said, but the fog rolls in, obscuring everything. 'I'm sorry, I didn't mean to...'

'Oh, you didn't, Gordon,' she says shaking her head. 'It's just so hard to talk about.'

'Take your time, love,' he says, patting her hand gently. 'I was a teacher, you know, so I'm used to young ones who have something they need to say. There's no rush.'

Ruby smiles, and he wonders if he's told her he was a teacher before. She takes a deep breath, and he recognises someone on the edge of telling a secret, making a confession.

The sound of a key turning in a lock and the front door opening startles them both.

'Who?' begins Gordon, and then he hears a voice calling, 'Hey, Dad. I got away early. I thought it would be a good idea to come down and help with the search since I grew up here.' There are some thumps as Malcolm brings his suitcases in and puts them down in the hallway. 'I told Lila to bring Del down in a few days. I don't want her here while all this is going on. I hope there's a cold beer in...'

Malcolm walks into the kitchen and sees his father and Ruby. He stops. His mouth drops open, obvious shock on his face.

'Oh my God, J—' he begins to say, and then he stops. 'I'm so sorry,' he says to Ruby, 'you just look so much like...'

'What?' says Gordon.

'Oh,' says Ruby.

CHAPTER THIRTY-TWO

ELIZABETH

Today, 4.00 p.m.

She is lying curled up on Joe's bed, holding on to the little shoe. The baby shampoo smell of his hair is on his pillow, and it makes it easier for her to breathe even though her side is aching, even though despair is eating away at her. She won't let go of the shoe, can't let go of it. Her mind keeps returning to the day she bought the sandals with Joe. He had arrived, as most foster children did, with one small suitcase of things, and she was horrified to find that most of the clothes were too small for him. He had been cared for, but he had been in a big family home for some months and he had grown a lot, as small children do.

The first night he spent in their home was wonderful. Howard was so careful with him, so patient. They both were, knowing that this was their last chance to really create a family.

'I can't wait to buy him new clothes, new shoes, everything,' Elizabeth said after the two of them had put Joe to bed, tucking him in with his ratty teddy bear that he had carried with him since he was a baby.

'I can't wait to throw out that disgusting stuffed toy,' said

Howard. 'I don't know why he only wanted that one after I bought him so many today.'

'It's his comfort object. I'll wash it for him and it will be fine.'

The next morning, Joe was subdued at breakfast and sat quietly afterwards, looking at the toys that Howard had bought for him but not really playing with any of them.

'What do we do?' Howard asked her. 'He seems so unhappy.'

'I think we just need to start as we mean to go on. You go to work and I'll be with him. Maybe we can go shopping in a bit.'

She was grateful that Howard agreed to leave so she would have the time to bond with Joe. She sat on the sofa watching him study and lightly touch the toys, his hand resting on the collection of superheroes that Howard had opened for him and posed into positions. It was overwhelming, she could see that.

'Do you know,' she said, and he turned to look at her, his big green eyes filled with confusion and sadness, 'there's a rule in my house.'

'A rule?' he said, his voice soft, and she understood that he knew about rules. She wanted to grab him and hold him, but she was wary of pushing.

'Yes. Before you can play, you need a hug, a joke and a snack.'

Joe looked at her, and then he nodded and stood up, coming over to her and putting his arms lightly around her neck. She tried not to squeeze too tight, and to let go only when he let go.

'Now a joke,' he said, his tone more confident.

'Where do cows go on Saturday nights?' she asked.

He studied her. 'I don't know,' he said, 'where do they go?'

'To the moooovies.' She laughed, and there was a beat, a second, before he giggled, and repeated, 'The moooovies... the moooovies!' He laughed each time he said it, and she watched, delighted at the change in him. 'Now a snack,' he said, when he had stopped laughing, and she took him into the kitchen to give him a chocolate chip cookie that she had baked.

The ice was broken and they played with the toys for a bit before she took him shopping, going to the children's shoe store and letting him choose a pair of sneakers and a pair of sandals. He loved the crocodile ones because he would be able to put them on himself. She had never enjoyed spending money as much as she did that day, wanting to buy him everything he looked at.

Now he is gone, and all she has is this small shoe in her hand, a painful reminder of what her life could have been. She cannot conceive of how to survive such heartbreak.

The bedroom door opens and she closes her eyes, hoping that Howard will just go away. It's obviously him. Anyone else would have knocked. *Not now, not now – please not now.* He can't hurt her, not here with all these people in the house, and what more could he do anyway?

Her skin shudders with loathing and she longs for him to leave. But he doesn't leave. Instead, she feels the bed dip as he sits down. She shifts her body as far away as she can from him on the single bed.

'Just go away,' she says, keeping her eyes closed, not wanting to see him. 'I'm sure they don't want us speaking to each other.' When he doesn't say anything, she opens her eyes, and focuses the full force of her anger on him, wishing she was like one of the superheroes Joe talks about, able to shoot flames from her eyes. 'Aren't you waiting for your lawyer to arrive?' She cannot hold back the bitterness she feels as she looks away, stares at the wall. She will not look at him.

'You're blaming me. I know you are. I've only asked to wait for my lawyer because I've done nothing wrong – and I'm trying to protect you.' So reasonable, so calm, his voice just above a whisper.

Elizabeth sits up, clutching the sandal tightly. Howard is

hunched over his knees, his hands clasped together, the very picture of despair. His usually neat hair is sticking up as though he has run his hands through it many times. This is the man who comes after the one who hurts. This is the man who is sorry, who wants to be forgiven.

She has no forgiveness left. 'It's your fault, Howard. You hurt him. You hurt me and you hurt him,' she hisses, anger replacing every other emotion. 'And now you've tried to tell them that I did something? You're a sick, sick man.'

'It's not my fault he's gone,' snarls Howard, a lightning-quick change, and the sorry man is gone, replaced by the Howard she's always waiting for. 'You want them to take me away, but it's not my fault he's gone.'

She moves further away from him, drawing up her legs. 'I don't believe you. It wouldn't be the first time you made a child disappear.'

'What?' he whispers, furious, standing up, jamming his hands in his pockets, his jaw tense.

'You know what I'm talking about.' She speaks quietly, but she can hear the hatred she feels for him in her words.

'That wasn't my fault either,' he says with a shrug. 'She ran away. Even the case manager said it wasn't our fault.'

'Don't you dare include me in this,' she spits. 'I was away. I was away and when I got back she was gone, and I know you did something to her, I know it.' She points towards him with the shoe.

'You're making shit up, Elizabeth,' he says, bending towards her, reaching for the shoe, which she pulls back and clutches close. He stands straight again, a hint of a smile on his face. 'You were the one who should have been watching Joe, so you're the one to blame.'

Her breath catches in her throat, a slice of pain goes through her side and she winces. She turns her head to stare out of the bedroom window. It's small and looks out onto the paved driveway. 'And I do blame myself,' she says, her words soft with regret, 'but where I really messed up was by staying with you, by defending you and covering up what you did after last time.'

Howard walks around the bed to look down at her, crossing his arms. 'What the hell are you talking about?'

Elizabeth cannot meet his gaze, focusing on the shoe instead, playing with the Velcro straps, ripping them open and putting them back together again, comforted by the slight tearing noise they make. 'She wouldn't have just run away, Howard. I agreed with you when we spoke to the case manager that she had been unhappy, but she wouldn't have just run away. She liked me. She wasn't unhappy with me. We got on really well.'

'Not well enough,' he sneers. 'And that was a long time ago. This is different, because I know who's taken him.'

Her hands stop moving and she looks directly at him. His eyebrows are raised and he has a look of triumph about him, like he's won something.

'What?' she asks, unable to believe what he's just said.

'I know and I'm going to get him back.' He nods.

For a moment she wonders if he has gone completely mad, but then she realises that he's going to tell the police it was Gordon. He's going to blame an old man. She gets off the bed, moves away from him, feels the slightly rough wall against her back. 'You're just trying to shift the blame because you've—' She stops short of an actual accusation. Howard's fists are clenched, his jaw tight and his grey eyes looking straight through her. The house is filled with police, but that won't stop him.

The door is closed, and she moves along the wall, closer to it in case she needs to run, to open it and just run. She wants him to go away, to be taken away, to be forced by other people more powerful than her to confess the truth. But what is that truth? What is it?

'You're not going to pin this on me, Elizabeth,' he says, stepping towards her, and her heart gallops in her chest, the pain in her side intensifying with her quick breaths.

Outside the room, someone calls, 'Mr Ealy?' and Howard's shoulders relax, his fists unclench and his face returns to neutral.

'Please go,' she whispers as she climbs back onto the bed, her body tensed and ready to run if he does not leave.

He leans down so that his face is just in front of hers, and she sits as still as she can, trying not to show any sliver of fear or revulsion. 'Just you wait,' he hisses, and then he straightens up and leaves the room, slamming the door behind him.

Elizabeth feels exhaustion creep through her body, stealing her ability to stand up and follow him. He cannot mean to accuse the old man. Surely the police will see through that. Surely they won't believe him?

She lies down again, listens to the hum of the old air conditioner on the wall and hugs the sandal to her chest, feeling a hot tear slide down her face and soak into the pillow.

CHAPTER THIRTY-THREE

MALCOLM

Today, 4.00 p.m.

He blinks a few times, making sure he is seeing what he's seeing. It must be a mistake. He must have made a mistake.

'Oh my God, J—' he begins, and then he stops. 'I'm so sorry,' he says to the young woman standing next to his father, 'you just look so much like...'

'What?' says Gordon.

'Oh,' says the young woman.

'You're early,' says his father. 'I...' He looks at his phone, and Malcolm feels bad for causing him more confusion. He was so clear on the phone about the time he was coming down, and he sent him a text. Now he's here early without warning, and his father is questioning himself.

'I'm sorry, Dad,' he apologises. 'I changed things. You haven't forgotten. It was me who changed my plans. I've been listening to the news all day and I thought that maybe I could help. I know so many places to hide around here.'

'Oh, you're here to help,' says his father, relief obvious in his voice.

'Yep, here to help with the search,' says Malcolm, 'for the little boy who's missing. I thought it would be better if Del came down when all this was over, you know.'

'Yes,' agrees his father, but Malcolm is not sure he fully understands. He looks away from his dad and steps forward, towards the young woman, who is staring at him. He almost called her by someone else's name. It's a surreal feeling looking at someone and knowing that you recognise them, and yet that you don't know them, because he's sure it's not possible. He holds out his hand. 'I'm so sorry, I thought you were... You just look so much like someone I knew once. I'm Malcolm, Gordon's son.'

'I'm Ruby,' says the young woman, shaking his hand.

'It's so strange,' he says. 'You look so much like her, but...'

'But my hair is shorter,' says the young woman, and Malcolm drops her hand and steps back.

'It *is* you... I can't believe it. I'm right, aren't I?'

'Yes, Malcolm,' she says quietly. 'You're right.'

'God, Jade...' he says as the memories come rushing back.

'I don't understand,' says his father, shaking his head. 'Malcolm, you said... Have I gotten mixed up? I don't understand. I thought your name was Ruby...' He turns towards her. 'I thought it was Ruby...' and Malcolm can hear how frustrated he is, confusion making him fearful.

'It's okay, Gordon,' she says, touching his hand. 'You're fine. You're not confused.'

'Okay, good,' says his father, 'because this is not Jade, this is Ruby. Ruby is here to interview me, because she's writing...'

'I wanted to write a piece on what's happening,' Ruby jumps in. 'Gordon was kind enough to invite me in, but I had no idea... Well, when he mentioned your name, I remembered you telling me you came from a small town on the south coast, but I thought it couldn't be possible that it was the same man.'

'I don't understand,' his father mutters, his eyes clouding

over with confusion. He pats his pocket for his glasses, even though he's already wearing them. Malcolm wants to explain it, but he can't stop staring, marvelling at what he is seeing.

'You look good,' he says.

She shrugs. 'I cut my hair, changed my name from one precious gem to another. Sad, but I wanted to remember who I used to be,' she says.

'Malcolm, Ruby – what is going on?' asks his father, and Malcolm can see he is getting agitated.

'Dad,' he says, 'do you remember how about ten years ago I told you and Mum a story about how I helped someone?'

'Damn stupid idea,' says his father. 'You always were one for strays.'

Malcolm laughs, relieved that his father remembers this, that he can access this memory right here, right now. He is struggling himself with what he is seeing, with how this has happened. But there is no doubt that this is the young woman, the same young woman who was so broken he was afraid she wouldn't survive, so broken and yet so determined not to get help from anywhere.

'This is her,' he says, touching Ruby lightly on the shoulder. 'This is the young girl I found at the bus stop.'

'The young girl he took in and cared for for a whole month, Gordon,' says Ruby. 'I didn't know he was your son. You got old,' she says to Malcolm.

'You look lovely,' he answers.

'This is her?' asks his father. 'But... how did you land up here, lass?'

'I don't know,' shrugs Ruby. 'I came here to... I mean, I know I said I wanted to interview you, Gordon, and I do, but there's more to it than that.'

'Ah yes,' says his father. 'You were going to tell me some-thing, you were going to explain.'

'You never told *me*,' says Malcolm. 'You never really told me what happened.'

'I know,' agrees Ruby, nodding her head. 'I should have. I owed you that explanation and I owe it to you as well, Gordon. I can explain, if you'll let me. I can explain everything.'

Malcolm feels the car journey, and the last few exhausting days as he tried to get ready to take some time off, creeping up on him. He's glad his daughter is not here right now. There is a missing child and there is someone here from his past, someone he never thought he would see again. Never thought he would see, but always wanted to see.

'I need a beer. Do you want one, Dad?'

'I need one,' says Gordon. 'I need to sit on the sofa as well.'

Malcolm looks at Ruby. 'For you?'

'Just water for me, thanks.'

Malcolm grabs two beers from the fridge, still not able to believe that Jade – or Ruby, as she is now – is here, in his father's house. He walks slowly behind his father, who settles himself on the sofa with a slight groan. He hands him a beer and takes a long drink of his own, enjoying the crisp, cold rush in his mouth. He and Gordon are silent as Ruby sips her water, and Malcolm can see her working through the story in her head.

'You look alike,' she says. 'You have the same blue eyes, nice eyes.'

'I have more hair,' laughs Malcolm.

'Watch it, son,' jokes Gordon, and Malcolm experiences a small burst of happiness. He spends a lot of time worrying about his father these days. He is here for a few weeks now because he cannot leave him in this house, without someone to help him, any longer. He is here to make some changes, but he could never have expected his past, the past that changed him, to be here as well.

Every day she was in his apartment he waited for her to do something to betray his kindness, and every day she reminded him that there are some human beings you can just trust. He was struggling at the time at work, hating his job but desperate to make management. After Jade left, he decided that life was too short, and that things that were meant to be would be.

She was lucky he was the one who stopped to help, and because of that he realised that he had nothing to lose by taking a chance on pursuing his dream of running his own company. Maybe whatever force in the universe had led him to Jade would lead him in the right direction with his own life. And it has, he knows it has.

'If I had seen this story on the internet or the news, I know I never would have believed it,' says Ruby. 'I would have said, that can't happen.'

'In my experience, the strangest things are always possible,' says Gordon, taking another small sip of his beer.

Malcolm realises that he's nearly finished his and puts the bottle down on the table. He wants to be present to hear what happened to this young woman. To hear who hurt her enough to make her want to hide, and to hear how her life has changed since then.

'My name used to be Jade, Gordon,' she says. 'But you remember how I was saying that after my foster mother, Monica, died, I was sent back into the system?'

'Yes, yes,' says his father, nodding at her words. 'You said that another couple offered to adopt you and you were happy about that.'

'I was,' agrees Ruby, 'especially after I met her. I only met her at first. She told me her husband was away on business. He was away for a long time, months, actually. I thought he was never coming back, but I didn't mind that. She lived in a beautiful house with views of the harbour, and we got along really well. She bought me so many things; clothes and books and a computer, things I had never dreamed of owning.

'But it wasn't just that she bought me stuff. It was something else about her, something open and kind. She listened when I talked... listened without jumping in or giving advice. And she was so kind... so lovely. I remember my first day at school after I moved in with her. It was lunchtime and I realised that I had forgotten to ask her for something to eat. We were both rushing that morning, both just getting used to being together, and she wasn't quite sure how to get to my school, and in the middle of everything, I forgot about lunch. I went to my bag to check if I had a muesli bar I could eat, and I found a lunch box tucked at the bottom. She had packed me this beautiful lunch – a perfectly made cheese sandwich and some strawberries in a little container and even a small chocolate and some crackers. And with it there was a note that said, "Hope you're having a good day." I had been packing my own lunch for a long time, and I can't describe how much it meant to find someone had done it for me, had taken the time to think about what I might like to eat. That was what she was like. All she wanted to do was take care of me.'

'Lucky,' murmurs his father. 'That was lucky.'

'At first, yes,' says Ruby, a small smile on her face. 'When it was just me and her, it was wonderful. I was not an easy kid, I know that.' She shakes her head at the memory of her younger self. 'After Monica died, I was so, so angry. I ran away from quite a few foster homes. I never expected to feel comfortable anywhere ever again. But she was so nice, and easy to be with, and I felt like... like she almost understood.' She shrugs. 'And so for a few months it was good... but then he came home. I could tell she was shocked – that she wasn't expecting him. I hadn't asked about him because I didn't care, and she never talked about him except to lie to my case manager about him being away or busy. I knew there was something else going on, but I kept her secret. And then one day he was just there, and after the initial shock she was smiling and laughing a lot more and acting like he really had just come back from some extended business trip. And that's when all the rules began.'

Malcolm feels his heart skip a beat. Every family has its rules, but the way Ruby says the word tells him this was different.

'Rules...' he says.

Ruby nods. 'About how I should speak and eat and sit and what I should watch on television and how well I was supposed to do at school and how I should answer the phone. I didn't pay attention to a lot of them because I thought they were just rubbish that he was making up to kind of get some control of me... of her, of us. She kept trying to moderate him, to tell him I needed time to adjust, but from the moment he walked in, she changed... kind of shrank and became less herself, less the woman who was so caring and more someone who was afraid and nervous and stressed.'

Gordon sits forward and clasps his hands together, and Malcolm can see that he understands that Ruby is trying to tell them something important. 'And what happened if you broke the rules?' he asks. Malcolm is surprised that his father has found this very important question in his ageing, failing brain.

She looks down at the glass of water in her hand, turning it in slow circles, and Malcolm wants to tell her that she doesn't have to explain this, that there is no need for her to lay herself bare for them.

'It wasn't good,' she says. 'It wasn't good.'

'I'm so sorry,' whispers Gordon. 'So sorry.' Malcolm lays a hand on his father's shoulder, grateful again as he has been many times over the years for the gentle way he was raised. His mother fussed and worried, but no matter what happened, his father was always calm and collected, always willing to listen.

'It wasn't like I'd never been hit before, you know,' says Ruby, looking up from her glass. 'I'd been hit in other homes, but he was so... mercurial, I guess. And the worst thing was that

I was never allowed to tell her. He turned it into our secret. He yelled at me in front of her, but he only hit me when she was out or couldn't see, and then he would be completely devastated and cry and apologise and tell me he was getting help for his temper. I never could tell when it was going to happen. Sometimes I would hold my knife the wrong way and he would say, "Jade, do it like this," and I would do as he said and it would be fine... but sometimes, he would completely lose it, screaming that I was never going to amount to anything, that I would end up on the streets, that I was no better than an animal. She tried to stand up for me when he yelled, but he would turn on her and tell her she didn't deserve children. It was like a switch went off in his brain, and then all of a sudden it would be over and he would apologise and buy me something... a necklace, or a leather jacket... and I would think that it was worth his weirdness for all the stuff. But I was fifteen and I didn't know I was selling my soul. I know it was partly my fault for not telling my case worker. I know that.' She smooths her short hair, tucking a wisp behind her ear, nodding her head slightly.

'No,' says Gordon firmly. 'No. It was never your fault. You were a child in need of love and it was never your fault.'

'I'm so sorry,' says Malcolm. 'So sorry you had to go through that.'

Ruby brushes at her cheeks, and then leans over and grabs a tissue from the box on the coffee table.

'It was nearly eleven years ago,' she says. 'Eleven years, and they were both much younger then, but they haven't changed. I knew as soon as I saw them on television this morning that they haven't changed.'

'Who?' asks his father, confusion obvious on his face.

'The Ealys,' she says softly. 'I was fostered by Howard and Elizabeth Ealy, and they were going to adopt me until I ran away.'

'Oh God,' says Malcolm, the thought making him feel sick. 'He did that to you? He did... The father of the missing kid?'

'Foster father,' she says. 'And yes. He did.'

'But... but why? What happened?' Gordon asks, his face pale, horror in his eyes. 'I remember Malcolm telling us about it, I remember like it was yesterday. He said you were so badly beaten he couldn't make out your features.' He shakes his head.

'I think it was because I wouldn't accept his apology,' Ruby says. 'He seemed to think that if he apologised, that if he begged for forgiveness and got it, then it was okay, that what he had done was okay. Elizabeth always forgave him for his behaviour, and I have a feeling that he hit her as well, away from me, in secret so no one else could see. And then he always, always said sorry and needed to be forgiven. That was the most important part of it, that he heard that he was forgiven so he could pretend it had never happened. It became this secret that the two of us kept together. And it was easy to keep because whenever it happened it would come out of the blue and I had no idea what had triggered it, so I could dismiss it as something that wouldn't happen again. And inevitably, I always blamed myself for making it happen, so I was ashamed to tell anyone because I knew they would say I deserved it. I feel silly saying that now, but back then...' she sighs heavily, 'back then I didn't know any better.'

'So what happened the night I found you? Had he ever hurt you that badly before?' asks Malcolm. His hands are on his knees and he can feel that he is squeezing hard. Inside him, anger is mounting at a man he has never met.

'No... he hadn't,' she says, and she picks up her glass of water, drains it. 'Do you have anything aside from beer to drink?' she asks.

'Sherry,' says his father. 'Flora used to have a sherry on Friday night. I keep forgetting... Well, there's a fresh bottle. Or I have whisky, do you drink whisky?'

Ruby shakes her head.

Malcolm gets up off the sofa and goes to the timber cabinet where he knows his mother kept her bottle of sherry. He has never been able to understand the appeal of its sickly-sweet taste. As he picks up a small crystal glass, he is assailed with memories of Flora sitting right where Ruby is sitting now, a book open on her lap as she sipped the sherry on a Friday night. He misses her so much, but not as much as his father misses her. Since she died, his father is a different man.

He hands the glass of sherry to Ruby, who drinks it down and pulls a face at the taste.

'We need to go to the police and tell them about what he did to you,' says Malcolm.

'I know,' she says, 'but what if something else happened to Joe? I mean, maybe he's changed.'

Malcolm and his father share a glance, and Malcolm remembers something Gordon told him before he moved away to live in Sydney. 'When someone shows you who they are, son, believe them,' he said, and Malcolm has done just that. While he does believe in second chances, he is always aware that most people will show you their true nature early on. He watches for it with clients, with women, with everyone.

'I don't think he has,' says his father. 'I've only known him for a couple of weeks, only spent a little time with him, but I don't think he has.' He tips his beer to his mouth, the words hanging in the air, and Ruby nods slowly, accepting this fact.

'I guess I hoped he had. I really hoped he had. I didn't come here to say anything; I just needed to see that the little boy came home safely. What happened with me couldn't have happened with him, could it? He's too young. He wouldn't have pushed back against the rules like I did. At least I don't think he would have.'

'And what did happen?' Gordon asks. Malcolm can see his

dad is getting tired. He doesn't want to hear the details of what happened to Ruby, though he knows he needs to ask.

'One night,' she says, and then she stops speaking, presses her hands against her eyes, before looking up again as she takes a deep breath, 'I refused to forgive him, refused to accept his apology. Elizabeth was away for the night with her sister, celebrating her birthday, and we were watching a movie on television. It was *Love Actually*,' she says, 'because it was close to Christmas. I was a bit upset because Elizabeth had promised we would all watch it together and I had this vision of a kind of traditional family experience. I knew kids at school who all watched it every Christmas with their parents, even though they considered themselves too cool to be watching such a cheesy movie. But then her sister's husband booked a night away for the two of them – a girls' night out and a room at a hotel – and she was desperate to go.'

'That was Flora's favourite movie,' says his father.

'It was,' agrees Malcolm.

'It was a great night at first. I couldn't stop looking at the Christmas tree in the corner of the room and the pile of presents underneath. "You'll just have to wait and see," Howard laughed every time he caught me looking. I was sitting next to him on the sofa and we were eating popcorn and I thought everything was okay. He'd been calm and happy the whole night, but then I stood up to go to the bathroom and brushed some specks of popcorn off my top and onto the floor. "Clean that up," he said.

'And I said that I would but I was just going to the bathroom first.

'I can't even remember him standing up. The slap seemed to come out of thin air, hard and fast.' Ruby reaches up and touches her ear, and Malcolm can imagine her shock and the pain she must have felt.

'I should have just cleaned everything up then, but I got so angry at him, so angry at myself that I had believed he was fine

to sit next to that night, that I just screamed, "I'm telling Barry."
He was my case manager; you know, my social worker, and he
checked in with me once a month to see how I was doing. I
hadn't told him about Howard's behaviour. I liked Elizabeth so
much...' She flushes slightly, and Malcolm wonders if she
blames herself for this.

'You wanted to be part of a family,' he says. 'Everyone wants
that.'

'Yes,' she says, her eyes filling with tears. 'It was all I
wanted. But when I told him I was going to tell Barry, when he
knew I wasn't going to keep his secret, he went completely
crazy. First he begged me not to tell, and then when I said again
that I was going to, he followed me to my room and started
hitting me, just hitting me over and again. I begged him to stop,
begged him.

'Eventually I passed out, and when I woke up, the house
was quiet and I knew he had left. I could have called the police,
but I was afraid to. I didn't want to tell them what had
happened and have Howard deny it, because I knew he would.
He would find a way to lie about it and Elizabeth would
inevitably end up believing him, because she was his wife and I
was just some foster kid.

'I had a hundred dollars from Elizabeth because she'd told
me to get something for Howard for Christmas, and so I shoved
that in my pocket and just walked out the door. I didn't want to
go to the hospital, because I knew that after I got well, I would
be back in the foster system, and I never wanted to be there
again. I wanted control over my own life.' She crosses her arms,
jutting out her chin. 'My plan was to make it to Kings Cross and
find a shelter or sleep on the streets until I recovered.' She
shrugs her shoulders. 'I had no idea, you know, no idea at all. I
just wanted to be alone, and at least it was warm. But then I
stopped at a bus stop because I was so tired, and I thought I

could get on a bus and ride all night because I knew you could do that. But I fell asleep and then...'

'Then I found you,' says Malcolm.

'Well I'll be...' says Gordon. 'Who would have thought a thing like that could happen.'

'I got lucky,' says Ruby, with a small smile.

Malcolm stands up and goes over to her. He leans down and puts his arms around her, and Ruby hugs him hard. She smells of jasmine, and he is assailed by the memory of the metal tang of blood the night he found her.

'The kindness of strangers,' she says when she lets go. 'Whenever I think of you, I think that some people come into your life for a reason. You were there when I needed someone, and you had no idea if I was a good human being or someone who would lie to you and steal from you.'

'My mum always taught me to look for the good in people, didn't she, Dad?'

'She did,' agrees his father. 'She was so good herself, you see.'

'She must have been,' says Ruby, 'to have raised a son like Malcolm. And now we need to help this little boy. I don't know where he is, but if he's alive, we need to find him, and help him get away from Howard, and from Elizabeth, because I don't think she will ever leave him.'

'Ah now,' says Gordon, 'that's where I think you're wrong.'

CHAPTER THIRTY-FOUR

GORDON

Today, 4.30 p.m.

'Why, Dad?' asks his son. 'Why do you think Ruby is wrong?' Malcolm touches him on the arm as he speaks, something he has started doing when they are together. Gordon can almost feel his son saying, 'Pay attention, Dad,' willing him to stay in the moment, to remember where he is and what he's talking about.

'She told me she wants to leave – she told me so.' Gordon feels too overwhelmed to explain, but he knows this fact, and he knows his son will believe it's the truth.

'You need to talk to the police, Dad, you both do,' says Malcolm, standing up and swinging his arms, and Gordon can feel his son's physical need to do something.

'I can't,' says Gordon, looking up at his son, trying to communicate his worry. He is fearful that he will get it wrong, fearful that he has it wrong. Something nudges at him, something he is supposed to remember, and he sighs, folding his arms and dropping his chin to his chest. He feels like this so often these days, like he is forgetting something. 'Latch the gate,' he says suddenly. 'I should have latched the gate. I'll remember when Del is here. I promise.'

'I'm sure you will, Dad, don't worry about it,' says Malcolm. He leans down and picks up his beer, drains the bottle and then stares at the label, starts scraping at it with his fingernail.

'So what now?' asks Gordon. He has a terrible headache and he would like to rest, but he knows there's no time for that now. Joe is still missing – or worse.

'I keep thinking,' says Ruby, as she swipes at the screen on her phone, 'I keep hoping he's still okay, still... alive, that maybe he just ran away and he's hiding. But now that they've found his shoe, I don't think there's any hope, no hope at all.' She drops the phone into her bag, disappointed that it has given her no new information. She looks so terribly sad that Gordon would like to comfort her, but he can feel the fog rolling in.

'He's hurt him, I know he has,' says Ruby, her voice thick with tears. 'I never told anyone what he did. I just disappeared and changed my name. I lived on the streets until I was too old to go back into the system and then I legally changed my name. I was always afraid of him finding me.'

'He was such a lovely little chap,' says Gordon, rubbing his hand over his eyes to try and force the fog to disappear. 'He loved the birds, you know, and I made him cold hot chocolate like I make for Del. I told him about how you used to go and play in the bush around the estuary, Malcolm. Funny to think that a child would never be able to do that these days. Everyone is always so worried about what's out there that can hurt a child, but honestly, nothing can be worse than your own home some-times. Nothing.' He stares out of the window.

'You told him about the bush by the estuary?' asks Malcolm, excitement in his voice. He puts the beer bottle down on the coffee table and starts pacing around the room.

'I did, when they came over.' Gordon watches his son, his

head moving as Malcolm goes back and forth across the living room.

'When...' asks Malcolm, stopping in front of him, 'when did you forget to latch the gate, Dad?'

'This morning,' says Gordon, because he remembers his walk. 'I saw Joe and I told him I was going for a walk, and then I found the path and...' He waves his hands. He doesn't need to tell Malcolm that he sometimes cannot find the path. That's a truth for another day.

'And he was okay when you saw him?' asks Ruby as she too stands up. Gordon feels like something is happening, but he has no idea what.

'He was, sad but physically fine. I wouldn't have left him there otherwise. I told him Malcolm was coming. I told him that Malcolm could help.'

'What if he...' says Malcolm.

'Followed you?' says Ruby.

'Yes,' says Malcolm animatedly. 'What if he followed you and you didn't see, and he got out of the back garden because you left the gate unlatched.' He looks down at Gordon, who struggles to understand what his son is saying. Is it his fault? Is it his fault that Joe is gone?

'But then where is he?' asks Gordon. 'Where is he?'

'He could be hiding,' says Malcolm. 'He could be hiding around the estuary, where you told him I used to play.'

'They've been looking all day,' says Ruby. 'Surely they would have found him?' She and Malcolm seem to understand each other.

'Kids,' shrugs Malcolm. 'Maybe they called and he didn't want to be found.' He starts pacing again. 'I need to go and take a look. Jade... Ruby, you have to go and tell the police what he did to you.'

'No, no,' says Ruby, shaking her head and stepping away from Malcolm, her hands up as though to stop him. To Gordon, she sounds terrified. She has grown up knowing she cannot trust the adults around her to keep her safe, and perhaps she has some mistrust of the police because of this. 'I can't do that. He'll say I'm lying. Please don't make me go alone, Malcolm.' Dropping her hands, she folds her arms around her body, comforting herself.

'I tell you what,' says Malcolm, running his hands through his hair. 'Come with me to check where I used to play, and then I'll come with you to the police.'

'Okay,' says Ruby, relief in her voice. 'Okay.'

'Dad, you need a rest. Shall I help you to your room?'

'I could use a nap,' says Gordon.

He finds himself a little unsteady on his feet as Malcolm guides him to his room and helps him lie down on the bed. 'I should have called the police again,' he says to his son. 'I should have kept calling them until someone came to help her and the boy.'

'Dad, the first thing they did was call me and tell me that they were worried about you being on your own. They weren't going to listen to you.' As he speaks, Malcolm pulls up the light grey blanket that has been on the end of Gordon's bed for as long as he can remember. Flora crocheted it when she was pregnant and had no idea how big it was going to be, simply making square after square. It has holes in some places now, but Gordon doesn't like to think of getting rid of it. Malcolm tucks the blanket around him the same way Gordon used to do when Malcolm was a child.

'They didn't want to listen to me,' Gordon says, his head sinking into the pillow. 'I'm sure that all those years ago, Ruby thought they wouldn't listen to or believe her. Why is it that the most vulnerable people in society are the ones no one ever wants to hear from?' He closes his eyes, not wanting to see the way his son is looking at him. He *is* vulnerable now, and he prefers to remember a time when Malcolm looked up to him and imagined that there was not a problem in the world his father couldn't solve.

'I don't know, Dad,' sighs Malcolm. 'I don't know.'

Gordon moves his head on his pillow, enjoying the feel of the cool cotton on his skin, and closes his eyes. He is asleep before Malcolm and Ruby leave. The day has worn him out, Ruby's secrets have exhausted him, and his fear over what has happened to Joe is too much to think about any more.

CHAPTER THIRTY-FIVE

ELIZABETH

Today 4.30 p.m.

In the dim light of the bedroom, the curtains drawn, she thinks about the last time she felt this level of devastation. She never imagined she would have to feel this way again. At first, because she protected herself by not fostering again for a long time – not until Joe – and then because she thought it couldn't possibly happen again. But the truth – the terrible truth – is that the only thing she can be completely sure of with Howard is that it *will* happen again.

Jade ran away. After that wonderful night in the hotel with her sister, Elizabeth returned home, and at first, she didn't worry that Jade wasn't there. It was the last day of the school term. She was looking forward to the Christmas holidays in a way she had never looked forward to them before, and her small suitcase was filled with gifts from the hotel spa for the fifteen-year-old girl she felt such love for.

It was only after she had unpacked and put on a load of laundry that she went into the teenager's room and found something wrong. It was too tidy, too clean. Howard liked Jade to keep the room neat, but Elizabeth believed that it was her space and that she should be able to decide when she wanted to clean up. A mild worry niggled at her, and she called Howard.

'Ah, you're home,' he said. 'Did you have a good time?'

'Lovely,' she said. 'And was everything okay with Jade?'

'Well,' he sighed, 'I did tell her to tidy her room, and she wasn't happy about that.'

'It's very tidy now,' said Elizabeth. The clean room was disturbing, all traces of the teenage girl stashed away so that the room could belong to anyone. Something had happened while she was away, and she knew she had to tread carefully.

'Good,' he said, 'that's very good. She must have gotten it done after I went to bed.'

Elizabeth felt her stomach cramp. She hadn't wanted to leave for the night, unsure if Howard and Jade would be okay, but Natalie had been insistent.

'I'm here from the USA and Sean is treating us to the most amazing hotel and to dinner; you have to come and stay with me.'

'It will be fine,' Howard told her. 'The two of us are getting on a lot better now. It'll be good for us to bond without you there. I'm going to be her father after all.'

Elizabeth had desperately wanted to believe him, wanted to believe that the few times he'd lost his temper with Jade were in the past. The relationship between Jade and Howard had not been an easy one. When he had eventually returned home, he had been shocked to see the young girl. He had walked in one morning with flowers and pastries from Elizabeth's favourite bakery as though he had simply returned from the fictional trip she told everyone he was on, and found Jade in the kitchen.

'You're home,' Elizabeth had said quickly. 'This is Jade. Remember I told you about Jade?'

Howard nodded and smiled widely as though he did know about her. 'I wasn't sure what pastries you liked,' he said, 'so I bought Elizabeth's favourites.' He walked up to Elizabeth and kissed her on the cheek, handed her the flowers; no words of apology, his perfect husband mask firmly in place. She was relieved at his calm reaction. *This will be fine*, she told herself, and that night, when she explained that there was a chance they could adopt Jade if things went well, he was positive about becoming a family. 'An older child will fit right in,' he said.

For a few days, Howard and Jade were polite and careful with each other, and then one night at dinner, Jade was slouched over her food, her mind on something that had happened at school, and Howard said, 'If you sit up straight, your food digests better, and don't hold your fork like that.' Elizabeth started to say something, but a glance from Howard rendered her silent.

Perhaps because she wasn't really concentrating, or perhaps because she was still being careful with Howard, Jade sat up straight and moved her fork in her hand so she was holding it the same way Howard and Elizabeth were holding theirs. And Elizabeth caught the look of smug victory on Howard's face as he said, 'Thanks, Jade,' and the young girl nodded. And then suddenly he was pushing Jade on everything, and sometimes she pushed back, stomping off to her room, slamming doors, refusing to do what he asked. There was shouting, and every time Elizabeth tried to step in between them, she would pay for it later, in secret.

Howard developed a pattern with Jade. A screaming argument would be followed by a thoughtful gift and days of peace. Her room was a particular bone of contention. Some days Elizabeth believed that Jade purposely left it in chaos to rile Howard up. She understood the need to push back against his rules for living.

'But did you see her this morning before you left for work?' she asked him, needing to know if the tidy room had been Jade's choice, and not because Howard's temper had flared, forcing the girl to do what he wanted. How bad could the argument have become?

'No, I left early for the gym, as you know. She was still asleep.' There was a tightness to his tone, something that she knew meant she shouldn't push him.

'Did you...' She paused, but then spoke quickly. 'Did you two have a fight last night or something? Did you... lose your temper?' She needed to ask the question, because she knew it was possible.

'Of course I didn't, Elizabeth. Why would you ask me that? I know how important it is for this to work. I have been nothing but kind to her.' His wounded tone didn't quite manage to convince her, but she knew better than to press. Howard yelled at Jade, but a lot of parents yelled. It wasn't a reason to run away, was it? He never raised a hand to the girl, of that she was certain, and she hoped Jade had never noticed that occasionally she had a slight bruise, a red, burned cheek. Howard was always devastated when he lost control, and so grateful that he was forgiven.

'Okay,' she replied. 'I'm sorry. It's just that her room...'

'Looks the way it should,' said Howard. 'Now, I have a meeting to get to. I'm glad you enjoyed your night away.' He hung up the phone before she said anything else.

Jade never came home again. She left everything Elizabeth had bought her, every piece of clothing, every expensive gadget, even the silver bracelet inscribed with her name.

Elizabeth remembers the hours passing that day, time ticking away as school ended and she waited for Jade to walk through the door. When she called Howard at work at five to say that Jade hadn't returned, and according to the school had not attended that day either, he was dismissive.

'She was fine last night,' he told her. 'She'll turn up,' he said. But she never did.

'She's left everything here, everything we bought her,' Elizabeth said as she paced around Jade's room, opening drawers and cupboard and moving things, hoping to find some clue as to where the girl could be. She knew she shouldn't be in her room touching her things, but worry compelled her.

'Perhaps she didn't want anything from us,' he said.

'What? Why would you say that? Do you know something you're not telling me, Howard?' She stopped pacing, stared out of the window, where she could see a ferry crossing the harbour, the water sparkling in the sunshine.

'Elizabeth,' he said quietly, menace in his voice, 'I have told you all I know. If this girl has chosen to run away, then she didn't want to be a part of a family with us. We have done what we could. You need to leave this now. You have no idea what kind of a life that girl led before she came to live with us. She could be mixed up with all sorts of people, and if she has chosen to be with them over us, then it's a good thing it happened before we went ahead with adoption. I don't want to talk about this again. It would be terribly sad if you ended up on your own because you'd pushed me away as well.'

'But I didn't... didn't... push her away,' she sputtered, turning from the window and sinking onto Jade's neatly made bed, the duvet perfectly smooth. Nothing identified this as a room belonging to a teenage girl. It didn't even smell like her rose-scented body spray any more. She took a deep breath, her heart racing with the knowledge that Jade wasn't just late, that she wouldn't simply turn up. She opened the drawer of the bedside table and lifted out the silver bracelet she had bought her, feeling the inscribed letters as her fear for Jade, who was somewhere in the city alone and vulnerable, made her feel sick.

'You didn't push her away?' he asked, his voice silky smooth. 'Imagine how she felt about you swanning off to spend the night with your sister when we had promised we would all watch that movie together. Where are your priorities?'

'Oh,' she said, dropping her head into her hand, guilt filling up every cell of her body. This was her fault. 'I shouldn't have gone.'

'No,' he agreed. 'You always struggle with what's most important, Elizabeth. You pick your family over me – and now you've picked them over this young girl who needed us so much.'

The next day, she called the case worker, Barry, and told him that Jade had not come home.

'Ah,' he said, resignation in his tone. 'I did worry that nothing would keep her in a foster home.'

'But we got along so well,' lamented Elizabeth.

'Jade's a tough one,' said Barry. 'I'll let everyone know she's gone, and the police will start looking.'

'I tried so hard with her,' Elizabeth said. 'I liked her so much… loved her, even, and she was—'

'Please don't blame yourself, Elizabeth. Jade has struggled since her last foster mother died.'

Barry tried to reassure her, but when there was no news and Jade remained missing, Elizabeth was devastated. She contacted Barry again and again, desperate to know if Jade had been found. She kept the girl's room the same, all her things waiting for her, despite Howard telling her to let go.

They were interviewed by a constable who came to the house, an older woman who sounded bored even as she asked the questions about the last time they had seen Jade.

'Do you think you'll find her?' Elizabeth asked desperately, and the constable sighed and shrugged her shoulders. 'She's a regular runaway. She doesn't want to be found. We'll keep an eye out… but I can't guarantee anything.'

Elizabeth spent days searching Kings Cross and any other areas where she thought a runaway might go, needing to know that Jade was safe. That was all she wanted – for the teenage girl to be safe.

When one day she said to Howard, 'I don't think we'll ever

see her again,' she couldn't miss the relief on his face. Now she wonders if he knew a lot more about why Jade chose to leave.

She didn't want to foster again for over a decade, was too heartbroken over what she regarded as her failure, but then Howard encouraged her to give it one more go. 'We can tell them that younger children are better for us. It would be amazing to be able to help shape a future.'

And it seemed that that was the right decision, because Peter contacted them so quickly about Joe and told them they were hoping for a permanent placement.

'We can finally be a family,' Howard said.

But then Joe arrived, and she could see Howard watching him, waiting for him to make a mistake. Why did he want a child in his life at all? Was it only about control? Was Elizabeth herself so subdued, so easy to manipulate now, that he needed someone else to test his will against?

She turns over in the bed, listening to the cicadas outside, drowning out the sound of people talking. It doesn't matter any more. She knows in her bones that Joe is never coming home again. Not ever. And perhaps that will suit Howard.

He saw how quickly she and Joe had bonded. 'You know it's not a guarantee that he will be with us forever,' he said before they left to come on this holiday from hell.

'Of course it is,' she replied without thinking.

She regrets those words now.

CHAPTER THIRTY-SIX

MALCOLM

Today, 4.45 p.m.

Malcolm moves quickly through the garden of his father's house and out through the back gate with Ruby. It is unlatched – open. 'This is the quick way to the beach,' he explains.

'Do you have an idea of where he might be?' asks Ruby.

'You know, I could be wrong, but the bush over by the estuary has a lot of little hidden pockets. I'm sure they've searched everywhere – I mean, a lot of the people helping are locals – but there was a place that felt like only me and my friends knew about. It's off to the side and kind of behind some rocks. It's a long shot, but everything is worth looking into.'

Ruby struggles to keep up with him. He is so much taller and he takes such long strides, she resorts to a skipping run just to make sure that he doesn't get too far ahead of her.

'Sorry,' he says, noticing and slowing down. 'Lila used to complain that I walked too fast.'

'Is Lila your wife?' asks Ruby.

'Ex-wife now,' he replies as they make their way down a

path between two houses and out onto the beach. 'This way,' he says, turning left.

Only a large sandbank separates the river and the ocean. Dense bushland lines the side of the river. Malcolm feels his childhood rushing back at him as he always does when he returns to Gilmore beach. Long hours spent in the water, salt on his sunburned skin, and the feel of an ice-cold drink as he and his friends watched the summer sun set are the things he associates with home, with safety. But his safe space is not safe for everyone, and certainly not a place a young child should be alone.

'Could he really be in there?' Ruby asks.

'Let's find out,' he says.

As they walk, they lift their hands to wave at SES volunteers searching the beach and surrounding bushland, identifiable by the flashes of orange amongst the green-brown of the bush.

When they get to the water, Malcolm sits down and takes off his shoes. 'No sense in ruining these – we'll have to wade through.'

Ruby does the same thing, quickly pulling off her red leather strappy sandals.

'I'm sorry about your divorce,' she says.

'It's okay,' says Malcolm, standing up and dusting sand off his short pants. 'I think some relationships are better as friendships. Lila and I get along really well, but we didn't have that... spark, I guess. Hold your shoes above your head, you'll need them when we get to the bush.'

They step into the water.

It is only up to his ankles, but then he takes another step and feels his foot move down, and soon the water is up to his waist. He looks back at Ruby. 'Okay?' he asks.

'Okay,' she says.

The current is quite strong, and they push against it until

they make it to the other side, then they sit down and replace their shoes. Malcolm looks around him, feeling the security of the place he grew up, a place that has not changed in decades. There are still bushes growing out of the water, still scattered bits of shell on the sand, which has green algae growing over it in some spots, black mud coming through in others. The rich salt smell of the sea relaxes him, despite what they are doing. He is in his favourite place and he hopes that it will still feel like that after today. It will never be somewhere he thinks of fondly again if it is where a little boy has lost his life.

He knows from listening to the radio that they have located a single shoe said to belong to the child, knows that the possibility of drowning has been at the forefront of all the volunteers' minds.

He stands up and looks over the bush, left and right, trying to remember the path he used to take with his friends. What was unclear suddenly becomes clear as he sees himself as a twelve-year-old boy, walking in single file with his two best mates.

'This way,' he says excitedly to Ruby. 'I have no idea why I think he could be there. I mean, I used to hide there sometimes, but I was much older.'

Together they tramp through the sandy bush, the heat beating down on them.

'We should have brought hats,' says Ruby.

'And water,' he agrees, 'but I just wanted to get here.'

'I've searched over there,' a man calls, and they see him standing in the middle of the bush in front of them.

'Just taking another quick look,' Malcolm says, raising his hand in a wave, and the man waves back.

They keep walking, and Malcolm, a little ahead, asks over his shoulder, 'Do you have someone, Ruby?'

'I do,' she says, and even though she is behind him, he can hear the smile in her voice. 'We're engaged.'

'That's great. I hope he's good to you; you deserve to be happy,' Malcolm says, feeling a rush of happiness at this young woman having someone to care for her in her life.

'He's wonderful,' says Ruby.

They round a corner to see a collection of rocks. 'There.' Malcolm points. 'There's an overhang that kind of feels like a cave.' He walks purposefully towards it.

When they get to the rocks, he stops and wipes his hand over his forehead, where sweat is beginning to drip into his eyes. He really needs a hat. It's still very hot despite it being late afternoon. In the distance he can hear the other searchers calling for Joe, their voices sounding tired and desperate.

He walks slowly around the rocks, hearing Ruby stepping on twigs and branches as she follows him. And then he hears her say, 'Malcolm,' her voice slightly panicked. 'Malcolm.'

CHAPTER THIRTY-SEVEN

GORDON

Today, 5.00 p.m.

He opens his eyes in the dim room and lies very still for a moment. He knows by now to do this as his brain tries to catch up on where he is. A few weeks ago, he woke up in the middle of the night and thought it was morning and that he was late for school. Panic set in and he moved too quickly and found himself crumpled on the floor. He has not told Malcolm about his fall, not wanting to worry him. Now he thinks for a moment. He is in his bed, that much is obvious, and it's not night because he can see light coming in through the curtains. He turns his head slowly to look at the clock that has been beside his bed for nearly twenty years, and the large red numbers tell him that it is 5 p.m. Why is he lying down this late in the afternoon? He'll get no sleep tonight. He counts to a hundred and then tries to count down from 100 as he moves his feet back and forth, warming up his body to move like he would an old car.

He becomes aware of sounds in the house, something like footsteps and clutches the duvet he is lying on top of. Who would be in his house? He lies still, working through the possibilities, until finally: Malcolm. Malcolm came early and talked to Ruby. He remembers now. Yes, he remembers. Malcolm has gone to look for Joe, he has gone with Ruby, with Jade. Who is Jade?

There is something he knows, but it feels like all his thoughts are trapped behind fogged glass. He takes a deep breath, trying to calm himself down, because if he gets into a panic, the fog becomes thicker and he loses everything. Malcolm is here – he knows that for sure. Malcolm will know what's going on.

More footsteps, the sound of doors opening and closing as though Malcolm is looking for him.

'I'm in here, son,' he calls, taking his time as he sits up on his bed. 'In here.'

His bedroom door opens, and Gordon stands up to greet his son.

But it's not his son who is standing there blocking out the light from the hallway. It's not his son.

CHAPTER THIRTY-EIGHT

ELIZABETH

Today, 5.10 p.m.

She startles awake and sits up quickly, grabbing her phone and looking at the time. She is relieved to see she has only been asleep for fifteen minutes. No one has come to tell her if there is any news, something that makes her want to scream with frustration. He's been gone for a whole day now. If he is alive, he is hungry and thirsty, definitely sunburned and probably dealing with a sore foot because he lost his shoe. If he is alive. *Please, please let him only be suffering a sore foot, let him be sunburned and thirsty, but let him be alive. Please.*

In the bathroom, she looks at her face in the mirror and then strains to see what the mark is on her cheek. She turns on the light despite it still being full sunlight outside, and peers at herself. A small, sad smile appears on her face when she realises that it's a crocodile, the raised rubber decal from Joe's shoe. She fell asleep with her cheek on the sandal. Tears come quickly, and she covers her mouth so that no one else in the house will hear.

She needs to get something to drink, something icy cold and sweet, so when she is calm, she washes her face and makes her way to the kitchen.

'Ah, Elizabeth,' says Constable Brown, who is in the kitchen, his arms crossed as he listens to a volunteer talking about where they are going to search next. The man he is talking to immediately stops speaking and nods at Elizabeth, leaving quickly as though he doesn't want to be near her. The constable relaxes his arms and says, 'I thought I would let you rest. We have Detective Inspector Gold here to speak to you, if you don't mind.'

Elizabeth fills a glass with water and drinks deeply. 'I don't mind,' she says, refilling her glass. This is not the time to go hunting for a sweet drink.

The detective is in the living room, standing by the window and looking out onto the front lawn. She is a small woman in a tailored blue suit, her black hair in a high ponytail.

Elizabeth looks around the room, expecting to see Howard, but he's not here and she doesn't want to ask where he is. She doesn't care. Once this is over – whatever happens – she will never be with him again. She cannot be his wife any more. If she leaves, she will have nothing. She hasn't worked properly for years, and everything is in both their names. It will be a long, arduous fight to get what belongs to her. She will have to start her whole life again.

The detective turns from the window and offers her a tight smile, 'Mrs Ealy,' she says, holding out her hand, and Elizabeth leans forward to shake it, feeling the woman's strong, sure grip. 'I was hoping to speak to your husband as well,' she continues, 'but we're having a little bit of trouble locating him.' She sounds slightly embarrassed about this, and Elizabeth understands that she should be. 'Do you know where he might be?'

The hand holding the glass trembles, some water spilling.

How could they have lost sight of Howard? Where would he have gone?

'He's not with me. He was for a bit, but he left. He said...' She tries to recall his exact words, and then she realises, remembers. 'Gordon,' she says. 'He thinks Gordon has taken him. Gordon from across the road. Oh God... Oh no... oh no...'

CHAPTER THIRTY-NINE

MALCOLM

Today, 5.15 p.m.

'Malcolm, Malcolm,' he hears her call, and he realises that he has disappeared from view. He didn't notice that as he walked around the rocks, he actually stepped down a little and out of sight. The sand of the estuary slopes away slightly. She sounds frightened.

'I'm here,' he says, emerging from between two rocks. 'There's a small overhang just past here, come on.' He holds out his hand and Ruby takes it, letting him lead her through the gap.

Malcolm is instantly assaulted by childhood memories of him and Ralph and Blake, out here until it got dark, eating candy and reading comic books. He still keeps in touch with his childhood friends, and he will forever be grateful that he got to grow up in a beautiful place like Gilmore. But the sea and the bush hold their dangers, and he prays that they are not too late to rescue this little boy. He prays he is right about where he thinks he is.

'In here,' he says as they get closer, and then he peers

around the overhang, and his heart leaps as he sees what he's been looking for. 'I knew it, I just knew it.'

Ruby stands next to him, and for a moment they both breathe in the sight. They don't move any closer. Lying on the sand underneath the overhang, slightly shaded from the harsh sun, is a little boy with dark hair.

He is completely still, and Malcolm feels his breath catch in his chest, fear squeezing his heart. This is not what he wanted to find. The child is curled up, one foot bare, his skin darkened by the sun. Malcolm is almost afraid to go near him, to touch him, in case he is not looking at a sleeping child. Why has the boy not heard anyone call for him?

'Oh no,' whispers Ruby.

Malcolm finds himself frozen to the spot, unsure and afraid.

And then from far away down the beach, a voice breaks through the air, another searcher calling for the child. 'Joe, Joe,' they hear, and the little boy twitches in his sleep suddenly, his body registering his name.

'Is he okay?' Ruby asks, her voice high with panic.

Malcolm shakes himself and takes a step forward to check. As his foot crunches on some broken sticks, the little boy opens his eyes, finally woken by the noise, and sits up quickly, pushing himself back against a rock, terror in his wide green eyes.

'It's okay,' says Malcolm softly, crouching down. 'It's okay.' He holds out his hand as you would to a frightened animal, trying to communicate that he will not hurt him.

'Go away,' shouts the little boy. 'Go away. I'm not going back.' Malcolm sees his face turn red, even under the sunburn, his body rigid with determination. He recognises a child on the way to a tantrum. Del doesn't have them often, but he knows that when she gets going, nothing gets through until she has worn herself out. He needs to get this little boy to safety. He needs to let him know that he is all right.

'Joe, it's okay,' he says. 'It's okay.' He wants to yell with joy, because an angry five-year-old is an alive five-year-old.

'No, no, no,' Joe shouts, pushing himself further back as Malcolm tries to reach for him.

Ruby puts a hand on Malcolm's arm, letting him know to move back. 'Joe,' she says, 'my name is Ruby, and this is Malcolm. Malcolm is Gordon's son; you know, the man with the birds?'

'Gordon's son?' asks Joe, scepticism in his tone.

'Yes,' says Malcolm. 'I have a daughter your age. My dad is her grandpa and Del likes to watch the birds every morning. Did he tell you about Del?'

The little boy nods his head. 'He makes her cold hot chocolate,' he says.

Malcolm wants to grab the child and rush him to help. He wishes he and Ruby had some water. How long since Joe has had a drink? How long has he been hiding here?

'He does,' he says, 'and it's her favourite. Now if you come with me, we can get you some water and take you to your mum. And I will even ask Gordon to make you some cold hot chocolate to drink. You must be hot and thirsty.'

The little boy nods his head. 'I want some water,' he says.

'I don't have any, but if you come with me, I'll get you some, I promise,' says Malcolm.

Joe looks down at his dirty foot and then shakes his head. 'I can't go back... It will be very, very bad.'

Malcolm runs his hands through his hair, frustrated.

'Joe,' says Ruby, 'I know the man you were living with, Howard. I know he can be mean. I'm not going to let him be mean to you, okay? You don't even have to see him.'

Joe looks up. 'Really?' he asks.

'Really,' says Malcolm. 'I absolutely promise.'

The child doesn't reply, but something in the way he is looking at them tells Malcolm he may be ready to come with them. He holds out his hand. 'Come on, Joe. Your mum really wants to see you. Lots of people have been looking for you all day.'

'She's my foster mum, not my real mum,' whispers Joe.

Ruby stands. 'Maybe we can find someone with water,' she mutters, and she goes to look.

Malcolm is still holding his hand out, and Joe is still studying him, deciding whether to trust him. Malcolm doesn't want to just grab him and risk scaring him. The voices calling for Joe have faded, but if Ruby can find someone, she can wave them over. They will have water.

'No one in sight,' she says, crouching down next to Malcolm again. 'Joe, you need to come with us,' she says. 'We will keep you safe, I promise.'

'Come on, Joe,' says Malcolm. 'I can carry you.'

'I followed Gordon,' says Joe.

'You did?' asks Malcolm.

Joe nods. 'He was going for a walk and he left the gate open. He didn't see me because I was like a mouse, creeping on my tippy-toes, and I followed him.'

'Why didn't you follow him back from his walk?' asks Ruby softly.

'Howard is mean,' says Joe. 'He hurt me. I ran away. I wanted to stay on the beach forever.' He turns around and touches his back. 'It's sore,' he says, and Malcolm's heart breaks for him.

'He won't hurt you again,' says Ruby firmly.

'He will. He said he was sorry, but then he hurt me, and he told me that he would take away all my toys if I told Peter that he was mean.'

'Who's Peter?' asks Malcolm.

'Peter is my friend,' says Joe. 'He said I can live with Lizbeth and Howard, but he didn't tell me that Howard would be mean.' He shakes his head, as though baffled by this fact. 'I don't like having a foster father,' he says, a tear tracing its way down his dirty cheek.

Ruby shuffles a little closer. 'Can I tell you something, Joe?' she asks, and the little boy nods his head. 'I also had a foster mother and father. Foster parents are supposed to take care of you, not hurt you. I promise you that I will tell the policemen and women who are looking for you that Howard did a bad thing. He won't be able to hurt you again.'

Joe nods. 'Did your foster dad also do a bad thing?' he asks. It's an innocent question, but the simplicity of it slams into Malcolm. He looks at Ruby, who touches her chest, covering her heart.

'Yes,' she says, 'he did.' He can hear the tears she is swallowing so that she doesn't distress the child, and he feels one fist clench at the thought of the man who has hurt her and this little boy.

'But my toys,' Joe says. 'I only took the Hulk, because he's the strongest.' He turns a little and digs in the sand, uncovering a plastic figurine.

'I like the Hulk,' says Malcolm. 'He's very strong.'

The little boy nods.

'I promise that you will get to keep your toys, Joe. I absolutely promise, okay. Just come with me and we can go and get them.' He hopes he is not lying to this child. He has no idea what will happen now, only that he will make sure that Joe does not have to go back to the people who were supposed to take care of him and didn't.

'The Hulk can't keep me safe from Howard,' says Joe, shaking his head, the weight of this betrayal heavy on his small shoulders.

'But we can. The police can. We will all keep you safe from Howard,' says Ruby.

And finally, Joe leans forward and puts his trust in them, letting Malcolm pick him up.

'Thank you, God,' he hears Ruby whisper.

They make halting, slow progress through the bush, and when they get to the part where the river runs into the sea and they need to wade across, Joe clutches Malcolm tightly around his neck. 'I couldn't swim,' he says, clinging and scared. 'The water came up and up and I couldn't swim.'

'I will keep you safe,' Malcolm murmurs over and again, his tone low, his voice soothing.

Ruby carries their shoes. 'The tide must have come up after he crossed over,' she says.

'Yes,' agrees Malcolm, remembering that he and his friends had to be aware of the tides if they didn't want to swim across. The current can be quite strong, and he knows that if Joe had tried to cross the water at high tide, he would have been swept out to sea. He closes his eyes briefly in pure relief that there has not been a different outcome to this day.

'You okay?' he asks Ruby, for whom the water is nearly at chest height. He feels the sand moving underneath his feet with the swirling of the tide.

'I'm good,' she says, determined.

Finally they are back on land, and only minutes away from his father's house. Malcolm wants to shout with joy when he sees another volunteer, standing looking out at the ocean with a pair of binoculars.

'I'll get some water,' Ruby says, and she takes off at a run, nearly bumping into the volunteer and explaining in breathless words. The volunteer is an older woman, her skin burned by the sun, her grey hair hidden by a large yellow hat, but she has water and she moves quickly to Malcolm and Joe.

'Hello, love,' she says softly. 'We've been looking for you.'

'I couldn't swim,' says Joe, leaning forward as she holds the bottle of water out to him.

'The sea can be a bit scary,' says the woman, her voice soothing both Malcolm and Joe.

Joe drinks, gulping the water down, as the woman murmurs, 'Slowly, slowly.' She holds out her hands. 'Why don't you come to me, love, give this nice man a chance to put his shoes on and dry off a bit?' but Joe buries his head in Malcolm's shoulder, refusing to be parted.

'It's okay,' says Malcolm, tightening his hold on the little boy. He weighs about the same as Del does, and as he walks across the beach with Ruby next to him, he thinks about his daughter, who has only ever known love and safety and security. What must this child have been through to run away to such an unsafe place? Was it as bad as what Ruby went through? Despite the heat, he shivers at the thought. Not everyone should get to be a parent.

Not everyone.

CHAPTER FORTY

GORDON

Today, 5.15 p.m.

'Mal... Mal,' says Gordon.

'No, just me, just Howard Ealy, the man whose child you've stolen – abducted.' The man spits the words into the air, filling the space with venom.

'What? Is this about Joe?' Gordon takes a step forward, wanting to get out of the bedroom, but Howard takes a step forward as well, forcing him to stumble back. He feels the bed against the back of his legs. Where is Malcolm? Where is Ruby? Ruby? Jade? Where is everyone, and what is happening? The glass is back, the fog around his thoughts is thick, but he can feel something clearly. He can feel fear. This man is here to scare him, to hurt him. His brain is confused, but his body knows the truth.

'You need...' he says, and he finds himself breathless with panic. 'You need to go.'

'Where is he?' demands Howard, his voice soft and menacing. He moves forward again, and Gordon slumps down onto the bed. Howard stands above him, fists clenched. 'I'm warning you, you had better tell me the truth.'

'You hurt him,' says Gordon, 'you hurt him and he's only a little chap.' He tries to sound defiant and as though he isn't scared, but he is terrified. One blow from this man could kill him, that much he knows. Just one blow. Howard leans towards him, puts his hands around his neck. Gordon immediately puts his own hands over Howard's, trying to prise his fingers off as Howard squeezes hard and then harder. He feels his breath catch in his throat. He's choking. 'Please...' he gasps.

'Where is he?' The hands squeeze harder as Gordon meets the man's dark grey eyes, reads the hatred there. 'Tell me now.'

He is squeezing so hard Gordon cannot speak. How can he tell this man anything if he cannot speak? Black spots appear in front of his eyes, and he thinks briefly of Malcolm, sees him at age six running in and out of the waves, sees Del doing the same thing, and then he feels Flora beside him, feels her light touch as she says, 'Come on, my love, time for a walk.' He wants to reach out to her, wants to tell her that he cannot speak, that he cannot breathe, but he can't do anything.

And in an instant, he is back to this morning, to when he took his walk, to who he knew was behind him as he left his back garden. He didn't turn, didn't say anything, because he knew the child was trying to keep his presence a secret, and in the foolish way he sometimes went about things these days, Gordon let him follow him. He was supposed to latch the gate and he was supposed to make sure the little boy was behind him when he turned to go back home. But when he found the path – when he finally found it – he didn't remember that he was not alone. And now this man will kill him for the lapse.

He lets his body go limp, because it's what he deserves. He should have remembered that the little boy followed him to the beach. It's all his fault.

Sound rushes through the open window, something like shouting – clapping? He is dying and he knows it. And then his neck is released and he collapses back onto the bed, and everything is gone.

CHAPTER FORTY-ONE

ELIZABETH

Today, Now

She doesn't get to finish her sentence, because the noise level outside rises – people shouting, and then something like clapping – and the detective and the constable turn and rush to see what is happening. Elizabeth clutches the blue sandal and then she touches her still-imprinted skin, feeling the small crocodile on her face. 'Oh God,' she whispers. 'Please...'

All thoughts of Gordon disappear at the noise, the sound of laughter and clapping. It can only mean one thing, and she is off the sofa and out the door before she can even take a breath. She moves through her garden, the little shoe clutched in her hand, pushing past people, some of whom try to talk to her, to explain, but she cannot stop to listen. Her head swivels frantically around, looking for him, looking for Joe, because he is here, she can feel him here, and she wonders at this, at her body knowing something when the child did not come from her body.

Just outside the front gate, a tall man is standing with Joe in his arms. He is not dressed in one of the vests that the SES volunteers wear, and he has no hat or water bottle. But he is holding Joe, or Joe is holding him. The little boy has his arms wound tightly around the man's neck, as a young woman beside them holds a bottle of water for him to drink from.

'Joe,' Elizabeth says, 'oh Joe,' as she gets to the man. She holds out her arms for him and hears a rush of clicks from phones and cameras. Joe buries his head in the man's shoulder.

'He's afraid,' says the man, and she hears such judgement in his voice that she drops her arms.

'He's not going to hurt you, Joe,' she says, despite knowing that she should say nothing, despite something telling her that she needs to keep quiet to protect Howard, as she has always done. She senses someone next to her, and glances quickly to her side to see Peter, his mouth a grim line. Peter is in a smart shirt despite the heat, and he's wearing a tie. The formal clothes mean he is here to take Joe, of course he is here for that, dressed up and official. Whatever she says now will only work against her, but there is no stopping this truth, no stopping her decision. She repeats herself, loud and clear, for the police who are standing next to her, for the press who are recording everything, for Peter who is here to break her heart. She repeats herself for Joe and for herself. 'He's not going to hurt you ever again, Joe, I promise,' she says.

Joe studies her for a moment, and then he sticks a grubby foot out to her. 'I lost my crocodile shoe,' he says.

'I have it,' she tells him, and she gently slips it back on, making sure not to tighten it, because she can see that there is some blood on his foot, and that means there is a cut that needs to be seen to.

'I bet you need a snack,' she says, holding out her arms again.

He nods. 'But first a hug and a joke,' he says, and he lets go of the man and turns to her, letting her take him in her arms. His whole body is damp with sweat, a strong seaweed smell clinging to his clothing as his legs tighten around her waist and his small hand rests lightly on her back. She feels him settle into her body, into her soul, because he is back where he belongs.

She holds him tightly as Constable Brown moves people aside so she has a clear path back into the house.

'Elizabeth, I think...' begins Peter, his shoulders back and his chin forward. He is ready for her to disagree with him, to try and stop him taking Joe from her, and he's right to be. She will not let the child go.

'Not now,' she says firmly. 'In a few days, but not now,' and to his credit, the young man doesn't argue.

'Can we get one of the paramedics in here, please?' says the constable as they reach the front door.

'Knock, knock,' says Elizabeth.

'Who's there?' asks Joe, glee on his face, and she wonders at his resilience. He has been gone for a whole day, he is hot and thirsty and hungry, his little body sweaty and burned, but despite everything, he is just a little boy enjoying a joke.

'Boo,' she says, feeling her cheeks crease into a smile.

'Boo who?' he giggles, actually giggles, as they walk into the house, into the cool air conditioning and Constable Brown closes the door behind them, shutting everyone else out.

'Don't cry,' she says. 'It's only me.'

'Only me,' crows Joe.

'Only me,' she says.

CHAPTER FORTY-TWO

MALCOLM

Today, Now

He leans against the wall watching the press send information and make calls. 'Alive, yes, alive,' a man says excitedly.

'Not sure who found him, but getting the name now,' a woman yells into her phone.

'Where's my cameraman?' another man calls.

Occasionally he glances at Ruby, at Jade, remembering the frightened, badly hurt fifteen-year-old girl he took home one night just before Christmas, ten years ago. He is sweaty and thirsty and he could use a shower, but he wants to stand here for a bit longer, wants to enjoy the party atmosphere that has arisen because a missing child has been found alive. Even as the afternoon heat clings to the air, everything somehow feels lighter and fresher.

Ruby turns to him and smiles. 'Any minute now, someone is going to want to interview us, and I really need a shower.'

Malcolm laughs. 'We should get our phones,' he says. 'I can't believe we walked out without them.'

'I'm sure it's already on the news. You'll be a headline,' she says.

'As will you,' he nods. Together they turn to make their way across the road. 'I can't wait to tell my dad. He'll be so happy,' Malcolm says.

'He tried so hard to help,' says Ruby.

'I know,' sighs Malcolm. 'I feel bad for not believing him and for not telling him to keep going to the police. All this could have been avoided. Kids don't hide for a whole day without a reason.'

'Malcolm,' says Ruby, her voice touched with panic, 'Malcolm, look.'

He looks where she is pointing and sees a man walking around the side of his father's house as though he has come out of the back door.

'Who's that?' he asks, quickening his steps.

'Howard... it's Howard,' she says, frantically. 'He's been in your father's house.' Her face pales as she gestures desperately.

Everything he now knows about this man comes hurtling towards Malcolm. If he is capable of hurting a fifteen-year-old girl and a little boy, what could he do to an old man? His heart beats his fear as Howard notices him and Ruby coming towards him and turns as if to walk back down the side of the house. Malcolm knows he is probably heading for the back gate. In a few rapid steps he is on the man, his hand clamped on his shoulder, stopping him.

'What were you doing in there?' he asks, his jaw tensed.

'Let go,' shouts Howard, trying to shake him off, but Malcolm is bigger than the man with the neat beard and the dead grey eyes, and he holds on tightly. 'The police want a word with you, mate,' he hisses. 'We found Joe and it's not looking good for you.'

'What the hell is wrong with you?' yells Howard, rage

colouring his cheeks, as he squirms to try and get away from Malcolm's hold.

Drawn by his yelling, a policewoman comes over to see what is happening. 'This is the little boy's foster father,' says Malcolm. 'You need to talk to him.' He shoves Howard towards the policewoman, who quickly mutters something into her radio. Malcolm doesn't let go, not until another policewoman comes across to help her colleague, saying, 'If we could just have a word with you, please, sir.'

'Let me go... This is harassment, let me go,' shouts Howard as both policewomen take a hold of his arms.

'Just calm down, sir,' says one of them.

'You hurt him,' spits Ruby, and Howard looks at her, shock evident on his face. It's clear he recognises her.

'Jade,' he says. 'You're—'

'Not dead from my injuries,' snaps Ruby. 'You need to arrest him,' she says to the policewoman. 'I want him charged with assault. He hurt me a long time ago and he hurt the little boy – he hurt Joe,' she says, her voice loud enough to attract attention, her fists clenched at her sides, her cheeks pink with fury.

Malcolm can see her eyes burning with a furious desire for Howard to be punished. The night he found her comes rushing back, the terrible bruises on her face and body, her fear of calling the police in case they sent her back to this man. What must it be like to confront someone who has done something so hideous to you?

'She's lying,' spits Howard, one eye twitching slightly, pulling out of the policewoman's hold and moving towards Ruby.

'Okay, whoa, whoa, let's just talk,' says the officer, using her body to push back against Howard as Ruby steps to the side to avoid him.

'Gordon,' says Ruby, turning to Malcolm, her expression horrified. 'What if he's hurt Gordon?'

Malcolm looks at his father's house. 'Oh God, Dad,' he says, and he darts into the house, followed by Ruby, who shouts, 'Gordon,' as Malcolm shouts, 'Dad!'

The house is cool and dark after the glare of the sun and the heat. Ruby looks in the living room while Malcolm makes his way to his father's bedroom.

At first, he feels relief when he sees his father on the bed, because he assumes he is still asleep despite the noise from the street, but then he sees that his father's head is at an odd angle, that his hands are not relaxed in sleep but slack in his unconscious state. He kneels down by his bed, his head on his father's chest, his fingers at his neck.

'Ruby, Ruby...' he yells, anguish in every syllable. 'Ruby, you need to call an ambulance. Dad... wake up, please. Dad, can you hear me? Can you hear me?' He gives his father a small shake, not wanting to hurt him. He listens again to his chest but cannot hear a heartbeat, cannot feel a heartbeat over the sound of his own fear.

He hears Ruby shouting as he stands up and tries to remember how to do CPR. He only knows to push down on his father's chest, so he does, even though Gordon's bones are fragile.

'He hurt him,' he hears Ruby screaming. 'He hurt Gordon, and we need an ambulance, quickly.'

Malcolm keeps pushing down on his father's chest until he feels someone grab him. 'Let me do it,' says the policewoman, and she is instantly next to his father, her hands moving up and down as she mutters a rhythm to keep him alive.

'Dad,' moans Malcolm, rubbing his arms as his body chills in the cool room. The policewoman keeps going, pressing down, counting under her breath, 'One, two, three...'

Malcolm hears Ruby burst into tears, and he turns to look at her as a siren screams through the air. They are both pushed aside as two paramedics enter the house.

Only minutes later, they are out the door with Gordon on a stretcher, an oxygen mask on his face, Malcolm following behind.

'I'll lock up the house,' Ruby calls after him, and he waves at her as he climbs into the ambulance. He cannot think about anything now but his father. He takes a seat beside him and holds his hand, stroking the paper-thin skin, remembering stroking his father's hands as a boy, touching the calluses he had from chopping wood for the fires they used to light on the beach on a summer's night. 'Dad,' he whispers as oxygen is forced into his father's lungs and the ambulance races through the streets.

He doesn't even have his phone to call Lila and tell her what has happened. And what will they tell Del? How will they explain this to Del, who adores her grandfather?

'Nearly there now,' says the paramedic, and Malcolm looks up at him for the first time, seeking some reassurance. 'He's hanging in there,' says the man, nodding.

'He's eighty,' says Malcolm. 'I don't know what that man did to him. I don't have a phone. I need to call...' He fades off. At least Del is with Lila, at least he did not bring her here to this town on a day when a little boy was missing and a psychopath was on the loose.

'Please hold on, Dad,' he implores. He's not ready to say goodbye. He needs some more time to tell his father that he's grateful for everything he did for him. He's grateful that he taught him how to be a man with honour and integrity. He would never have stopped to pick up a young girl at a bus stop if not for his parents' lessons in kindness.

'He used to be a teacher,' says Malcolm.

'I know, mate,' says the paramedic. 'He taught me geography. We all liked Mr Perry, he was one of the best.'

'Yes,' agrees Malcolm, his voice catching, 'one of the best.'

EPILOGUE

ELIZABETH

One year later

'That's not his car,' Joe says.

'No,' agrees Elizabeth. She moves her hat forward, grateful that today is still relatively cool, the summer breeze keeping the temperature down. Joe has insisted on being out here to wait for Malcolm to arrive.

'I'm going to get something to drink,' Elizabeth says. 'Do you want something?'

'No, I'm going to wait here,' he says.

'You need to come in with me,' she replies.

Joe sighs, and for a moment she has a vision of him as a teenager, rolling his eyes at her when she asks him to do something. 'I'm six, you know,' he says. 'I won't leave the garden.' Last year he couldn't open the latch on the front gate without standing on tiptoes, but this year he has the height to do it easily.

Elizabeth hesitates. She will only be gone for a moment, but she knows that a moment is all it takes. She is trying to pull back a little, to stop hovering as much. At the beginning of the year, Joe was grateful to have her at his side every minute of the day. He slept in her bed for a couple of months after he was found, waking in tears and telling her there was a spider, demanding a drink or a cuddle. With Peter's help, they found him the right therapist and found a way through. She has had to tell him over and again that it is okay to talk about all the things Howard did that he didn't like.

'Seems like that's a message for you too,' Natalie said, when Elizabeth told her this. Elizabeth was surprised at the relieved burst of laughter that came from her own mouth – as though she had just been waiting for someone to tell her this.

Her parents and sister are relieved that she is no longer shackled to an abusive man. They were horrified at the things Elizabeth finally felt able to share with them. 'You should have told us,' her mother said. 'I would have sent Sean over,' her sister said, but Elizabeth knew that the only person who could free her from Howard was herself.

Truthfully, she clung to Joe as much as he clung to her in those first few months.

Things began to change once he started school. She had been worried about what he would take with him into his second year of primary school. He was starting at a new school because it was close to where she lived – where they lived – with her parents. But he seemed to settle in from day one, finding friends and taking part in everything the school had to offer. He loves soccer and art classes, and has playdates scheduled for almost every weekend. She is grateful that he feels safe, that he feels secure where he is.

She really is very thirsty, so she jumps up and darts into the kitchen, which Petra has had renovated this year. She is doing up the house one room at a time over the winter months when she doesn't have holiday renters in it. Elizabeth was so excited to see it was available for a couple of weeks when she knew Malcolm would be here as well.

She fills her glass with water as she watches Joe through the window. He is so much bigger, so much stronger than when they were here last year. He turns and looks at her and waves, so she waves back and grabs a juice box for him to have while they wait.

Del is coming with Malcolm to stay for two weeks, and Joe and Del have spent a lot of their recent playdates organising everything they are going to do, from sandcastles on the beach to refilling the bird feeder in the garden. Elizabeth was surprised that Joe wanted to come back here. She would never have chosen to come, but he asked her if they could when he found out that Del was going to be here. 'Are you sure?' she said. 'It was a bit of a scary time for you – for us,' she added, not wanting to bring up everything that had happened.

'Del will be there and Howard won't,' he said simply. He sounds a lot older than he is sometimes, as though the child in him has been forced to grow up quickly, which she knows is the case. Her favourite moments with him are when he sounds like a six-year-old. She doesn't even mind when he misbehaves, because pushing back, small acts of defiance, mean he feels safe enough to express himself.

Out on the blanket again, she reflects that she could so easily have ended up completely alone, and she feels a rush of love for the child competently pushing his straw into his juice box, a rush of grateful love. Peter didn't want to allow her to keep Joe. There were so many things stacked against her. But Joe refused to leave her side, and eventually she was able to convince Peter that she was capable of caring for him. They still have a few official hoops to jump through, but the adoption is now guaranteed. Jenny had tried to push her claim for custody up until a few months ago when she found out she was pregnant and her interest in her first child waned. She told Peter she would stop fighting the government over the adoption. Elizabeth hopes and prays that Jenny manages to stay away from drugs and raise her second child. Her relief at no longer having to fight Jenny is palpable because Elizabeth knew Jenny was one of the final obstacles to the adoption. Everything has fallen into place and she knows Joe is meant to be hers.

She has moments of imagined horror when she thinks about what would have happened if Joe had never been found.

'There is a lot you've lied about,' Peter said bluntly when he came to see her and Joe five days after they returned from Gilmore.

'I know,' she agreed, 'but you can't take him from me, you just can't. I'll agree to anything.'

'My hands are—' he began.

'No, don't say that,' she said, lowering rather than raising her voice, knowing that Joe was in the next room with her mother. 'He loves me and I love him and I promise you he will never see Howard again. Neither of us will.'

'I'll do my best for you,' Peter said, relenting, 'but it's going to be tough.'

'I can do tough,' said Elizabeth, relief and joy making her cry.

Agreeing to live with her parents for two years while the divorce is finalised and she finds a way forward was a big step in the right direction. Joe has three adults in his life who are available at all times.

Howard was charged with domestic violence and assault. Ruby was triumphant on the day he was sentenced to five years in prison. It doesn't feel like enough, but then no number of years would be enough.

Elizabeth has not seen him since the day Joe disappeared. He was given bail after agreeing to live with his parents, and she had to take out a restraining order against him after he wouldn't stop messaging her. For months she was terrified that he would turn up at her parents' house, but he stayed away. She still jumps at strange sounds, still hesitates to open the front door when the bell rings, but she is working on accepting that she is safe.

Natalie flew over from America and stayed for a month, helping her pack up her things in the house and move in with her parents, helping her find a lawyer, and just being there to listen as she talked for hours, for days, about what had happened to her life.

She is beyond grateful to have Ruby back in her life. She wanted to adopt the young woman once, and she will always feel she failed her by leaving her alone with Howard – even though she never could have imagined what he would do to her. Deep down she knew, even though she tried not to know, that he had done something to make her leave. Joe calls her his foster sister anyway, because they are both foster children. She is sure that Ruby's impassioned pleas to Peter on her behalf helped her retain custody of Joe and allow her to move forward with adoption plans.

Ruby and Lucas are on their three-month honeymoon, travelling across Asia. They had a beautiful wedding, small but filled with people who love them, and she and Malcolm were both so grateful to be invited. Malcolm walked Ruby, wearing a pink dress covered in cream netting, down the aisle of the little church, and afterwards, at the wedding lunch, most guests had to wipe away tears as she described how he had found her hurt and alone, and what he had done for her; giving her time to heal, but also restoring some of her faith in humanity.

Now, a sleek black Mercedes pulls into view, and Joe jumps up and down and claps his hands. 'They're here, they're here,' he says.

Malcolm parks the car in the driveway and he and Del climb out. Del looks like her mother, with blonde hair and blue eyes, and she is bossy and funny and Joe adores her.

'I told my dad that we want to go to the beach now,' she calls over to him, 'but he says we need to unpack first. I said we can unpack later.' She speaks as though she and Joe have been together in the car on the ride down.

'Okay,' says Joe.

Elizabeth takes his hand and crosses the road.

Malcolm opens the back passenger door and leans in as Elizabeth feels herself holding her breath.

'Here we go, slowly,' he says, his voice soft and laced with patience.

It takes Gordon time to get out of the car. Elizabeth wants to rush forward and help, but she waits as he emerges gradually, standing up and then holding onto the door as Malcolm positions his walker for him. He is so much older. Only twelve months ago, she turned to him for help and advice, and now... She lifts her chin, smiling so that there can be no tears. He is here and that's all that matters. It was touch and go and Malcolm was told to prepare himself, but Gordon fought on and here he is now, his face tilted to the sun.

He moves forward with his walker, one small step at a time, as Del and Joe chat.

'Hey, you,' says Malcolm, and Elizabeth smiles.

He was the first call she made when things had settled down, when the press had lost interest and everyone was allowed to move on with their lives. She needed to thank him. She called Ruby next, girding herself for the conversation, sure that the young woman would be filled with anger towards her, but Ruby was just wonderful – open and forgiving and kind. Elizabeth had not protected her and Joe the way she needed to, but most people seemed to understand that it was not her fault; she was struggling to protect herself.

Malcolm settles Gordon on a chair in the front garden, and Elizabeth sits down next to him as he watches the birds.

The first thing she did when she got here yesterday was to refill the bird feeder, because she knew Gordon was coming. He lives in a home now, where he is cared for by some wonderful people, one of whom will be staying here with Malcolm and Del to help.

The birds flutter up into the tree as Malcolm moves past them, and then swoop down to the feeder again.

'This is a nice place,' says Gordon, and Elizabeth nods.

'It is, isn't it,' she replies, leaning towards him.

'I'm Gordon,' he says with a wide smile.

'Hello, Gordon. I'm Elizabeth, and that's Joe over there, talking to Del.'

'He looks like a nice chap,' says Gordon.

'He is,' she agrees as Malcolm comes to stand behind her. He squeezes her shoulder a little and she reaches back and touches his hand. They have a strong friendship now, and maybe it's becoming something more than that, but she is concentrating on making sure that Joe is fine and that she can support him the way she needs to.

'Mum... Mum,' says Joe, his hands on his hips.

'Yes, sweetheart,' she answers.

'Del says they're going to have fish and chips for dinner and I want that too.'

'And you will have it, young man. We're having dinner together. Now what about a walk on the beach for you two so that Malcolm can unpack?'

'Yay,' both children shout.

'Thanks, you're the best,' says Malcolm, and he kisses her cheek. She touches the place where his lips met her skin, wondering if this holiday might tip the balance between them from friends to something else. Does he feel the same way? She hopes he does.

It's not something she's going to think about right now. Instead, she takes Joe's hand and Del's hand and together they cross the road so she can grab water bottles and more sunscreen, despite it being late afternoon.

'And Mum, Del wants an ice cream at the beach, and Mum, we want to build a sandcastle, and Mum...' Elizabeth laughs as Joe talks and the whole world gets to hear that she is his mum.

MALCOLM

Malcolm heaves a suitcase onto the bed so he can unpack Del's things into the chest of drawers that she always uses when they stay here. He unpacks in silence, listening out in case his father needs him and relishing just being able to be quiet for a few minutes. Del asked a question every two minutes all the way from Sydney. *And what is my bedtime? How many times can I go to the beach in one day? How many ice creams can I have every day? When will Joe get there? Will we have dinner with them every night?*

He didn't mind the questions, but even as he patiently answered every single one of them, his mind was occupied with how his father would look when he saw him. It's only been a few months since he came down to visit him, but he can feel time slipping away every time he sees his father's rapid deterioration. The disease has a strong hold now, and Malcolm's heart breaks for the man who raised him so well. The worry is tiring and he could use a nap, but he won't sleep until the carer gets here. His father needs constant attention.

He picks up a collection of shorts and slides them into a

drawer, marvelling at the sweet, flowery scent that still lingers there from when his mother was alive.

He stops what he's doing and listens for a moment, but his father is quiet in the front garden, surrounded by his beloved birds. Malcolm chose the care home where Gordon now lives for its wonderful staff, but also because they have large bird feeders in their gardens, so he can still spend as long as he likes watching his feathered friends.

He smiles, thinking of his father in the garden, and then he thinks about Elizabeth and the children, who will be back from the beach soon. Does Elizabeth feel the same way he does when they're together? He thinks she might, and he has a dinner planned for a couple of nights from now, just the two of them, at the nicest restaurant in town, so he can tell her how he feels, because he feels like this may be love, and he's too old to let the opportunity go by.

When he walked Ruby down the aisle to marry Lucas, he saw the way the young man looked at his bride-to-be. Something in his glance felt familiar – something soft and deeply felt – and Malcolm realised that his own face must look the same way when he looked at Elizabeth. It was a revelation after he had accepted that he would remain single, not needing anything except work and Del.

He doesn't just need Elizabeth; he wants her in his life – her and Joe. Even as he can feel himself losing his father, he is gaining a new family. Ruby and Lucas are part of that family as well. The coincidence of Ruby-who-was-Jade turning up at his childhood home still amazes him, but he knows enough to know that amazing things like that happen all the time. The day he nearly lost his father a year ago comes rushing back at him, and he closes his eyes briefly, letting it go so that he can enjoy just being here now.

Sliding the last of Del's clothes into a drawer, he lifts the empty suitcase and stores it under the bed. He will unpack his own stuff later. Now he could use something to drink, and he's sure his father could as well.

In the kitchen, he fills a glass with water and looks at Gordon sitting in the sunshine, watching the birds. His father will be happy for him and Elizabeth, even if he doesn't quite understand. They speak about her and Joe often, and Malcolm finds he doesn't mind telling Gordon the same things again and again when it comes to Elizabeth. He could talk about her all day.

'When you know, you know,' his father once told him when Malcolm asked how he knew he was in love with his mother.

With the glass of water in his hand, Malcolm goes out to his father, who is always right.

When you know, you know.

GORDON

He watches the woman and the two children cross the road. They look like a nice family. He should tell Flora about them. He has no idea why they are living in Dawn and Louie's house. Perhaps they are cousins. Dawn once mentioned something about cousins from Queensland.

He looks around to find Flora, but she must be inside, in the kitchen. Perhaps she's making dinner. He should tell her he feels like a nice steak. You can't go wrong with a nice steak.

'Hey, Dad, here's some water for you. It's warm here in the sun.'

Gordon turns to look at the man standing next to him. 'Malcolm,' he says.

'Yep, I'll just go and grab us a snack.'

'Tell your mother I'd like a steak for dinner,' says Gordon.

'I will, Dad,' Malcolm says, and satisfied that he's getting what he wants, Gordon concentrates on the birds on the feeder, smiling at the cockatoos, who like to push the other birds around. He likes sitting here, likes watching the birds. Is this his house? He thinks it must be his house. Of course it is – he recognises the bird feeder and the garden. Flora will be out in a minute with a cup of tea, and she'll sit with him and together they can watch the birds and enjoy the sun. He feels like he's loved Flora forever, but he knew from the moment he saw her that she was the one for him. When you know, you know.

He smiles at how good life is. It's simple, but good. He has school and his students and Malcolm and Del... Del is his granddaughter. He's lucky to have a granddaughter.

Somewhere in the distance, a car door slams and the birds take off from the feeder in fright, wings whirring through the air.

'Nothing to worry about,' Gordon reassures them, 'you're safe here,' and believing him, they settle again as he watches.

A LETTER FROM NICOLE

Hello

I would like to thank you for taking the time to read *The Foster Family*. If you enjoyed it, and want to keep up to date with all my latest releases, just sign up at the following link. Your email address will never be shared and you can unsubscribe at any time.

www.bookouture.com/nicole-trope

It is a fact of life that not all human beings are capable of caring for those who are the most vulnerable. The capacity to put another's needs above your own and to be prepared to make sacrifices for someone else is not something that everyone has.

When parents or guardians fail, the foster system is there to care for children who are not being adequately cared for, but it's not a perfect system. It is filled with dedicated professionals who want to help, but they are only human, and human nature and lack of funding get in the way of a satisfactory outcome for everyone.

If children in need were only fostered by perfect families, very few would be taken care of. On the outside, Howard and Elizabeth appeared the ideal choice for a foster family, but they were obviously battling their own demons. I know that some readers will have wanted to give Elizabeth a good shake and tell her to just leave, but it's never as simple as that. Unless you find yourself in an abusive relationship, you can never fully understand why someone chooses to stay. I have known many strong, intelligent, resourceful women who have stayed longer than they should have for a myriad of reasons. Everything is more difficult when children are involved. Elizabeth stayed until a near tragedy, but I can see a brighter future for her and Joe.

Gordon has become a favourite character. Sometimes when I was writing him, I could actually feel his confusion. No matter how much I wanted to, I couldn't change the outcome for him, but what I hope is that he understands he is loved and surrounded by those who love him for the rest of his life.

There are many wonderful, amazing foster families who are giving needy children the gift of a home, and I can only admire them. I have written a story of one family that is deeply imperfect to begin with, but as just Elizabeth and Joe, they will have a wonderful life.

If you have enjoyed this novel, it would be lovely if you could take the time to leave a review. I read them all and experience true joy when readers identify with characters and stories.

I would also love to hear from you. You can find me on Facebook and Twitter and I'm always happy to connect with readers.

Thanks again for reading.

Nicole x

facebook.com/NicoleTrope

twitter.com/nicoletrope

instagram.com/nicoletropeauthor

ACKNOWLEDGEMENTS

I would like to thank Christina Demosthenous for her advice and continued support. I hope we will be working together for many more books to come, even as her star rises at Bookouture.

Thanks to Victoria Blunden for the first edit. I am loving having your perspective at the beginning and hope we can keep working together.

I would also like to thank Jess Readett for all her hard work and enthusiasm as she ramps up the attention for each of my novels.

Thanks to Jane Selley for the copy-edit and Liz Hatherell for the proofread.

Thanks to the whole team at Bookouture, including Jenny Geras, Peta Nightingale, Richard King, Alba Proko, Ruth Tross and everyone else involved in producing my audio books, selling rights and answering any questions I can think of.

Thanks to my mother, Hilary, my first reader, who overlooks mistakes in rough drafts.

Thanks also to David, Mikhayla, Isabella and Jacob and Jax.

And once again thank you to those who read, review, blog about my work and contact me on Facebook or Twitter to let me know you love my books. Every review is appreciated.